M000076824

# After She Said Yes

# After She Said Yes

A Novel

Kaya Gravitter

Published by Tablo

I dedicate this book to all women. May you always have the strength to stand up to any man who tries to silence you.

# Chapter 1

*Hurry up, Aurora. You gotta leave before he sees you.*

Aurora was about to leave for work. She looked into the mirror that was hanging on her cream-colored walls in the doorway entrance of her apartment. She put her dark wavy hair into a ponytail, and then fluffed her fringe bangs. She touched the bags under her blue eyes, hoping the dark circles would go away. She picked up her big black-rimmed glasses that were sitting on the entryway table. She put the glasses on, and they fit snugly on the small curve of her flat nose that she had inherited from her grandfather. After she un-tucked her white long-sleeved blouse to hide the small of her curves on her slender body, she pulled down the blouse as much as she could to cover her hips.

"Where are ya goin' dressed like that?" Gannon, her husband, said in his sly southern drawl. Gannon's red hair was a mess. He was still in his pajamas.

"L-l-like what?" Aurora flinched.

*I used to love seeing him next to me in the morning when I first woke up. She looked down at her outfit. But now...* Along with the blouse, she was wearing black pants and black Chanel flats with small white ribbon bows on the front of them.

"What do you mean? I'm going to work."

*Why do I put up with this?*

Gannon's cheeks became red and flushed. "Not dressed like that you ain't. Why'd you have makeup on?" He raised his red eyebrows and opened his brown eyes wide. "Who are you gettin' dressed up for?" He laughed, but Aurora knew that he wasn't joking.

*I only have a little mascara on my eyelashes.* She pushed her index finger against the bridge of her glasses.

"No, of course not," Aurora said, shocked. "I dress like this all of the time, Gan. I wear makeup for myself. I don't know why you care so much." *How can he see this small amount of makeup, anyway?*

"Can't you just do as I say?" Gannon said. "It would make me feel better for you to stop showing off your body."

"But I'm..." Aurora looked down at her outfit again but couldn't see her curves under her loose clothing.

"Put on a different shirt or at least a jacket. You know it's cold in Madison."

Aurora looked out the small window next to the door and heard a gust of wind. She shrugged her shoulders in agreement with Gannon's comment.

"I grew up in cold weather, not in Alabama like you, Gannon." Aurora had grown up on a small crop farm in northern Wisconsin. Her grandparents bought the land when they moved to the United States from Germany.

"Well," she sighed, "if it would make you feel better."

"Thanks, baby."

Gannon opened up his arms and pulled Aurora into him, his arms muscular and cold. She stood there, stiff and enveloped in Gannon's chest. A tear ran down her blushing face.

"You are too pretty to cry." Gannon dried the tear and pushed her bangs behind her right ear. Aurora froze.

"Don't leave home again without asking me what to wear. You know better. Besides, your body is too sexy for anyone to see it." *How is this sexy?*

"Okay," she stuttered, "I won't." Gannon gave her a black suit jacket to put on and she flashed him a fake smile. She grabbed her purse, keys, and coffee mug.

As Aurora stepped out of her house to lock the front door, she took a deep breath and inhaled the crisp air. As she exhaled, she tried to release the tension that had been building in her chest. She grabbed her phone from her purse, put her headphones in, and listened to Enya to relax her nerves. Her polished thumb, a glossy red, swiped the volume up across the screen. She walked up State Street in downtown Madison, Wisconsin, starting from the college to the state capitol building. This part of town was filled with restaurants, bars, and vintage clothing stores.

While she was a block past her house, she stopped and set her coffee mug on a park bench. She rolled her eyes as she took off the black suit jacket Gannon had urged her to wear. She draped the jacket over her arm, trying to dismiss the thought of Gannon from her mind. As Aurora continued to walk, she stared at the trees bursting with color. The colors reminded Aurora of the cold autumns in her hometown. In the summers, the fields were covered with crops of some sort, usually corn or hay rustling in the wind.

Aurora took out her headphones as she walked into her work building. The glass-fronted building was sandwiched between an art museum and an old Italian restaurant called Amore.

"Good morning, Mrs. Tousey," Tiffany, Aurora's assistant, greeted her. She was a short brunette with curly hair wrapped in a bun.

"Morning," Aurora replied as she opened her office door.

Next to Aurora's office door was her nameplate. *Aurora Tousey. Happy Living Magazine, Editor-in-Chief.*

Aurora's office had white walls with one painting made of colored squares of black, pink, and yellow. Her desk, where she spent many late nights editing, was pushed to a corner of the room. On the left of her desk was a full glass window overlooking the marbled Wisconsin state capitol building. She loved the way natural light was brought into the room. She also loved to watch people walk by and imagine their life stories. The window by her office door overlooked her assistant's desk, but she usually kept the shades on that window closed. She liked her privacy.

On the wall behind Aurora's desk hung her diploma in a dark brown wooden frame. In another frame was her first article published in *The New York Times*.

--

Aurora's phone rang. She pulled it from her purse. Shahrazad popped up. *What could she want?* Aurora picked up.

"Hey, Rora," her friend said while sighing. Shazzy and Aurora had met in college during a public speaking class. Shazzy was shorter than Aurora. Aurora thought she was curvy and beautiful. Shazzy had black shoulder-length bouncy curls. Some would call her chubby, but she owned her body shape. Aurora wished she could love her body as Shazzy did. Aurora and Shazzy met through mutual friends a few years before at a party of one of Aurora's college friends. Aurora loved that Shazzy was so smart, but also loved to live life on the edge. She wanted a spontaneous spark in her own life. Shazzy brought that, but sometimes Shazzy brought too much spontaneity.

"Hey, what's up?" Aurora leaned back in her chair, cradling the phone against her cheek. "You okay, Shazzy? Don't you have patients today?"

"I have a break now. I was wondering if I could stay the night at your place tonight." Though Shazzy was a doctor, she was from a conservative Iranian family. Since she was unmarried, she still lived with her family, since that was her "family's" values.

"I mean, sure. I just need to ask Gannon first," Aurora said. "But why do you need to stay over? Is everything okay?"

"I got into a fight with my parents...."

"What happened this time?"

"One of my parents' friends saw me on a date with a boy."

"And?"

"A white boy."

Aurora exhaled through her teeth. "Shazzy."

"Well, we were kissing."

Aurora rolled her eyes. *I think she usually does more than kissing.*

"I was raised Muslim," Shazzy said. "You know my parents are strict, but I hate being told what to do. I'm thirty years old!" Shazzy tried to be promiscuous because her Iranian parents were old-fashioned, so she always lashed out in her personal life any way that she could.

"I don't know how you manage to sneak out. I mean, I can't--" Aurora cut herself off. "Uhh, well anyway, what if Gannon says no?"

"I don't want to stay alone."

*Shazzy appears to be so tough on the outside, so why does she want to stay at my place?*

"Come on, Aurora. I am not asking you to go out and party. I am just asking to stay over." Aurora could hear the shakiness in Shazzy's voice. "Besides, I will be in good company and will bring wine."

Nights when Gannon would go out of town for work, Shazzy would call Aurora. Some nights Aurora wanted to spite Gannon, so she would let Shazzy drag her out to a dive bar called The Outfit. The faux leather seats were torn, and the neon sign only displayed the letters, "The OU-F--." After a night of dancing and drinking, the hangovers would make Aurora feel nauseated and irritable.

"No, I don't really want to drink tonight," Aurora said. "I just got this book from the library."

"Don't be so boring!" Shazzy said. "You are a career woman; you need to enjoy yourself. Come on! It will be fun."

"Reading a book and drinking a cup of hot chocolate is reward enough."

"Aurora, really?" Shazzy said. "That sounds pathetic."

Aurora sighed.

"Fine. I will call Gannon," Aurora said. "You have patients to get back to and I need to get back to work. Also, don't bring the wine unless you plan to drink it while Gannon is asleep."

Aurora called Gannon after she hung up with Shazzy.

"Hey, Gannon."

"Hey… I am a bit busy with this designing thing for work. Can I call you back later?"

"Well," Aurora said. "I will talk quick."

"Fine."

"Can Shazzy stay over tonight?"

"Why? Doesn't she live with her parents?" Gannon said.

"Yes, but it is kind of complicated," Aurora said. "She got in a fight."

"Aurora, I have work to do."

"I know, but she really has nowhere else to go."

"Uhhhh."

"Please," Aurora pleaded.

"Fine," Gannon said. "I have a deadline tonight. I just don't want any noise."

"Okay."

"It's good you asked me. You know I don't want you to hang out with anyone I don't approve of."

"Like Tessa?"

"Exactly like that! It is for your own good. You will thank me someday."

"Well, see you later," Aurora said as she hung up.

# Chapter 2

It was cold and still that late October night. Outside, the moon reflected the ice-frosted leaves. Covered in dew, the grass resembled the icing on a freshly glazed pastry. When Aurora went to bed, Shazzy was asleep in the guest bedroom and Gannon was working in his office. Aurora struggled to sleep that night. She had to work early the next morning. She often found herself restless and over analytical.

Aurora got up from her bed to go to the bathroom. The lights were off, and she did not have her glasses on. Aurora's bare feet felt cold on the hardwood floor. The hallway to the bathroom felt like a dark tunnel. When she got to the end of that tunnel, she couldn't see much besides a smeared canvas in front of her eyes in the living room. Instead of turning right to the bathroom, something made Aurora look back.

She heard a sound that made her turn her head. *That moan sounds too familiar*, Aurora muttered to herself.

All she saw was a blur. She walked further toward the moving objects. Her heart started to beat faster. She squinted her eyes and saw the side of a man's face as the lamplight reflected his strawberry blonde hair. She heard a whisper, "Take off your shirt." She took in a big breath of air as if she were punched in the stomach. She knew that slightly crooked nose from a mile away, and could recognize that light southern accent anywhere, even as a whisper.

*Is this really happening?* Her heart started to beat faster. Her breaths got shorter.

Aurora stopped. She felt a tightness in her chest. The hair on the backs of her arms stuck up as straight as the quills on a porcupine. She stood there as her blood froze in her veins. She could neither speak nor breathe.

She felt numb and cold. Shivers ran down her spine.

She stared at both of them for a few moments before she could say anything. When words started to come out of her mouth, she began to whimper. She couldn't utter a word.

It was her husband kissing Shazzy.

"You have got to be kidding me!" Aurora finally managed to yell.

Gannon jumped off the couch.

"It ain't what it looks like, Rora," Gannon stuttered as he smiled, taking a step toward Aurora.

"It didn't mean anything," Shazzy said, her eyes wide and her face pale. Then she yawned. "We are both really drunk."

*Shazzy... But Shazzy doesn't get drunk. She is a lush. A heavyweight.*

Shazzy continued, "Aurora, don't worry."

"Are you really telling me not to worry? You are nothing to me. You are both nothing to me," Aurora said. "Shazzy, the thought of your voice right now mimics the sound of nails being scraped on a chalkboard."

"Rora, this is my mistake," Gannon said. "I thought she was you."

"Really, Gannon? Really?" Aurora said. "The difference between Shazzy and me is like the difference between real milk and soy milk. Are you seriously thinking I am going to believe that your'e 'sorry' this time?"

Both Shazzy and Gannon stared at Aurora in amazement. Aurora shook her head as she stared into Gannon's eyes. *Those are the same dark black eyes I fell in love with during my first month*

*in college... those eyes persuaded me to marry him.* The truth
behind those eyes was finally staring right at her, and she
couldn't run away or brush it off anymore. *Such an idiot,
Aurora! I am such an idiot!*

"I know why both of your eyes are brown," Aurora said.
"Because you are full of shit."

"What?" Gannon said. "What did you say to me?" He got
off the couch, clenching his fists.

She knew Gannon was a flirt with other women before
marriage, but she thought she could change him or he would
change himself. But she knew deep down that she could not
change a man like Gannon. *Wishful thinking for a guy who flirts
with about every waitress we have ever had.*

"Shazzy..." Aurora said. "You were asleep when I went to
bed."

"I know I was, but...".

"Is this the real reason why you wanted to stay here
tonight?" Aurora said as she stared down Shazzy. Aurora threw
her hand up like she was throwing away garbage. Aurora
continued before they could utter another word. "Gannon!
And you! You were working!" Aurora said. "This has to be a
joke."

Aurora stood there, her knees buckling. She could barely
stand or breathe.

As she stared at Shazzy and Gannon, she became sick to her
stomach. It was as if someone were cutting out her intestines
with rusty kitchen scissors. *Is this a horror film? Or am I
dreaming? I must be dreaming.*

Aurora ran back to her room. She slammed and locked the
door. She put her right hand on the door and slowly rubbed it
as if she were rubbing her hair like her grandma used to do to
her as a child.

*Aurora, you will be fine. Everything will be okay. You will be fine.* She fell to the floor.

She felt like she was out of options and had nowhere to turn. "God!" She screamed. "I do not know what to do! I am talking to you because I have nothing else to lose. I know I haven't gone to church in a few years because I felt you never answered my prayers, but..."

Aurora got on her knees with her hands folded, hyperventilating, "I do not know if you are there, but please forgive me and just give me a sign that I will get through this." She heard someone slam the front door as they ran out of the house. *Was that Gannon or Shazzy?*

She heard someone knock on the bedroom door, but she covered her ears. They kept knocking on the door.

"Rora, let me in," Gannon said in a mellow voice as if he had done nothing wrong.

She always gave in to him after a fight, and he would somehow put the blame on her. This time was different. She would put up with all of the abuse he gave, but she thought that cheating was a line that if he crossed, she would leave him and never turn back.

She crumbled there on the floor, like a piece of paper about to be thrown into the trash. She stood up and dragged herself onto the bed. She felt numb. She felt empty. She stared at the ceiling and closed her eyes.

# Chapter 3

Aurora woke up the next morning at 6:00 a.m. sharp. She rubbed the crust off of her eyes. She got out of bed and looked around her apartment, realizing she was alone.

She went to the bathroom to wash her face. She looked in the mirror and saw she had bags under her eyes. *I probably only slept a couple of hours*, she muttered to herself. *Just pretend nothing happened. You have to go to work. You are a boss. You have deadlines.*

She attempted to maintain her same daily routine by turning on the coffee pot and changing into her gym clothes. As she sat on the bench by her front door, she paused as she tied her shoes and remembered the night before. *Nope, not today, Satan.* Aurora went to the gym. As she was on the treadmill, running with each breath, the breaths became harder, like the night before. She knew sticking to her routine would get her back on track. After the gym, she came home and showered, then headed to work.

--

Aurora wasn't normally busy at work on Wednesdays. She always kept that day open for work meetings, but this Wednesday, she tried to stay as busy as possible. Aurora kept rearranging and organizing her desk and color coordinating her pens. As soon as she saw the picture on her desk of her and Gannon on their wedding day, she threw it in her desk drawer.

Next to her computer was a pile of articles she had to sift through, but the images of the night before kept replaying in her head. She often caught herself staring at her computer or out the window. Then she would shake her head back into reality.

Tiffany knocked on Aurora's door. "Gannon is here to see you." She peeked her head through Aurora's office door.

"He's what?" Aurora cleared her throat and sat up straight. "I mean, what did you say?" Aurora's face went white. *Oh, God. Take me now.*

Tiffany hesitantly walked in and closed the door behind her.

"Mrs. Tousey, are you okay?"

"Oh yeah, I'm fine," Aurora said. "I'm just overwhelmed with all of the work I have to do today." She sat back down and pretended to type something on her keyboard.

There was an awkward silence and Tiffany looked at her while tilting her head.

"Why are you giving me that look?"

"Well," Tiffany said. "I know you are not busy on Wednes —"

"Please," Aurora cut her off. "Please, next time knock before you come in. There is a reason why I chose the shades." Tiffany started to walk out the door.

"Wait, Tiffany... I am sorry. It's just.... Never mind." Aurora signaled with her hand for Tiffany to leave.

Tiffany opened the door and signaled for Gannon to come in.

Gannon came in walking with his head down and lightly closed the door behind him. *I wonder where he went last night.* She wanted to have time to organize her thoughts to decide what to do next. She wanted time to heal and never see him again, but Gannon would never let her think after a fight. She could hear his nagging voice in her head: *You are worthless. No one will ever be with you. I am the reason you are successful.* That time, she ignored the thoughts.

She started to breathe heavily as she saw his arms, which were full of yellow roses. *You have got to be kidding me.*

"Rora," he said as he put out his hand to try to touch her. She pulled away.

"Gannon, you know I am allergic to flowers."

"Oh, I forgot." *Why is it that he never remembers anything about me?*

"Gannon, how could you forget? We have been together for years."

Gannon set the flowers on Aurora's desk. Aurora inhaled a large breath of air while turning her head away from the flowers.

Gannon ruffled his fingers through his hair with his nostrils flared as he clenched his jaw. One of the nostrils was slightly larger than the other and it drove Aurora crazy. Aurora could feel sweat accumulating everywhere on her body as she grew angrier.

"Rora, I was so drunk last night," Gannon said, his cheeks flushed. "I thought she was you." She looked at him and rolled her eyes. *Really? You have been with me for how many years and you thought she was me?* Aurora thought.

With angst, she continued, ignoring what Gannon had said completely: "Gannon, why are you here?"

Tiffany knocked on the door and cracked it open. "Is everything okay, Mrs. Tousey?"

"She is fine," he said, as he always said when someone suspected her of being abused, upset, or depressed. Aurora's eyes grew wide at Tiffany. Then she flashed a fake smile at

Tiffany through the crack of the door.

"Here." Aurora grabbed the flowers from her desk. "I got you some flowers for being such a great assistant."

"Thank you!" Tiffany said as she smiled, staring at the roses.

Then Aurora closed the door.

Gannon began to pout and stepped towards Aurora. "I came to apologize." He tried to grab her hand, but she slapped it away.

"You know I'm at work," Aurora said. "I like to keep my personal life outside of work. Can you please leave?"

Looking frustrated, Gannon said, "Well, I guess so, but I...."

"I said 'please,' Gannon. Don't make me ask again and call security. I don't want to see you." She clenched her jaw and ground her teeth. "And those flowers mean nothing to me."

"Aurora, I am not giving up that easily." Gannon looked deep into Aurora's eyes. "It isn't my fault for what happened."

"Then whose is it?" Before Gannon got a word in, Aurora continued, "It must be my fault, huh? Just like when you... When you abuse me? That's my fault, too."

"Well."

"Then Shazzy's? Honestly, Gannon, get out of my office." Aurora started to breathe heavily. "Get out of my life!"

Gannon stepped in to try to hug her. She pushed away.

"Get out before I call security or maybe even the police."

"But Aur…" Gannon pleaded.

Aurora pushed him out of her office and shut the door. She put her back against the wall and took a deep breath.

She went to her desk, grabbed their wedding picture, and threw it in the trash.

# Chapter 4

The following day, Aurora went to meet with her best friend, Tessa. Aurora had texted her that morning about meeting up, telling her friend that it was important. Tessa was in her senior year of dental school. Aurora stood on the lawn next to the brick building where Tessa's class was. She leaned against an oak tree that seemed to tower over her small frame. She looked up as she heard a gust of wind ruffle the colorful leaves.

After ten minutes of Aurora waiting and kicking around leaves, Tessa came out of the building.

*I am so nervous. What if she yells at me for just blacklisting her?*

"Hey, Tessa," Aurora said as she lowered her head.

"Aurora?" Tessa said. "Is everything okay? We haven't talked in forever. I thought Gannon didn't want you to see me anymore."

Tessa was blonde and walked with spunk in her step because she was a jock and ran track in high school. During their undergrad, Tessa always tried to get Aurora to run with her, but Aurora would always quit ten minutes in. Aurora preferred to bike if anything.

"I am sorry. I know we haven't seen each other or talked in a while, but I..." Aurora started to choke on tears.

"I know you are not here to just tell me sorry," Tessa said as she pulled Aurora in for a hug. "What's wrong?"

"Gannon cheated on me," Aurora said as she took a deep breath and wiped the tears from her face. "I caught Gannon with a woman the other night."

"Oh, Rora," Tessa said.

"I was wondering. Before you say I told you so..." Aurora said.

"I won't say that."

"Well, you know I hate asking for help. I paid for all of my college and expenses on my own and covered the expenses of my life with Gannon and never asked anyone for a dime."

"Really?" Tessa said. "He paid nothing? That lazy ba – "

"Tessa," Aurora said. "I know I was so stupid to ever pay for anything for him. I am just asking you... Asking for your help."

"Of course! What can I do?"

"I just need a place to stay. I can pay for rent. I will even stay on your couch. I just don't know who to talk to about what happened. I can't tell my family or any of my friends."

"But you can tell your best friend," Tessa said.

"Yes," Aurora laughed as she shed happy tears. "My best friend.... I guess I have been so distant lately. Gannon just got so bad that I felt like I was in a hole I could not get out of."

"It's fine. I get it." *Does she really get it? I guess I won't get into that now*, Aurora thought.

"So, do you still live in the suburbs?"

"Yes," Tessa said. "I still live an hour away, like I mentioned the last time we bumped into each other. I am working for a dentist now."

"That's a long commute, but that's fine," Aurora said. "I have been staying in a hotel the last few nights. You know, since I left my place. I just cannot stand to be alone anymore. I haven't eaten anything in three days."

"No problem," Tessa said. "I would love to have you stay with me. It will be just like college again."

When Aurora and Tessa met in college, they lived across

the hall from one other. Aurora had needed help setting up her Wi-Fi. She asked Tessa for help in her own awkward way, but she usually tried to avoid small talk or introduce herself to people she didn't know. Aurora could tell by Tessa's mannerisms that she was the same way. They became friends after that, and would do everything together, like going to parties, eating, and studying.

"Thank you," Aurora said.

"It's okay. Pretend you never asked, and that I asked you." Tessa said. "Is that all you wanted to say?"

"Well," Aurora said in a silent voice. "No. Gannon was abusing me."

"He was what?" Tessa stammered. Her voice began to attract the attention of onlookers.

"Such a horrible human being. Remember the summer of freshman year when I took a trip with you and Gannon to Chicago?" Tessa continued.

"Yes. I remember." Aurora was standing stiff and tense.

"Well, I saw how Gannon was always poking fun at you or making you feel stupid. I hated that. That is probably why he hated me. I saw through his narcissistic personality by his always making excuses for you and me not to hang out."

"He didn't hate you," Aurora said as she kicked some leaves on the ground. "But he didn't like you either."

"He did hate me then, and he still hates me." Tessa rolled her eyes. "He had to, because no one just stops seeing their friends for no reason," Tessa said. "I am sure he hated me because I saw through his crap. I never liked him. Who knows what he would say if he knew we were talking now."

"He won't," Aurora said. "But you told me how he was before I married him. I just didn't want to listen. I am sorry I let him get between us."

"It's fine. I am just happy you are not with him."

"I am sure."

"I am happy that you will be staying with me."

"I am just glad you said yes." Aurora took a deep breath and smiled as she relaxed her stance. "I was expecting the worst."

"You always expect the worst, Rora." Tessa smiled and let out a soft and comforting laugh. "Some things never change."

--

Aurora went to her and Gannon's apartment with Tessa after work the next day.

"I'm not going to miss this place," Aurora said as she and Tessa walked into the living room. "It was like my own little hell here."

"Funny thing is," Tessa said, "this is the first time I am allowed in your place, and it is to pack your things."

"Please, Tessa," Aurora said. "You know I felt guilty about that every single day."

"I know. I am just messing with you."

Aurora looked at her wedding picture hanging on the wall.

"Wow," Aurora said. "That is probably the last time I remember being happy." Aurora pointed at herself in the photo.

In the photo, Aurora was wearing her dream wedding dress, which was an off-white lace dress, like the dress Kate, the Duchess of Cambridge, had worn to marry Prince William. Aurora's hair was up in a French twist and she was wearing a white lace veil. The ceremony was a picture-perfect fall wedding. They were at Gannon's parents' estate, The McMaster Plantation, just outside of Auburn, Alabama. It had a beautiful garden in it. Aurora was sickened when she thought it was probably built on the backs of slaves, but she never said anything about it though it bothered her deeply. The garden had been around since it was created in 1862 when Gannon's great-great-grandparents first purchased the land after coming to the United States from Ireland. In the photo, Gannon and Aurora were walking in the garden down the wedding aisle that was covered in white rose petals. The garden flourished with pink peonies, which were Gannon's mother's favorite flower.

"I doubt I will ever have a wedding like this again," Aurora said. "Not like I ever want to again, anyway."

"Don't talk like that," Tessa said as she got closer to the photo. "But wow. To think you were only twenty-one when you and Gannon got married."

"Yup, and Gannon was twenty-three," Aurora said. "Everyone said we were too young to get married, but we didn't care. I just loved him so much, but it was only that Gannon didn't want to lose me to my career." Tears ran down Aurora's face, and she wiped them away with her sweater sleeve.

"Aurora," Tessa said as she tried to console Aurora.

"It is just that everything changed on the day I married him," Aurora said. "Everything changed after I said 'yes'."

"It's okay," Tessa said. "It is done now."

"I was just so stupid," Aurora said as her cheeks grew red and her voice began to crack. "Giving up my dream of working at *The New York Times* for him."

"Aurora," Tessa said. "This is upsetting you. We don't need to talk about it."

"It is what it is," Aurora said. "He literally ran to my gate and begged me not to leave. I mean, he got down on one knee and asked me to marry him. I was so young and naïve."

"No, you were not," Tessa said. "Do not blame yourself."

"He didn't even have a ring to propose with."

"Aurora," Tessa said as she touched Aurora's arm, "there is no need to talk about this anymore. It is only making you upset and it is in the past now."

"You're right," Aurora said. "Let's start packing."

Aurora stared at the couch where she and Gannon would sit and binge watch Netflix. All she could see was a vision of her friend and Gannon kissing. Aurora clenched her jaw and fists as she thought, *I wonder how long Gannon and Shazzy have been doing this with one another.*

Aurora and Tessa went to her office to pack up some of her things.

"Wow, Tessa," Aurora said. "I will never forget the time he kicked my desk chair out from underneath me and bruised my whole left hip. It took months for that bruise to go away."

"Aurora, I can't believe I never knew."

"I know it is uncomfortable to hear, but it happened," Aurora said. "I still have photos of the bruises on my phone."

"Why did you never show them to the police?"

"I don't know." *If people only knew why it is just so hard to up and leave an abusive relationship.*

"Well, you need to get yourself a lawyer," Tessa said. "And when you do, as hurtful as it will be, show this to them."

"Come here and look at my phone," Aurora said. Aurora pulled up the picture that showed the bruise marks on her hip.

"Oh Aurora," Tessa said as she put her hand to her mouth in awe.

In one photo, from another time, Aurora's left forearm had a large purple mark from where Gannon had thrown her against a countertop.

"I only took them because I wanted to have proof if I ever had the courage to leave," Aurora said. "And he would always threaten me that if I tried to tell anyone, he would tell everyone I am crazy and that I cheated on him. I just want proof of what he did to me."

"Tessa, it was such a normal occurrence," Aurora continued. "When one bruise would disappear on my body, a new bruise would form. It was like my body was a blank canvas he painted and colored with bruises."

"I am so sorry," Tessa said. "If I had known, I would have done everything I could to help prevent this."

"It is not your fault," Aurora said. "After every fight, I would just put a bandage on our relationship and hope it would heal itself, like my bruises and scars. But the scars on my heart never healed – they only grew more with time. And now look where I am. I made it out. Finally."

# Chapter 5

Aurora stepped on the scale in her bathroom and to her demise, she found out that she had lost fifteen pounds in two weeks after she decided to weigh herself.

Earlier that day, she had heard employees at her job talking about how she had lost so much weight in a short period of time. One of her tall blonde employees asked Aurora in her valley girl accent, "How have you lost weight so fast, Mrs. Aurora? What is your secret?" She touched Aurora's arm. "Oh my God, you have to tell me your secret."

Aurora just stared at her employee blankly. "Well, it is just working out and eating healthy." *Or not eating at all.* "But hey, enough about me, you have a deadline, Jessica. So you should get back to work. As Aurora shut her office door, she muttered, *I just can't eat anything.*

Aurora took her feet off the scale and set them on the cold, white mosaic tiles of Tessa's bathroom floor. Tears started to roll down her face as she put her hand against the wall to maintain her balance. She felt the ribs while rubbing over her shirt and lifted it up to look at herself in the mirror. She quickly pulled her shirt down and took a deep breath.

Aurora walked out of the bathroom to find Tessa cooking something in the kitchen.

"Let me make you some soup or something, Aurora," Tessa said.

"No," Aurora said. "The idea of food makes me sick."

"I hate seeing you like this."

"It's fine. I will be fine. You eat what you want," Aurora said as she looked for something in the fridge.

"This protein drink is all I can eat," she said as she grabbed it out of the fridge, showing it to Tessa. "I can only drink the butter pecan one today."

"That is not enough, Aurora!" Tessa hesitated. "At least try to drink a couple more a day."

"I said, it's fine!" Aurora said. "I will be fine. I manage to work still, so I will make it through."

"Aurora, you are not fine," Tessa said. "You are far from fine. You have to take care of yourself."

"It's easier said than done," Aurora said.

"That is true. I mean, I don't know how you feel or how to help," Tessa said. "But taking care of yourself is quintessential to your surviving, and if you can't do it, then I am not going to let you wither away and die on me."

"It is not that serious."

"Yes, it is!" Tessa exclaimed. "You are skin and bones. I know you see it when you look in the mirror. Aurora, you've got to try to eat something. Force yourself."

"Come on, now," Aurora said, startled.

"I'm sorry," Tessa said. "I am just worried about you and I wish I knew the right thing to say or do to help you. You just came back into my life. I don't want to lose you again."

"Tessa, you won't lose me."

"Aurora, I just know that if you don't gain any weight, I am going to take you to a hospital," Tessa said. "Have you thought about seeing a therapist?"

"I don't think I will be able to accept help from anyone," Aurora said. "No one can help me at this point besides myself. I want to eat: I just can't."

--

Aurora only was able to drink one small bottle of a nutritional beverage a day for another two weeks. Each shake equaled about three hundred calories. The muscle on her body went soft since her stomach had no fat left because her stomach was eating it. Her backbone showed through the back of her shirt when she would wear tight clothes. Tessa saw that Aurora was on the brink of dying from her starving herself, and she was already skinny.

"You look terribly ill, Aurora. I am going to take you to the hospital."

"You can't," Aurora said. "I have to work tomorrow."

"I think your boss will understand."

"No. He won't," Aurora said. "He never cares about these things or cares about his employees, even though I run his magazine."

"Okay then," Tessa said. "If he needs you that bad, then he will not fire you for missing one or two days."

"Fine, you can take me." Tessa went to Aurora's room and helped her pack an overnight bag. "I am worried I am going to die." Aurora broke down in tears.

"You were beginning to scare me with not eating," Tessa said. She and Aurora were on the way to the hospital. "Well, I mean not being able to eat."

"I have just been tortured for weeks by the thought of how I put up with all of what he did. I am madder at myself than anyone else. I was such an idiot. Why did I ever marry him or put myself in this situation? Why did I say yes to him in that stupid airport?"

"Aurora, you will be fine. I promise," Tessa said. "Besides, you have me again, and I am not going anywhere."

"That is true," Aurora said. "You are someone who is not feeding me, per se, but feeding my soul."

"What is that?"

"Well, I know I have to be stronger to get back at him. Gannon keeps trying to contact me, but I ignore his calls, voicemails, texts, and Facebook messages."

"Why didn't you tell me this?"

"I don't know. I just enjoy torturing him for my own benefit," Aurora said. "I want him to know I am ignoring him because out of everything in the world, Gannon hates nothing more than being ignored or not being in control."

"Does it actually make you feel better?" Tessa asked.

"I want to feel better about this, but I can't. I feel nothing, Tessa."

# Chapter 6

Aurora was in the hospital for a week. She got on some new medication and saw a counselor while she was there, and they put her in contact with a domestic abuse center that helped people who went through what Aurora did. The center was Domestic Abuse Intervention Services, a non-profit organization in Madison, known as DAIS.

DAIS was important to Aurora because she started to meet with a support group from the organization, which was one of the many services they offered.

--

A few days after getting out of the hospital, while Aurora was engulfed in her work, a mutual friend of Aurora and Gannon's reached out to Aurora. He was tall and slim with green eyes and sun-kissed skin. Melih, pronounced Mel-lee, would come over for house parties at Aurora and Gannon's townhouse on occasion, but would never drink. He was from Istanbul, a highly populated city in Turkey. Though some people from Turkey did not practice Islam, Melih did. He liked the spirituality that religion made him feel and he thought alcohol would get in the way of that. Many people respected him for it. Aurora always did. She respected it more after the doctor she was seeing, after she left the hospital, told her to stop drinking with her anxiety medication.

Melih called Aurora before lunch.

"Hey, Melih." *Hmm... I wonder why he's calling.*

"Hello, Aurora," Melih said. "How are you?" When he talked, it sounded mellifluous, as if honey were dripping from his lips. Whenever he would say a vowel, it sounded similar to a French melody in your ear. His words were soft, but with a strong undertone. Aurora thought he had a lovely accent when he spoke.

"I am fine," Aurora said. "How are you?"

"I am good," Melih said. "I'm on my lunch break now." He was a successful petroleum engineer.

"Oh, nice. Me too." She said as she stared at her small bottle of nutritional protein she had been sipping on since the morning.

"Dat is good. I am sorry for vhat Gannon did, but I have to say, I'm not surprised he did it."

"That doesn't make me feel better."

"It really upset me the way I saw Gannon treat you at your house that night you vere going to play guitar for us," Melih said. "I am sure you remember."

"Unfortunately, yes, I do." Aurora sighed.

What Melih said reminded Aurora of that night. She had tried to get everyone to snap their fingers to the same beat, but it was a struggle for everyone to get the beat down.

"Aurora, you're horrible. Just stop," Gannon said bluntly. Everyone stared at Gannon. The room became quiet.

"But I just want everyone to –" Aurora started, her voice barely a whisper.

Gannon cut her off, "Aurora, don't make me repeat myself. Just stop."

Aurora inhaled a big gulp. A tear fell down Aurora's face and she felt the hair rise on her arm.

Everyone urged her to keep going, but she was already too

embarrassed.

She swallowed her pain and tears like she always did from Gannon.

Melih continued the phone conversation, "Vell, before that, he was so focused on the girls arriving, as vell." Aurora rolled her eyes

Melih continued, "He kept telling me to keep calling the girls because he was eager for them to arrive." Aurora recalled that one of the girls was Shazzy.

"Well," Aurora said. "That makes sense."

"How is dat?"

"Well, my mom always says, 'love is blind, but the neighbors aren't,'" Aurora said. "I finally know what she means."

"I guess so."

"Yeah."

"I have to tell you some-ting," Melih said. "I vanted to tell you for a vhile."

"What's that, Melih?"

Aurora's heart started to beat fast. She thought Gannon had done something else. She felt a knot in her stomach.

Tiffany knocked on Aurora's office door. "Ms. Tousey, you have a work lunch to get to."

"Vhat?" Melih said.

"Oh, I am sorry!" Aurora said. "I have to go. I am late for a meeting. Talk later?"

"Okay, dhen," Melih said.

--

She expected that Melih would tell her something horrible. Though, Aurora thought it was hard to top all of the things

Gannon had already done. She assumed Gannon had been cheating on her for a while, and Melih would break the news to her. Aurora wasn't sure why she cared so much. *Do I enjoy this pain? I don't understand.*

Aurora wanted to forget about Gannon, but she knew she would have to go through with the divorce eventually. She knew she couldn't go back to Gannon. The divorce wouldn't be too hard on legal terms because they got a prenuptial agreement before the wedding. Gannon was from old southern money and Aurora was from a working-class family. Though Aurora didn't want his money, she signed it to prove to him and his family that she loved him for him.

# Chapter 7

Aurora started to move on with her life and forget about Gannon. She was still staying with Tessa. Aurora would spend most nights reading by herself or watching romantic comedies on Netflix with Tessa. She had seen every single one, even the one-star movies. She was trying to distract herself as best as she could. She wanted to message her friend Melih to see what he wanted to tell her, but she didn't want to pry or annoy him. She also realized that if it was any information about Gannon cheating, it would only make things worse and all of her progress would be purposeless.

Aurora had not been out in weeks since she found Gannon with Shazzy, until one afternoon when Tessa sent a text to Aurora while Aurora was at her desk editing an article for her magazine. She kept staring at her protein shake on her desk and forcing herself to drink it. *I am so sick of the taste of this*, she thought as she swallowed down the lukewarm butter pecan-flavored drink. She heard her phone ding.

"Hey, you want to go out tonight?" Tessa said.

"No, not really…"

Aurora thought about how she had been sulking for months and wanted to dress up and feel pretty again. *What do I have to lose?*

Aurora took another sip of her protein shake.

Aurora hesitated, "You know what, yeah, let's go out, but I want to remind you that I cannot drink alcohol because the doctor said it does not mix well with my anxiety medicine."

The day went on, and Aurora kept thinking about how ugly she was. She wasn't confident at all. Gannon had made her feel like she was so ugly and fat. She thought since she saw herself that way, the rest of the world did too.

Aurora went to the bathroom later that day after her lunch break. The tiles on the wall were black, but the lighting was very bright. While was washing her hands in the sink, she looked at her face closely in the mirror. She then pulled back her cheeks. *Wow. These bright lights in here hide no flaws.* She let out a large sigh.

She stared at the bags under her eyes. She got depressed about how thin she was. *Why did I let a man do this to me?* She then unbuttoned her suit coat and could see her ribs through her shirt. She started to cry. *I do not even know who I am looking at anymore. Who am I? What have I become?* She thought she was seeing a skeleton in the mirror. She immediately regretted telling Tessa she wanted to go out with her that night. She first grabbed some tissues to dry her tears.

Aurora called Tessa while she was still in the bathroom, looking at her reflection in the mirror.

"Tessa."

"Yes, Aurora?"

"I don't think tonight is good for me," Aurora said.

"No way!" Tessa said. "You said you were free tonight! You told me yesterday."

*Crap.*

"Uh." Aurora said. "I forgot I have a business meeting tonight." She looked at the coffee stain on her shirt in the mirror.

"Dude, no you don't," Tessa said. "Let's go out. Please. You need this. I am sick of seeing you so unhappy."

"Fine," Aurora said. "I am just…"

"Just what?" Tessa said.

"Sad."

"Come on, Aurora."

Aurora looked at herself again and lifted up her shirt and saw that one of the old bruises Gannon left was finally gone.

"You know what," Aurora said. "I just don't feel beautiful today." She tried to put her hair behind her ears.

"You are gorgeous!"

"You are just saying that because I am your best friend. So your opinion is biased."

"It may be biased, but I am not wrong," Tessa said. "How about this? I do your makeup and your hair tonight and we can go to that Korean place tonight!"

"Okay. Fine," Aurora said. "You win." *This will be the first time I eat an actual meal in God knows how long...*

"No, we both win. I promise you will have fun tonight."

"Okay then. I have to get back to work."

"Okay!" Tessa said. "I will see you after work."

--

Aurora got home from work and saw Tessa on the couch. Above the couch, there was a collage of Aurora and Tessa on the wall. Aurora was cheesy, so she loved to get cheesy gifts like that for people. Tessa owned a small two-bedroom townhouse in the outer suburbs of Madison. The kitchen was at the entrance. Also by the entrance was the kitchen table, which Tessa and Aurora used as a makeshift shelf to place their things. It was just far more convenient than getting an actual shelf to hold their keys and purses. Tessa loved to sit on the couch in the small living room after work and watch *Gilmore Girls* while sipping on a cup of coffee. Tessa was always so relaxed but peppy at the same time, and she didn't even smoke weed. However, Tessa was also very blunt.

Tessa said in her peppy voice as she saw Aurora come through the front door, "Heyyyy. Excited for tonight?"

"Ecstatic."

"Really?" Tessa asked.

"No. Not one bit," Aurora said as she took off her jacket. "You should know my sarcasm by now."

Aurora set down her things on the table and sat on the couch. "I don't know what to wear tonight."

"This is exciting!" Tessa said.

"Really?" Aurora said. "Well, of course it is for you! You love choosing outfits for people to wear."

People dressing was a hobby of Tessa's. It could have been a profession for her because she was so good at it, but she said she would rather be a dentist because she "loves teeth." She had a nice bright white smile, too. Aurora didn't know how Tessa's teeth never stained from all the coffee she drank.

"Okay," Tessa said. "Just don't get used to it."

"Do you have any black shirts?" Tessa said.

"Maybe like one. I always wear blue," Aurora said. "You know that."

"Okay, you can borrow one of my shirts. You should always have at least one black shirt. I'll even do your hair, but you have to do your own makeup."

"Uh... But I haven't worn makeup in months." Aurora used to love doing her makeup before Gannon made her stop. She thought it always expressed who she was without her having to say a word. "You know what. It will be fun to do my own makeup. Though I am sure if I do winged eyeliner it'll look more like more like squiggly lines a child drew." They both laughed.

"That is what I like to hear. You are at least happy to do your own makeup," Tessa said. "Now let us go pick out one of your outfits."

"Okay, mom," Aurora said, and then Tessa rolled her eyes at her.

Tessa did a blowout to her hair and Aurora's. Aurora was worried she looked like she was some model you'd find from an old 80's magazine. They both had on jeans and black three-quarter-sleeve shirts. They both looked hot. Aurora had put on gold eyeshadow and winged eyeliner. Nonetheless, Aurora was feeling pretty and feeling herself that night.

Aurora and Tessa decided to have dinner first before going out. They drove into the city and parked next to Aurora's office. They walked to their favorite Korean restaurant. They tried to walk everywhere as much as possible since it was a cheap form of exercise and burning off the huge amount of food they would eat. Aurora ordered the bibimbap, which was her favorite dish. She hadn't eaten it in so long, so it tasted amazing to her. Tessa would get her usual, the chicken katsu.

After dinner, they went to their favorite club in Madison called The Old Fashion. The décor reminded you of a speakeasy from the 1920s. There were leather booths and mahogany-colored curtains draped over the windows. The dance floor was made out of wood. They knew the drinks were always good and there were good-looking guys, which was the welcomed distraction Aurora needed. Aurora didn't really drink because it didn't mix well with her recent PTSD medicine she started taking, but seeing some hot men was just what the doctor ordered. The club was the hotspot for staffers from the state capital and lawyers from around town. This was the perfect place for successful and good-looking men. So Aurora and Tessa knew that there was no doubt Gannon would not be there.

Tessa and Aurora sat at the bar. Aurora's first drink was a virgin mojito. Tessa's drink was an old fashioned because that was the specialty at the bar. Frank Sinatra's song "The Way You Look Tonight" was playing in the background. It was swing music night.

Aurora and Tessa sat and talked with each other for a while about life while they scoped out the attractive men, though their talking seemed more like screaming because it was so loud inside. Aurora kept stirring her drink with a short black straw.

"Do you think that guy over there is cute?" Tessa asked. Aurora looked up.

"Really? To be honest?" Aurora said. "I am not interested in looking."

"Just look over there!" Tessa said. "It will not hurt you."

"Fine," Aurora said as she turned her head and locked eyes with the guy. She started to laugh. "Ha! Do you mean Mr. Jersey Shore over there?"

"Don't stare, Aurora!" Tessa said. "I meant the blonde guy next to him."

The two guys were now staring at Aurora and Tessa.

"Is Jersey Shore really walking towards us?" Aurora and Tessa looked at each other with deer-in-the-headlights looks. "Great. I unchained the beast."

"Crap!" Tessa said. "Let's pretend we didn't see him."

"Tessa, he looks like a guy who spends a couple of hours a day at the gym but definitely misses leg day."

He was attractive, but his bulging muscles overshadowed his face as if he had no neck. Aurora wondered how he could fit his arms through the shirtsleeves.

Aurora said in Tessa's ear, "He seriously looks like he just got out of the Jersey Shore and fell asleep in a tanning bed."

"He is right behind us, isn't he?" Tessa said as she felt the muscular man with a buzz cut approach them. "Crap."

"See," Aurora said. "This is why I didn't want to look."

The guy said, "Hey, where are your boyfriends?"

Aurora said, "We don't have any." *What? Why did I say that?*

The guy seemed excited and acted like he had won the jackpot. "What are your names?" he asked. "I'm Eric."

Aurora spoke because Tessa was the shy one when it came to talking to men. Aurora was never shy because she had always been in a relationship and didn't care if she embarrassed herself.

Aurora said, "I am Tanya, and this is my friend Veronica."

One thing that Aurora would do if she went out with anyone was use the name "Tanya." She never wanted anyone to know her real name. Aurora and Tessa would both use fake names, because if a "bro" asked them for their names, they would do it without hesitation, as if they knew what each other was thinking.

"Nice to meet you, pretty ladies." He then pulled his friend over. "This is my friend Jack."

Jack was easy on the eyes. He had blonde hair and a bright white smile. Though it was dark in the club, it seemed like he had brown eyes. He had to keep putting his fingers through his hair to push it out of his face. He was tall and skinny. *He definitely looks like a staffer from the capital.* He was definitely a politician type. Jack and Eric seemed completely opposite. Aurora wondered how they could have become friends. She then chuckled out loud.

"Hey," Jack said nervously.

Aurora raised her eyebrows, "Hey, what are you guys doing here tonight? Trying to find some chicks to take home?"

She laughed awkwardly to herself. *Wow. You are so smooth Aurora. Not...*

"No, my pal Jack just got out of a relationship," Eric said, "We are trying to find him a pretty girl to talk to."

Jack nudged Eric with his elbow and said in his ear, "Why did you tell them that?" It seemed Eric wasn't all that intelligent, and that Jack was the brain in their friendship.

Jack looked toward the girls. "Well, yeah, I did just get out of a relationship, but I am here to have fun."

Jack looked in Aurora's eyes, "What's your name?"

"Ahhh. Tanya."

"Wow, your name is almost as beautiful as you."

Aurora rolled her eyes, "I am sure you use that on every pretty girl." She put her hand to her mouth in dismay. *Oh! I just called myself pretty!* She smiled.

Jack said, "No, just to you. To be honest, I have been out of the game for a while. I don't know what girls like anymore."

"Well, I am a woman, so...."

"Ohhhhh, you are confident! I like that. How about we both stop talking and go dance?"

She shrugged her shoulders and remembered how unhappy she was when she looked at herself in the mirror earlier that day. *I guess I have nothing to lose. I mean, he seems awkward like me. I cannot let these moments keep passing me by unless I want to die old and alone.*

"Let me ask my friend first." Aurora could hear Eric and Tessa talking about working out. Tessa did not look too thrilled at the conversation. Tessa waved her hand at the bartender for another drink. Tessa kept looking down at her drink and stirring it.

Aurora tapped Tessa on the shoulder. "Is it okay if I go dance?"

AFTER SHE SAID YES

"Yeah, sure. I'll find you if I need saving." They both laughed. "Which will be pretty likely."

Aurora and Jack went dancing on the dance floor. Jack had to be over six feet, and Aurora was just over five feet. She was grateful she wore her dress boots that had a three-inch heel that night. They tried to dance, but it was extremely awkward because it seemed like Jack had two left feet.

Aurora felt someone who wasn't Jack grab her hand and pull her. She couldn't see who it was at first. Then she realized who it was.

*It's Melih? Oh my God. It's Melih dancing with me!*

She was shocked because she thought it was out of Melih's character to do something like that, but she liked it. She felt like a schoolgirl as the feeling of electricity ran through her veins. Her heart started to beat fast and her breaths became shorter and shorter. Melih's hands were warm and soft. His grip was strong but gentle. He interlocked his fingers with hers. His cologne and sweat smell was intoxicating to her. She looked up at him and smiled as she stared at his lips. *Is this really Melih? But he is too hot for me! He is Gannon's friend.*

"Hey!" Jack said as he pulled on Melih's arm. "I was dancing with her!"

"It's okay," Aurora said as she touched Jack's forearm. "He's my friend. Give me a minute."

"Sure," Jack said as he rolled his eyes. He stood there for a second and slowly walked away. Melih grabbed Aurora's hand tighter. He then started to spin Aurora.

"Well, hello Melih." She looked up into his eyes and smiled as she saw the lights reflected off of his eyes. She had never seen him like that before.

Melih still hadn't said a word. He just kept dancing with her. Melih was a great dancer and light on his feet. When he was a teenager, he had sneaked out of his home at night to attend ballroom dancing classes. That and he always wanted to be a whirling dervish as a child.

"What did you want to tell me the other day?" Aurora said.

Melih twirled her around his hand and pulled her close. "It vasn't about Gannon," he said.

*Finally, he said something!*

Melih said, "Rora, I am shy to say."

Aurora replied, "Don't be shy. What's up?"

"Rora…. I can't," Melih said. "You are Gannon's girl."

"What? I am not with him anymore. I am divorcing him."

"Really? He is telling everyone you are getting back together."

"Absolutely not!" Aurora yelled over the music in the background. "I have been ignoring all of his calls, texts, and messages for over a month now." Blood rushed to her cheeks. *Why does he care, anyway?*

Melih seemed confused. "Calm down. Rora." *I am calm. I am just anxious.* "It's okay, but it's weird he is saying dat. I am relieved you are not staying together. I hate Gannon for vhat he did to you. I can't hang out vith him anymore. He sickens me."

"You and me both," Aurora said.

Melih didn't even know everything that Gannon had done to her. He only saw the bare minimum of who Gannon really was.

Aurora gave Melih puppy dog eyes and said, "Is that what you wanted to tell me, Melih?"

"No."

"Why did you tell me this?" she said louder over the music. "Then what is it?"

"It is da same-ding I should have told you years ago," Melih said. "You know you vere my first friend vhen I came here to college."

"Okay. And?" Aurora said.

After Melih didn't respond, Aurora said, "Well?"

"Uh, vell…" Melih hesitated. I should have told you sooner. I feel guilty for not telling you because I could have saved you from marrying dat idiot."

"Tell me what, Melih?"

"What did Gannon do?" Aurora asked. "Or is it about Shazzy?"

"No."

"Did you want to tell me something else?" Aurora said.

Tessa grabbed Aurora, interrupting her and Melih, "Hey, that guy Eric was so lame."

Tessa checked out Melih from head to toe. "Who's this?"

"This is my friend," Aurora said. "My friend, Melih."

Tessa had never met any of Aurora and Gannon's friends because they would never invite her over. It was not Aurora's choice. Gannon hated Tessa, but he hated most people who loved Aurora and could see through his facade of a personality, which got in the way of his controlling Aurora.

Tessa said, "Aurora, let's go somewhere else."

Aurora said to Melih, "I'd asked you to join us, but it's just us ladies hanging out tonight."

Melih said, "I understand. I am here vith friends anyway."

"Well, message me sometime. You got my number." She rolled her eyes at herself. *How cheesy of a thing to say, Aurora. Wait, was that cheesy?*

"Okay, I will," Melih said as he walked away and waved. "Have a good night."

Aurora and Tessa left the club. Aurora didn't even say bye to Jack because she was in a state of euphoria. Her confidence level was high after going out that night. She was shocked she was getting positive attention from guys, especially from Melih. *That came out of left field.* Not only did Melih save her from Jack's two left feet, but he also saved her from worrying about what Gannon had done. Wherever else Aurora and Tessa went that night, it would not distract her from thinking about Melih.

# Chapter 8

Aurora had a lot to do at work for the coming month. She had a big gala coming up for her magazine, which they had every year since the magazine had started three years prior. They would choose a charity organization that they would team up with to raise money.

One morning, Tiffany knocked on Aurora's office door as Aurora was digging in her desk drawer looking for some lead to put in her mechanical pencil.

"Ms. Tousey?" Tiffany said, but it was muffled because the door was closed.

"Yes," Aurora said as she was still scavenging.

"May I come in?"

"Yes."

"Ms. Tousey, I had a question."

"Ha! Found it!" Aurora said as she pulled the lead from a tiny plastic box in the drawer.

"Excuse me?" Tiffany said.

"Sorry, I was looking for some pencil lead and I finally found it," Aurora said as she said up straight. "What is your question?"

"Well," Tiffany said. "I was writing up the talking points you gave me for the meeting."

"Okay?"

"Well, could you tell me a little bit more about why you want DAIS?"

"Why? What is everyone saying?"

"Well, uh," Tiffany said. "I am just curious."

The choices were between the non-profit organizations Domestic Abuse Intervention Services, known as DAIS. The second was the Center for Resilient Cities, which focused on providing clean water and food to everyone in need in Madison.

DAIS was important to Aurora because she was abused herself and met with a support group from DAIS, which was one of the many services they offered. Still, no one at work knew that Gannon had abused her. The people who were on the committee to choose the non-profit organization narrowed it down to two organizations. So naturally, Aurora wanted DAIS.

"I have insisted several times that I just really believe in their organization." *I will never mention that they are helping me to get over my abusive relationship and childhood.*

"I know, but…"

"If you must know, it is because I have a friend from college who was in an abusive relationship and they helped her a lot. I saw firsthand the work that they are doing," Aurora said. "A-a-and I volunteer, as well."

"All right," Tiffany said. "That is what I will tell them?"

"Tell who?" Aurora asked.

"I mean if Mr. Fratzenberg asks, or anyone at the meeting asks."

"Okay."

"Well, that's all I wanted to know," Tiffany said as she left.

Later on that day, Aurora went out to talk with Tiffany at her desk when she overheard her staff whispering about something. She overheard some staff talking about how everyone thought it was weird for how passionate Aurora was about the organization.

"I am thirsty," Aurora said. "I'm going to get some water." Aurora's face got red after hearing the other colleagues talking.

Aurora walked over by the water cooler in her office building to fill up her water bottle.

"Oh...." Aurora cleared her throat to let them know that she was there. "Don't let me interrupt whatever you were talking about." The people talking flinched in awe.

"We are sorry, Ms. Tousey. We didn't see you there," one of them said with a hesitation in their voice.

"We didn't mean to upset you," they continued.

"Oh. I am not upset," she said as her voice cracked and her cheeks flushed with red. "Why would I be upset?"

"Oh, nothing..." All of their faces became red and they all dispersed back to their cubicles.

She smiled at them and quickly stomped back to her office. *If only they knew what was going on with me, then they wouldn't need to gossip. No, wait. They would probably gossip more. Especially since I lost all this weight, too. I can't win.*

Since Aurora was in a place of power, she wanted to have others believe in DAIS, too. The only powerful person she was up against was her boss. His thick, wispy gray hair and strong jawline reminded her of George Clooney. He had the confidence that made you doubt your own self. The French cufflinks he always wore on the cuffs of his shirt under his suit sleeves were silver and engraved with the letter *F*, in old-fashioned calligraphy, which stood for Fratzenburg. You could tell the links had been passed down into his family for generations. She would always refer to him as Mr. Fratzenburg because he wanted it that way. It was as if he didn't have a first name.

The magazine was one of the many businesses that he owned. He didn't know the first thing about articles or writing, but he was an entrepreneur and businessman. So he knew money. The magazine was a gold mine for advertising, but usually, he was "too busy" to meet with Aurora whenever she wanted to meet with him. He treated his employees like peasants. So, Aurora knew it would be hard to persuade him.

She met with him in the conference room later that afternoon. The table was long with a glass top and Mr. Fratzenberg sat at the end of the table looking out the window with his legs crossed.

"So, Aurora, tell me why you think we should choose this?" Mr. Fratzenberg said.

"Well," Aurora said. "It is a place I have been volunteering at."

"And?" He said as he looked at her.

"Well, I know someone who was personally abused," Aurora said. "My best friend, actually."

"What?" Mr. Fratzenberg said.

"And when my best friend was going through this, she had no one to turn to. She was scared, and lost, and felt so alone. She couldn't even tell me."

Mr. Fratzenberg started to look intrigued as he said, "Continue."

"Well, if she had known about DAIS," Aurora said, "maybe she would have reached out to them to get help sooner." *If only he knew I was talking about myself...*

"But she got help eventually?"

"Well, yes," Aurora said. "She did eventually, and left the loser."

"But why DAIS?"

"Why not?" Aurora said.

"Okay. Today I am in a good mood," he said as he put his fingers through his gray hair. "Whatever you like then, Ms.

Tousey."

"Also," Aurora said, "I have seen some of these women at DAIS and I have heard their stories. This shelter would be an amazing thing."

"Okay. Okay. I get it," Mr. Fratzenberg said. "Let us go with that one then."

"Thank you."

"So," Mr. Fratzenberg said. "What will they do with the money we raise?"

"Well," Aurora said, "they have mentioned to me that they are looking for money for a new abused and battered women's shelter they were hoping to open."

"Okay then. Anything else you would like to talk about?" Mr. Fratzenberg said as he looked down at his Rolex to check the time.

"No."

"D-A-Y-S it is."

"It is D-A-I-S."

"It's okay," Mr. Fratzenberg said. "You know what I meant."

"Since you are here, I have one more thing to talk about," Aurora said. "I thought I would mention a pay raise."

"Well," he said, "let us not get ahead of ourselves."

"Right." *Things would be different if I were a man asking for a raise. I will just keep writing and editing about fake happy lifestyles while you make all of the money for it. I just want to write about something real.*

# Chapter 9

*Talking about the abuse at DAIS and telling them about my story indirectly made me realize how bad I want to move on with my life and get on with the divorce. Aurora, this is consuming your life.* She wanted to file the divorce jointly, but Gannon refused to sign the papers. She had to file for divorce on her own. She probably didn't need a lawyer for that, but she didn't have time to deal with all that drama in between work. She had his divorce papers served to him when he was at a work meeting. *That will get his attention.*

Before meeting with Gannon and his lawyer, Aurora met the lawyer at his office a few minutes earlier. Her lawyer, Erik Wulfblitzen, had a monotone voice. It seemed as if all of the emotions he had were drained from him. He was tall, and had gray wispy hair that resembled strands of silver thread.

"Why do divorces in this state have to be so messy?" Aurora asked.

"So lawyers have a job." Aurora gave him a stern look. Erik said as he hid his smirk, "Just kidding."

"It's fine," Aurora said. "I just feel this is dragging on forever." Once you filed the divorce papers, you had to wait one hundred and twenty days until your court date.

"So, when I am divorced, I have to wait six months before I can marry anyone again?"

"That is correct." She didn't expect to get married any time soon after divorcing Gannon. She just didn't want that looming over her head. She wanted to have him out of her life completely.

"That law is a bit outdated. Don't you think?"

"Maybe," Erik said, "but that is the law."

"So," Aurora said, "is there anything I should know beforehand?"

"No, this is pretty straight forward."

"He barely made anything in our marriage. I made and paid for everything. I know he has money, but he will not get it until his parents pass," Aurora said.

Erik opened his binder and looked through his notes and flipped through papers. Then he looked back at Aurora.

"Are you sure you don't want anything?" he said.

"I am sure," Aurora said. "He treated me like crap. I don't want anything from him. I feel it will all be tainted."

"Okay," Erik said. "You realize there is no going back, right?"

"I know. I'm sorry to spring this on you," Aurora said. "I didn't know that I wanted this until I just walked into your office.

Erik's assistant knocked and came in. "Your three o'clock is here."

"Okay," Erik said. "Send them in."

Aurora saw Gannon walk in, and she felt as if a black hole sucked all of her soul from her body. She gulped down a breath of air.

"So," Gannon's lawyer said. His name was Maxwell Redding, and Aurora thought he was similar to her lawyer, but he was younger and had blonde hair gelled and combed to one side. "Are we here today to discuss financial matters?"

"No," Aurora said.

Aurora's lawyer glared at her and whispered, "Aurora, let me do the talking."

"So why are we here?" his lawyer said. *We are here so I can prove to Gannon I am serious about divorce.*

"Well," Erik said.

"I have one question," Gannon said. Aurora's chest got tight as she took in a deep breath. "I want to know if in those six months, if Aurora and I decide to get back together, will that cancel the divorce?"

"Are you delusional?" Aurora asked.

"No, I just…" Gannon said.

"We are here today just so I can prove to you I am serious about divorce. I want to show you that you lost the best thing that has ever happened to you," Aurora said as she turned to her lawyer. "Are we done here?" Gannon's eyes grew big as he became shocked that Aurora was sticking up for herself.

"Well, I guess we…." Erik said.

"Okay, good," Aurora said as she got up to storm out of the office.

"Wait, Mrs. Tousey," Gannon's lawyer said. "We have further things to discuss."

"What do you mean?" Aurora said.

"Why don't you take a seat?" Mr. Redding said.

"I'd appreciate that you wouldn't tell me what to do," Aurora said.

"Fine," he responded.

"So," Aurora said as she sat down. "Do you mind telling me what you would like to say?"

"I would like to talk about the dowry clause in your pre-nuptial agreement," Gannon's lawyer said.

"The what?" Aurora said as she looked at her lawyer and whispered, "What does he mean? A dowry?"

"Why didn't you tell me this?" Erik said as he whispered to Aurora.

"I didn't know!"

Mr. Redding handed them all copies. Aurora read over what was in front of her. In despair, she sank back in her chair. *I feel like such an idiot. I thought this was a marriage license...*

"Look on page 8," Mr. Redding said as everyone turned to page 8.

"As you see here, it states that if the two parties do not conceive a child and heir to the McMaster estate, then the wife is subject to pay a dowry of fifty percent of all of their assets to the other spouse."

"What?" Aurora said. "I don't remember signing or reading this!"

"Your signature is on the bottom of the page, Mrs. Tousey," Mr. Redding said as Gannon slouched back in his chair and looked down.

"But I thought it was some marriage contract or something." She looked at Gannon with fire in her eyes. "Is this why you never wanted to have kids, Gannon?" Aurora turned to her lawyer. "You know what, scratch what I said about not needing to do anything about this divorce settlement. I will be contesting this prenuptial agreement."

"On what grounds?" Mr. Redding said.

"Please let me take this from here," Aurora's lawyer said. "From what I just heard from Mrs. Tousey now, she didn't know about this agreement. So just off of that, as you know, Mr. Redding, Wisconsin law states that a pre-nup is not enforceable when the terms of the agreement are biased in either party's favor."

"Okay," Mr. Redding said. "So, you want to contest it. What grounds do you have? Maybe she is not telling the truth."

"I am not lying! When I walked in here today, I didn't want

anything from him. I didn't even want to see him."

Erik cleared his throat to draw the attention to himself. "The pre-nup obviously favors one spouse," Erik said. "Also, Mrs. Tousey did not have a lawyer present, nor was she given the option to have one, as this prenuptial agreement was drawn up on the day of their wedding. In addition, I am sure there has to be something else in here," he said as he flipped through the pre-nup pages. "Well, I don't know now, but I will find it."

"Well, I guess we will be fighting this in court," Mr. Redding said.

--

A big gust of wind hit Aurora in the face as soon as she opened the door to walk to the parking lot. The wind sounded like Mother Nature was whistling. She quickly looked for her leather gloves in her purse. After the meeting with their lawyers, Gannon wanted to talk to Aurora.

As she looked up, she saw Gannon walking fast towards her. Her heart beat fast and adrenaline ran through her veins. She thought he was going to attack her, as she was used to when he would walk fast towards her.

After the lawyers left, Gannon was crying in the parking lot until he saw Aurora and yelled, "Baby, don't do this." Gannon stuttered, "I-I-I love you so much. You keep ignoring my calls and messages. I can't stop thinking 'bout you. Why would you leave me like this?" *I just want him to suffer like he made me suffer.*

Aurora hated confrontation, but she was getting frustrated at this point. "Gannon, we are done," Aurora said. "So, is your love for me your wanting me to pay you half of everything I have?"

"Aurora," Gannon said. "It is my parents. You know we are old southern money."

"If you are old southern money, then why do you need mine?"

"Come on now, Aurora," Gannon said. "You know that was my mother's idea."

"You are not royalty, Gannon," Aurora said. "Dowries like the one in that pre-nup are for royalty. You are far from it."

Gannon tried to get closer and touch her face. She flinched and threw his hand off of her. It brought back the trauma from one of the times he had slapped her so hard that he bruised her cheek.

Aurora raised her voice, as she started listing off things with her fingers: "One, you flushed my phone down the toilet. Two, even though they are crazy, you never let me see my family. Three, you abused me for months and constantly left bruises on me. Do not forget the time you kicked my desk chair out from underneath me and bruised my whole left hip. It took months for that bruise to go away. Four, you made me want to kill myself all of the time, and I have not felt that way since I left you. Five, you made me feel like I was the problem, Gannon. I am not the problem, Gannon. You are. We are done."

Aurora turned her back on him and began to walk to her car. She didn't want to give him a moment to respond.

"Rora, I'm sorry. I never meant to hurt you like I did. I gave up everything for you. Why would you leave me? I only agreed to meet today so I could see you." Aurora rolled her eyes as she walked towards her car and put on her leather gloves.

Aurora did not fall for his sweet talk for another second. That southern charm no longer worked on her. Something made her stop in her tracks as she was walking away. She didn't want him to say the last word.

She turned around and took a deep breath. "You didn't give up anything for me." She raised her voice and said, "I gave up everything for you, Gannon! You manipulated me to stay with you. I never knew who you really were before I married you. You abused me mentally, emotionally, and physically. How many times do I have to point these things out to you?"

Gannon gritted his teeth and knitted his eyebrows together as he said, "Yeah, I hit you sometimes, but you made me do it. Any man would hit a woman like you. I was never like that before I met you."

Aurora laughed hysterically. She wasn't going to give attention to what he had said, like you ignore a child after they have misbehaved. Aurora went silent and her words were monotone as she said, "Okay, Gannon. That is why we are getting a divorce. Because of the woman I am. Now leave me alone. I am leaving."

Aurora almost turned around again as Gannon said, "Rora, no! I am sorry. I didn't mean it. I am just p-p-pissed." He was acting like a child who lost his toy.

Aurora had enough of what was coming out of his mouth. She had no reason to listen to him or put up with what he had to say anymore. Aurora threw her hands up. She was fed up. She turned and looked at him again.

"Gannon, I am done," Aurora screamed. "Gannon, I hate you! Leave me alone!" Aurora turned her back and walked briskly to her car, almost running. She could feel Gannon running behind her, like the devil was chasing her.

"Are you going to try to abuse me in the parking lot?" Aurora said. "Come and try it!"

She ran to her car and slammed her car door, almost

breaking Gannon's hand by closing it. Gannon kept tapping on the window, screaming that he was sorry. Aurora started her car, pressed the gas, and drove away. Snow and a salty, icy slush flew up from under Aurora's tires and covered Gannon. She drove away as fast as she could and saw Gannon in the rearview mirror fall to his knees.

She started to cry. *You finally did it, Aurora. You finally confronted him.* She wiped the tears from her salty rose-colored cheeks. She was scared from her confrontation with Gannon, but proud she had stuck up for herself. She was happy the marriage was almost over.

Aurora was still surprised how her relationship with Gannon was so perfect before marriage. *Now how will I ever be able to trust again or feel safe with any man?*

Aurora thought back to her wedding day with Gannon. It made her even more upset and filled her eyes with more tears.

# Chapter 10

It was the week of the big gala charity event, and Aurora was extremely busy. In between Aurora's working and the divorce, she could not stop thinking about Melih. She couldn't stop thinking about how he pulled her close that night at the club. *Did I do something wrong that he hasn't talked to me since?*

Though Melih would not message, Gannon would not stop. He was relentless and kept sending the same messages along the lines of, "Don't do this, Aurora. Don't leave me. I promise I will change." *Blah. Blah. Blah.*

The food vendor pulled out last minute because the head chef accidently cut off one of his fingers. Aurora scrambled to find a new vendor on such short notice. She was supposed to have a beautiful elegant French meal, but she ended up catering the event with food from her favorite restaurant on State Street, Crandall's Peruvian Bistro. After big tests in college, she would always splurge by taking herself out to Crandall's. She would order their ceviche as an appetizer and delicious Peruvian meat stir-fry, called Lomo Saltado, as her entree.

It was an all-white dress code at the botanical gardens in Madison. Those gardens were where Aurora would go to read in the fall or just take a stroll in the spring to see the beautiful flowers bloom. They were lovely, as always, though during the gala they were covered in snow. Lights hung from posts and along the walking paths. Couples were walking outside side-by-side and holding hands to keep warm, while waiting for the event to start.

Aurora had decided to wear a classy white pants suit. She thought if Hillary Clinton could pull off a white pants suit, she could as well. Aurora had her hair in a nice updo and was wearing the pearl necklace her grandma had given her.

The hall where the gala was taking place looked like a winter wonderland. The tables were round with white tablecloths and white chairs. The centerpieces were short circular vases filled with water and tea light candles floating on the water's surface.

The event started, and Aurora made her introduction and shared a story of a woman who had gained help through DAIS. She actually told her own story, but no one knew that.

After her introduction, she had to talk to a few of the donors: college presidents and professionals from around the city. However, she just wanted to enjoy her sixty-five-dollar-per-plate-meal.

After thirty minutes of schmoozing and standing, she finally sat at a table in the back corner and relaxed.

At Aurora's table was a handsome man. He was wearing a white tux, like most of the men there, and appeared to be a few inches taller than she was. He didn't look like he had the best posture either, or maybe he was just bored. He had dirty blonde hair with it combed to one side, and he had a nice physique. It seemed to Aurora like he was slowly balding but still trying to look edgy, though he looked great in that tux. He kept looking at Aurora and smiling as he pushed up his Ray-Ban black rimmed glasses up on the slope of his button nose. Aurora thought he was cute in a nerdy way.

Aurora looked up at him and saw him leaving his chair to sit in the empty chair next to her.

"Hello," he said as he put out his hand for a handshake. "I

am Jason Waters, Esquire. I work as the policy analyst for the Children's Court Program."

Aurora pointed at his name tag. "Yes, I see that you are a lawyer. I am Aurora. I helped plan this event. I am the editor-in-chief for the *Happy Living* magazine." She hesitated. "I guess my name tag says that." She and Jason both laughed.

"Yes, I saw you do the introduction on stage, too. We also have your magazine in our office."

Aurora didn't seem surprised. "Oh, do you? That's nice. A lot of offices have it."

Jason giggled. "Yes, I always laugh at your section in the magazine. I like your sense of humor."

"I am glad people are actually reading them," Aurora said. "I didn't think anyone would notice me from a magazine."

Jason took a sip of whatever he was drinking. "I am an avid reader, and nothing happens in Wisconsin that I don't know about."

Aurora thought to herself, *Wow, such a know-it-all.* But somehow, she liked it. She was not used to being around smart, successful men. She looked down and laughed at her ridiculous footwear.

"I am just joking about knowing everything, but I am an avid reader." Jason sat up straight and cleared his throat. "So, this is a very lovely event. You did a great job with this. Everyone seems happy with the food. I know I am."

She was worried people would not be satisfied because of the last-minute food change. "Well, thank God. I am glad you like it." She continued, "So, what brings you here?"

"One of us from the office had the go. Since I am the only single one in the office with no kids, they usually make me go to these events."

"Oh, you are single." Aurora thought about her divorce.

"Well, I guess I am single, too." *I'm so stupid. I really didn't need to say that. I guess I am single?*

Jason seemed confused. "You guess?"

"Yeah."

"Okay, well, I actually wanted to tell you how beautiful you look tonight." Aurora's cheeks flushed a bright red color. "I mean, you are gorgeous and confident."

"Well," Aurora said. "Thank you." Aurora looked down at her food. She picked up a French fry and ate it.

"Are you all right?" Jason said.

"Yes, of course!" Aurora said. "I-I-I am not used to compliments. That's all."

"Really?"

"Believe it or not," she blushed. "Yes."

"Well," Jason said. "Do you want to go out and have a drink after this with me and my friends?"

Aurora was shocked, which caused her to almost choke on the fry. While gasping for air Aurora said, "Well, it is just... I don't drink. I don't drink alcohol." She took a sip of water.

"Oh, okay." Jason seemed bummed.

"I am kind of tired, too." Aurora said. "I plan to go home after this. It has been a long week."

Aurora continued in a peppy voice, "Well, maybe we can get coffee sometime, though."

Aurora was usually not that assertive, but she thought she had nothing else to lose. Melih wasn't messaging her. At the least, she would make a good networking contact or a friend.

Jason seemed cheerful. "I'd love that. I can give you my number and you can text me."

Aurora grabbed his phone from her clutch and gave it to Jason. "You can save it in here and text your phone. That way you have my number also."

Jason slowly started to stand up as he buttoned up his tux jacket, "Well, it was nice meeting you. I am going to go meet up with my friends."

Aurora watched Jason walk away just like she had watched Melih. She hoped he would actually text her, or she was going to feel pathetic. Though the only message Aurora really wanted was from Melih.

# Chapter 11

A week later, Aurora's parents came to visit her. They didn't come to visit her often, but it was her mother Elizabeth's birthday and Aurora's dad wanted to surprise her. Aurora didn't want to be around her dad. She avoided him at all costs.

Aurora felt a sharp pain in her chest while she was waiting for her parents. She took a Xanax from her purse and swallowed it down with a gulp of water. *Just remember, Aurora. You are meeting with them for your mother's sake.* Aurora's mom was petite like she was. Her mom had dark, gray-blue eyes, short curly hair, a button nose, and freckles that Elizabeth would call "beauty dots." She always had a smile on her face. Charles had gray curly hair; he had his German features of thin lips that you could barely see, a flat nose, and bright, piercing blue eyes. These were the traits that Aurora and her father shared.

Charles said nonchalantly, "So, when is your court date?"

"Well, you didn't beat around the bush with that question," said Aurora.

Charles rolled his eyes. "You don't have to be a smart ass."

"Charles, language!" Elizabeth blurted out. "Be nice to your daughter. She is going through a hard time. Be nice. We haven't been able to spend much time with her since she married Gannon."

Charles said proudly, "No, my daughter is tough." *Your beating me as a kid did not make me tough.*

Aurora ignored those comments, "Well, the court date is

March sixteenth. One hundred and twenty days after I filed. If everything goes right, I should be divorced that day."

Charles said as he laughed, "Too bad you won't be divorced by your birthday."

Aurora rolled her eyes. "Well, that is the last thing I was thinking of, Dad, but okay." Aurora started to quiver. "I know I always come off as so tough, but I have to tell you guys something."

Elizabeth seemed overly concerned and opened her eyes wide. She said in a soft voice, "Honey, what's wrong? Are you all right?"

"Well, I am fine. I just want to tell you something about Gannon."

"Well, what did that little effer do now?" Charles said as he clenched his jaw with anger. As Aurora saw her dad clench his jaw as Gannon would do before he would abuse her, she remembered that was what her dad would do right before he would beat her as a child.

"Well, he used to abuse me." *Just like you did.* "He was doing it since we got married, but...."

Charles clenched his jaw. "I am going to kill him. No one hurts my little girl." *But you did, didn't you? You hurt me.* Her heart beat faster.

"Dad, he didn't hit me at first." Aurora said. "He didn't act like this until after we were married." Though what she said didn't sound any better.

Elizabeth grabbed Aurora's hand. "Baby girl, we are so sorry. We didn't know. I wish we could have done something. We could have done something, but we rarely saw you. We didn't know."

"Mom, it's not your fault. You didn't know, and he never let me see my family or close friends, so no one knew. I was just trapped, but I am fine now."

Charles tried to be empathetic. "That's my girl. You are tough. Even that loser can't hurt you."

"Well, thanks dad. I am just glad I am almost done."

Elizabeth's mom pulled everyone in for a group hug, knocking over two glasses of water in the process. "We love you and we will never let anything like this happen to you again." Elizabeth continued, "Your father wants to tell you something."

"What is it now?"

"Aurora, I am sorry for what I did to you and your brother. I was really tough, and I am sorry about that."

"It's fine," Aurora said.

"I feel that the way I was to you pushed you to be with a bad person."

"It was the reason I was with him," Aurora said. "Before marriage, I thought he was perfect." She started to cry.

Charles gave her a hug.

"You have never hugged me before," Aurora said.

"I know, and I regret it. I am sorry," Charles said. "And I am sorry for what I did to you as a child. I feel this is all my fault."

--

Later that week, while Aurora was cooking spaghetti in her kitchen, one of Aurora's and Gannon's friend, Zarifa, called her to check up on her. Her nickname was Zara and she was from Russia.

Aurora was sitting at her desk at work and heard her phone ring. Aurora said, "Hello."

Zara said hello in a peppy voice, "Hello, Aurora."

"Hey Zara. How are you doing?" Aurora was worried that Zara was going to bring up Gannon or talk about him.

"Oh, I am good. Just checking how you are doing." Aurora was stirring the spaghetti pasta, then suddenly stopped when Zara asked, "Vee are going ice skating dis weekend. Vant to join?"

Aurora thought, *Definitely not. Gannon or Shazzy is going to be there.* Aurora assumed her friend Sara would be there because she and Zara were inseparable. They were also both studying to be neurologists.

"Well, I assume Sara will be there, right? Who else is coming?"

"Vell, me, Sara, Dan, and Melih." *Really, not Shazzy or Gannon? She must know. So, the skating can go one of two ways: awkward or more awkward.*

"Aurora?"

"Yes, sorry. I am cooking dinner." Aurora continued, "Okay, I will come. Just text me the time, place, day, and I will be there."

--

After eating the dinner she had made, Aurora made herself a cup of Earl Grey tea. She ran upstairs to change into her pajamas, then came back downstairs and sat on the couch to watch *Sex and the City*. The show was her guilty pleasure. She was sure she had watched each episode at least five times. In between sipping her tea and laughing at the TV show, someone called her.

"Hey, beautiful."

"Uh, hi?" Aurora said. "Who is this?"

"Oh sorry, it's Jason. The cute lawyer from the charity

event."

"Oh yeah? Humble, are we?" Aurora said as she laughed.

"So, I was thinking," Jason said. "Want to get a coffee tomorrow during our lunch hour?" Aurora took a sip of her tea.

"Okay. That sounds good," Aurora said. "Wait. How about we just get lunch and have coffee at the end?"

"I guess that makes sense," Jason said. "People usually eat lunch during their lunch hour." *I usually skip lunch these days.* Jason continued, "Lunch is too good to miss out on."

"That's true."

"Let's meet at the Colectivo coffee shop outside of the capitol building," Jason said. "They usually have food carts around. We can go to one of them. Is twelve okay?

"Sounds good," Aurora said. "See you then."

*I have this lunch date tomorrow AND I am going skating this weekend. I have to tell Tessa.* Tessa was in bed early that night sleeping. She had to get up early to study for school.

--

Aurora went upstairs and knocked on Tessa's door.

"Are you awake?"

"Yes," Tessa said. "What's up? Is something wrong?"

Aurora said frantically as she walked in, turned on Tessa's lamp, and sat on the foot of Tessa's bed, "Nothing is wrong. I have something exciting to tell you." Aurora smiled.

"Well, what is it?" Tessa said as she yawned.

"I have a date with a lawyer tomorrow."

"Ohhhh!" Tessa said as she sat up. "Tell me about it."

"Well, he was at the charity event I hosted."

"Yeah?"

Aurora said nervously, "Well, he is cute. Kind of nerdy looking. He is only a little bit taller than me. You know I am attracted to taller guys." Tessa rolled her eyes because Aurora was short, so really anyone was taller than she was.

"Well, anyway, I don't know what to wear on my 'lunch date.' I mean, is it a date if it's during lunch?"

Tessa laughed, "Yes, it is still a date. What are you going to wear?"

"That is exactly what I was going to ask you. What do you wear on a date with a lawyer?"

Though Tessa had great style, she didn't know what someone should wear on a date with a lawyer. "Well, just Google it," Tessa said.

"Okay, I got a couple of things to talk to you about," Aurora said. "You know that guy from the club that night?"

"Another guy... Is this the guy who was friends with that muscle dude?"

"No. The guy I introduced you to before we left. My friend Melih."

Tessa said, "Oh yeah, what about him?"

"Well, I kind of have a crush on him.... I am going skating with a group of friends this weekend and he will be there. I guess I don't even know if he really likes me, but...."

"Wow. You are dating two guys at once. You are one hot lady," Tessa said. "Just be careful, Aurora. You are still married."

"Don't remind me. It won't be for long," Aurora said. "Anyway, Melih hasn't messaged me at all or anything, so we are definitely not dating. People who are dating have to talk."

Tessa had a deer-in-the-headlights look as she said, "Well, let us hope it won't be awkward. Want me to come this weekend?"

"Yes, please! Then you can find out if he likes me or not or what his deal is."

"Sounds good."

Aurora went to her room, read articles, and looked at pictures of outfits she could wear on her lawyer lunch date. Finally, after an hour of rummaging through her closet, Aurora found the perfect outfit for her lunch date. She decided to wear a pair of her black Christian Louboutin red bottom heels that she had bought for herself as a graduation gift. She also chose to wear a black suit with a white pussy-bow-ribboned blouse. She had started to love wearing black since Tessa had pointed out she should own at least one black shirt.

# Chapter 12

The next morning, Aurora got ready for work and put on the perfect outfit after she finished her morning routine. She thought to herself, *I really need to start looking for a place in the city.* She made her morning coffee and put it in her thermos. She grabbed her keys, locked the door, and headed out for the long drive through the morning rush.

Work went slowly. Aurora was so anxious and could not focus on anything besides that lunch date. She thought, *Well, who does lunch dates, anyway?* She probably didn't know that a lot of successful people went out for lunch dates because she had been with a lazy graphic "artist" since college, whose idea of a romantic date was going to a club and dancing.

What made Aurora nervous was that Jason was a little bit older than she was, and he might not like how young she was. She also couldn't stop thinking about what Jason would do if he found out about her still being married. Maybe he wouldn't care because of his age. Maybe he already knew. She thought, *He is a lawyer, he probably does a security check on all of his dates. He probably already knows my social security number.... I am probably overthinking this.*

When it was ten minutes to noon, Aurora shot out of her desk, took her coat off the rack, put it on, then buttoned it as she walked out of her office door.

"Tiffany, I am going to lunch a few minutes early with a..... a business associate."

Tiffany looked at Aurora's schedule. "A business associate?"

"Yes."

"What does he do?"

Aurora did not like chit chatting. "He is a lawyer that was at the gala."

Tiffany raised her eyebrows. "Is he cute?

Aurora started walking away at this point, "All righty then.... Bye Tiffany. See you at one."

Aurora walked over to the coffee shop. She had to walk up State Street a few blocks. She knew she was going to be late. It was really cold out that afternoon, and she could see her breath. She walked fast and hunched over like a schoolmarm. *These red-bottomed heels were a bad idea.* When she had chosen her outfit the night before, she did not take into account that she would be meeting Jason wearing her black petticoat. Winters were cold and windy in Wisconsin. Just the thought of going outside would make you cold. *He probably won't even see my outfit! I am wrapped by my jacket and scarf.*

She arrived at Colectivo and looked around for Jason. The aroma of freshly baked buttery croissants teased her nose. She walked around a little bit until she tapped on someone's shoulder. "Hey, Jason." The man turned around, un-amused.

*Crap.*

"I am not Jason." The man rolled his eyes and turned back around.

"A-a-all right," Aurora said. "Sorry about that."

After that instance, she decided to sit down, so she could avoid another awkward encounter.

She texted Jason: "Hey, I'm sorry I am a bit late. I said hi to a guy I thought was you, but it wasn't. lol. Oops... I'll sit right next to the Costa Rican coffee basket. Come find me."

As soon as she looked up from her phone, she saw Jason walking toward her. She looked down right away and thought, *I don't remember him being that good looking the other night. Usually guys look more attractive in the dark, not the other way around.*

He didn't have on his glasses like he did at the gala. He was wearing a black petticoat, like her, but of a more masculine style. His hair was still styled the same as the other night, still hiding that he was balding. He had a strong jaw and light blue eyes. She couldn't believe that she had missed Jason's features when she first saw him. She almost stopped breathing. She hadn't been on a date with anyone other than Gannon since high school.

She looked up again because she could feel his presence right in front of her. Aurora's cheeks flushed with red and her heart skipped a beat.

He looked at her and smiled. "Hey. How are you?" Aurora could see the wrinkles from the laughing lines by his eyes.

"Sorry I am a bit late. I decided to wear heels in negative five-degree weather."

He looked at the shoes and giggled, "It is okay. Want to get something to eat from one of the carts then come back in for a coffee?"

"Okay. Sounds good."

They left the coffee shop. She looked down at Jason's leather shoes and noticed he was wearing two different colored socks. Aurora tried not to be distracted by it. "I sent you a text. Did you get it?"

"No, I didn't. I can check now," Jason said, grabbing for his phone.

"No, it's fine. I just wanted to tell you I was running late…. Oh, and I said hi to another guy who looked like you. Well, the back of his head did."

Jason clenched his jaw. "Oh, yikes."

"I was thinking we could try there." Aurora pointed in the direction of a line of food trucks that seemed to go on forever.

Jason looked at Aurora confused, but laughed. "Well, which truck? There are a lot of them."

"The Asian taco one." The truck was a light blue color with "Asian Tacos by Yang and Juan" written on the side in artistic graffiti.

"Sounds good."

The two of them walked toward the food truck. On their walk, they tried to maintain a conversation, but Aurora's feet were in pain and freezing, so she could barely hold a conversation. *Such a great first date*, Aurora thought. She was also annoyed with herself because she thought about how she had put all of the effort into looking cute and he would never even see her outfit.

Jason asked, "So, how was work so far today?"

"It was good. I have been very busy all morning," Aurora lied. She wanted to make it seem that she was doing anything besides focusing on their lunch date.

"Same here," Jason said. "I am preparing for a conference. Remember how I said at your gala that they always send me to these things?"

"Yes, I gotcha. Because you are single?"

"Right."

They waited in line and Aurora rubbed her hands together to warm them up. In between their talking, they would take a look at the menu board to see what they would get.

"So, what if you start dating someone?" Aurora said. "Would they cut you off the hook then?"

Jason enjoyed her witty question. "Well, I haven't been in a relationship since I got this job. I actually got this job a couple of months ago. That is why I moved here."

"So, where are you from?"

"I'm from Northern Wisconsin."

Aurora was intrigued. "I am from there, too!"

"What city? I'm from a town called White Lake. I went to high school there."

Aurora said, "What? I went to that school too. That school is so small, though. How do I not know you?" *Is he really that old?*

Jason said, "Really, what is your last name? I think I am a bit older than you." He asked her last name because there were only about twenty families that went to that school. So, people were either related or knew each other.

Aurora was relieved that she decided not to change her name when she got married. If she did, she might have had to tell Jason she was still married. "My last name is Tousey."

"There was a girl in my class with that last name. Her name was Kathy."

"That's my older sister!"

"Yes, I graduated with your sister!" He then thought for a second as if he were calculating her age in his head. "So, I guess that means I am ten years older than you."

Aurora did not give him a weirded out look like he was expecting. Aurora also wasn't picky about age because she thought that it would be hard to find someone her age that would want to marry a divorced or soon-to-be-divorced woman.

Aurora said, "My parents are fourteen years apart. So the age difference doesn't bother me. Does it bother you?"

"No. Not really. I mean, you are very mature for a twenty-seven-year-old."

She thought about how Gannon had aged her about twenty years. "I guess. I just have a lot of life experience from my busy career." She lied about that too. Though she had a busy career, the life experience actually came from her abusive marriage and childhood.

They got to the front of the line. "What would you like?"

Aurora said to Jason, "I'd like the chicken teriyaki tacos."

Jason ordered, "She will have the teriyaki chicken tacos and I will have the tofu tang tacos." Aurora flashed Jason a smile.

She loved that he ordered for her, but the thought of tofu grossed her out. She loved that togetherness Jason had, and the gray hairs that ran sporadically through his beard. He seemed like he was kind of boring, but Aurora didn't care because he was a man. Aurora was upset that Melih couldn't even message her, but Jason could ask her out right away. Aurora wondered why Jason was single, but she was sure he would tell her eventually. At least she hoped he would. Just like she thought she would have to tell him she was still married or getting divorced.

They got their food and ate the tacos very quickly, while standing. They walked briskly back to the coffee shop. Aurora couldn't even remember the conversation they had on the way back to the coffee shop because she could barely breathe from the cold winds. *I cannot wait to get a cup of coffee and sit down.*

They got to the coffee shop and Jason ordered them both small dark roast coffees. Aurora got them a place to sit. She took a big breath and looked around. She loved the smell of coffee shops, the sound of milk frothing, the clicking sounds from college students typing on their laptops, and the sound when the people reading would flip pages on their books.

Aurora took off her coat to show off her outfit. She then fluffed her fingers through her hair. She undid the one button on her suit jacket and sat up straight. She quickly looked through her coat pocket to grab her pink lip-gloss to put on.

Jason came and sat down with the coffees in his hand. Aurora raised her eyebrows and smiled at him. Jason said, "You like coffee, right?"

"Yes, I do. Thank you."

"Do you like it with cream or sugar?"

Aurora said, "Definitely not sugar. I can have it with cream or black. So, this one is fine. Thank you."

"I prefer my coffee black."

"Every time I hear that line, it reminds me of the movie *Airplane*."

"Maybe you are older than I thought to know of that movie?" They both laughed.

Aurora looked Jason in the eyes and noticed a freckle above his left eye. He took off his jacket and draped it over the chair as he sat down. He was wearing a gray suit with a red tie. Aurora took a sip of her coffee and burned her tongue.

"Ouch," She put her hand to her mouth.

"You okay?"

"What?"

"Was the coffee too hot?"

"Yeah...No, I am fine."

"All right," Jason said.

"So, where do you work?" Aurora said. "Somewhere around here?"

Jason said, "I actually work at the building right next door. It's connected to the coffee shop."

Aurora tried to keep the conversation going. "Oh, nice. So tell me, what exactly do you do at work?"

"Well, I analyze the policies of how children are handled in the court system and the laws surrounding it. Anyway, I don't want to talk about me. Tell me about you. What do you like to do?"

Aurora took a sip of her coffee. "Well, I like to read and write. I am not all that exciting. I like to work out and play guitar."

"Oh really? You play guitar? I have always wanted to date a musician."

Aurora giggled. "Too bad I am not a musician. It is just a hobby. I am a writer who is working as a magazine editor. I am not a published author yet, but I hope I will have a book published someday."

"Wow, Aurora. You have pretty big goals for a little person." She loved how he said her name but didn't like being called little.

Aurora pushed Jason's arm in a flirtatious way. She teased him back by saying, "I'm only a few inches shorter than you, it seems. So...."

"Good point, but I was trying to flirt with you. I guess that didn't work so well."

*I could tell he was flirting with me, but he must have been out of the game longer than I've been.*

"No, it was cute." Aurora started to blush, and her cheeks got red. She wore her emotions on her face.

"Not as cute as you." Aurora wasn't used to compliments.

She rolled her eyes. "Okay, sly guy." Though she really thought, *keep the compliments coming.*

Aurora looked down at the watch on her wrist. "I gotta go back to work now. Unfortunately, my office is not right next to here."

"I had a nice time. So, would you like to meet again?" Jason asked. Aurora thought the date had gone well.

*Well, why not? What do I have to lose?* She said, "Yes, I'd like to. Just text me."

Aurora left feeling confident – that feeling you have when

you are finally comfortable in your own skin. However, she was worried about getting into anything serious. She was not yet divorced, and things were complicated with Melih. She thought that Jason was just what she needed. He didn't seem complicated, but she wasn't sure. She wondered how a guy of his stature and his success would not be married or have kids. She wondered if he had kids. She also thought there may be something wrong with him. Aurora fell asleep that night contemplating all of these questions she had.

# Chapter 13

It was Saturday afternoon. Tessa and Aurora were doing their makeup together, like they always did when they got ready to go out somewhere. They had to allow almost two hours to get to where they were going because they were driving into the city. That day, it was extremely windy.

Aurora ran upstairs to ravage through her winter clothes. She yelled down stairs to Tessa, "Should I wear my gray yoga pants with some wool socks? Or should I wear jeans with long underwear underneath them?"

"Definitely wear the jeans with your thermal underwear. It is really windy out today."

Tessa was sitting on the couch and watching the Food Network as she was straightening her hair with a comb and air dryer. Tessa yelled up the steps, "You are lucky I love you, Rora. You know I like to stay inside cuddled up in my Snuggie when it is this cold out."

"I know! Thank youuu. I love you." Aurora came down the steps and almost fell because she had her fuzzy socks on. "Tessa, don't forget, you gotta see if this guy actually likes me tonight."

Tessa looked at Aurora, "Yeah, I can do that. So, you are dating two guys now? You are one hot lady." They both laughed.

"I wouldn't say that." Aurora sat on the sofa chair next to the couch and took a sip of her hot chocolate that was sitting on the end table. "Melih hasn't even texted me or talked to me since we saw him at the club the night I introduced you both."

"Just be careful, girl. You are still married." Sometimes Tessa was tough with Aurora just because she didn't want Aurora to get hurt again.

"You are right. I'll be divorced in a couple of months. I just don't want to let one of these guys go. You know, I am a hopeless romantic."

Tessa was finished straightening her hair and unplugged the hairdryer. Tessa said, "I know, but sometimes you think with your emotions and heart. You don't think with logic in these situations." Aurora thought that comment was tough, but Tessa was right.

"You have a point. Tessa, I also want to talk to you about something."

"Oh?"

Aurora said, "I want to start looking for a place. I can't keep driving this far to work every day. You know I appreciate your letting me use your guest bedroom."

"Aw, but I like having you as my roommate. I feel like we are in college together again, but I understand."

"I just have to check with my lawyer first, to see if it's okay to move in regards to my paperwork."

"Just let me know. You can stay here as long as you need."

--

The ride to the rink was windy, and Aurora found herself struggling to keep the car straight on the road. She had to keep a hard grip on the steering wheel. She was already a reckless driver. Her driving always drove Tessa nuts. When Tessa and Aurora arrived to the skating rink, Aurora wrapped her dark gray wool scarf around her face. She found it hard to open her car door because the wind was so strong. She opened the door and her stocking cap almost flew off. She barely had time to catch it before it blew away.

They walked into the ice-skating rink. Aurora was cold from the wind, her cheeks rosy. Her heart started to beat fast. *I cannot stop thinking of him and the night at the club. The way his sweat smelled so sweet. I thought Jason would be enough to distract my mind.* She looked around to see if Melih was there. *I don't know why I am so fixated on that night. I mean, maybe he was just being friendly, but he is so hot...* Aurora walked with Tessa to the front desk to get their ice skates. It was right next to the concession stand, where kids, some in hockey gear, were running up to buy soda and candy. Their moms were chasing after them telling them no.

Aurora and Tessa sat on a bench right outside of the ice rink. Aurora set her skates next to the bench. Before sitting, she put her mittens that were made of old sweaters, on the plexiglass window, overlooking the rink. She tried to find Melih or any of her other friends. She took her phone out of her pocket to see if she had arrived early or late. She looked around one more time, then sat down. Aurora thought to herself, *they are always late.*

Tessa was ready to skate at this point and was getting impatient. She didn't really want to be there anyway. "Aurora, I am going to get a coffee from the concession. Want anything?"

Aurora looked at her boots and kicked a dirty napkin she found on the floor. "Ahh, I will have a hot chocolate." She pulled some cash out of her pocket and tried to give it to Tessa. "Here you go."

Tessa refused the money. "No, it's okay. I got this." Tessa walked away to the concessions.

Aurora took the phone out of her pocket to call Zara.

"Hey, where are you guys?" Aurora said.

Zara answered her, "Hey. Vee are in da parking lot. Vee vill be in there in a second."

"Okay, sounds good. See you soon."

Aurora's heart started to beat fast. *He's literally right outside.* Tessa arrived back and handed Aurora her hot chocolate. "Here you go."

Aurora took a sip and burned her tongue. "Ouch. I always burn my tongue!" She put her hand over her mouth. She briefly looked to the right and saw in her peripheral vision that her friends had walked in.

She saw Melih and she started to get butterflies in her stomach, and those butterflies slowly started to form into a knot, as if they were forming back into a cocoon. She remembered that Melih had never messaged or called her. She then felt her cheeks turn red and her temples began to throb.

Zara saw Aurora and waved. She had on her black petticoat jacket that she was usually wearing with red lipstick and her gorgeous smile. She had short, wavy jet-black hair with bangs. Her emerald-like green eyes were accentuated by her beautifully shaped thick eyebrows.

"Hey guys!" *Don't look at him. Do not make eye contact!* Though she didn't notice it, all of his attention was on her. Aurora looked at Tessa. "This is my friend Tessa."

Pointing at her friends individually, Aurora said, "This is Dan, Sara, Zara, and M-m-melih."

"Yes." Tessa said. "We me…" Aurora nudged her to stop talking.

"Well." Aurora said. "I guess we should put on our ice skates and skate, right?"

Aurora took a big gulp of her hot chocolate that had cooled

down a lot. She thought as she sipped, *You are so hot, I bet you he could warm this hot chocolate up by touching it.* She rolled her eyes at herself.

Tessa scooted closer to Aurora and whispered in her ear, "Are you okay?"

"Yes, I am fine." Aurora said more quietly, "Did you notice if he was looking at me?"

"Not looking, more like staring." Aurora looked down and smiled.

Aurora looked at Melih through her peripheral vision as she bent forward to tighten the strings on her skates.

Aurora slowly got up to hang up her jacket, with her face toward the coat rack, facing the wall. She felt the hair prickle on the back of her neck, as she could feel Melih near her. Every time she heard him talk, her heart would melt like the snow in the spring. She stopped breathing for a moment as she felt Melih move past from behind her. She exhaled. She forgot that she was walking on skates, which felt more like stilts. She lost her balance and almost fell over.

Melih caught her.

It felt like electricity was running through her veins. Aurora took a deep breath, as her pupils grew small. For a moment, they stared into each other's eyes and said nothing. To Aurora, it was like his eyes were a galaxy or a new planet that had never been discovered, until that moment. *How have I not seen you like this before?*

"You hawe to be easy on dose skates," Melih said. "You should hawe good balance vhen you are valking." Aurora was still staring into his eyes.

"Aurora is fine." Tessa stood up and pulled up Aurora. "I got her."

All of Aurora's friends were looking at them. Aurora saw

everyone staring and said, "I am fine. Thanks."

Aurora held onto Tessa's arms and walked through the doors onto the ice.

Aurora started off by holding onto the rail, barely able to hold herself up. She slowly went from holding onto the rail to skating.

She saw Tessa laughing as she held on to Dan's muscular arm. Dan was very tall and strong. He used to be a running back for the Badgers football team. Aurora thought about Dan and Tessa: *well, that escalated quickly. I guess they are hitting it off. Good for them.* Aurora was happy to see that because Tessa was always working or engulfed in her studies. It was nice for her to let her hair down.

Zara came up on Aurora's side, skating backwards. Aurora said, "Wow, Zara. Where did you learn to skate like that?"

"Aurora, my lapochka, my sweetie," Zara said. "Everyone can skate in Russia."

"Of course."

"Hey, I saw Melih help catch you vhen you almost fell," Zara said. "Are you all right?" Aurora's mind went numb. "Are you all right, Rora? Is your ankle okay?"

"Oh yeah, I am fine. I wasn't raised skating like you guys. It takes me a while to remember how to use these," she said as she pointed at her skates.

"Ah duh, so how are you? Are you almost divorced?"

"I'm fine. I will be divorced in a couple of months."

"Dat's good." Zara grabbed onto Aurora's arm and looked her in the eyes. "We are sorry about what happened. We haven't talked to Shazzy since. Not Gannon either, but I never liked him."

Aurora had a flashback and saw Shazzy and Gannon on the couch. She was relieved that she didn't feel anything about what Zara had said. "It is fine. I am over it."

Zara looked shocked but smiled. "Vell, dat's great." She let go of Aurora's arm. "Vell, I am going to skate now, Rora." Zara skated away and Aurora felt a sigh of relief. *The pressure is off again. Thank God.*

Tessa and Dan skated up to Aurora. Tessa said, "How are you doing? Having a good time?"

"I am fine." Aurora was holding onto the rail. "Enjoy yourselves." Aurora smiled and quietly giggled as they skated away.

Aurora was skating again and Melih skated up quickly on her left. "Hey, Rora."

"H-i-I, Melih." Her face flushed with red. "Thanks for helping me back there."

"No problem. It vas my pleasure."

Aurora thought to herself as she clenched her jaw, *well of course it was.*

Melih grabbed Aurora's hand and held it close to his heart.

Aurora looked into his eyes as he pulled her close. Then she realized that everyone could probably see them. She abruptly pulled her hand away. "What are you doing? Everyone can see us!"

Melih took a deep breath as he said, "Aurora."

"Yes?" Aurora said.

"I told Gannon he was an idiot for doing what he did to you."

Aurora started breathing heavily. "You have no idea what he did to me." She now imagined Gannon hitting her and fell to the ice. She started to cry.

Aurora thought back to the one time that Gannon had punched her in the stomach and she fell to the floor and Gannon started laughing. The laugh had sounded like an evil villain and then she heard Melih in the distance saying, "Aurora, are you okay?"

Melih got to his knees. "Aurora, are you okay?" Aurora had a sigh of relief that it was only a flashback. Melih pushed Aurora's hair away from her face. "I am sorry, Rora. I would have told you sooner, but I vanted to vait until I saw you in person. It vas eating me up inside. I couldn't keep it a secret."

Aurora sat up and pushed Melih away. "Can you let me catch my breath, please?" Aurora breathed for a few moments.

Melih sat back up, while straightening his posture. "Well of course."

"Well, what if Gannon doesn't go to the court date now?" Aurora raised her voice. "Did you think of that?" She started crying. "I cannot be married to that abusive man anymore."

Melih said, "Abusive?"

Tessa arrived and said, "Rora, are you okay?" Aurora was crying and shook her head no. Tessa grabbed her hand to help her up. "All right then. Let's go home, Aurora."

Aurora stuttered, "No, it's fine." Melih tried to help Aurora but Tessa pulled her closer, "It's okay, I got her. Thanks."

They skated away and got out of the rink. From a distance it looked like Melih wanted to chase her and make sure she was okay. Until that day at the rink, none of her friends besides Tessa had known about who Gannon really was.

# Chapter 14

Aurora went back to work Monday feeling ill. She could not believe the breakdown she had at the ice skating rink. *I feel sorry for how I reacted toward Melih…I just had no control over my body in that moment. It was foreign to me. How has this not happened before, or did it and I just didn't realize what was happening to me?*

Just when she thought she was getting better, Melih triggered her bad memories about how Gannon used to abuse her. *I just cannot be tied to Gannon, but he will try as hard as he can to keep me.*

She didn't realize what Post Traumatic Stress Disorder was until the doctor at the hospital told her at one of her checkups that she may be suffering from PTSD, and he wanted her to relay her symptoms or any events that may have triggered a bad reaction during their next appointment. She wouldn't realize until the next appointment that that is what she was suffering from. She thought it was something that happened to people in the military.

Aurora could not eat or think the rest of that weekend because she thought that there was nothing worse that could happen to her besides having to be stuck being married to Gannon. She couldn't stop thinking about what she would do to herself if she could not leave Gannon. *As long as we are married, he will have some sort of control over me.*

Since Aurora was so stressed from all of the overthinking she had done over the weekend, she knew that she would have to get something out of the way on Monday. She wanted to start looking for a new place to live and needed to contact her lawyer.

*I need to get my life together. No one except me will do it for me.* She kept exhausting big bursts of air and growling at everything that went wrong.

"Tiffany, come in here." Aurora said frantically from her desk at work Monday morning. "Please."

Her assistant came in and closed the door behind her. "Is everything okay? How can I help you?"

Aurora didn't realize that she was making such a scene by yelling out her office for Tiffany. Her anxiety was so bad that morning. "Well, I am fine." Aurora cheeks were red and her hair was a frizzy mess. "Can you call my divorce attorney and schedule an appointment with him as soon as possible? If he can't do a meeting, just have him call me."

"Divorce attorney?"

"Yes," Aurora said as she pulled her lawyer's business card from her purse. "Go give him a call for me."

Tiffany went back to her desk and called Aurora's attorney's office. Aurora sat at her desk.

*Why hasn't Tiffany called through to me yet? Why isn't he answering?*

Several minutes later, Aurora jumped up and looked at Tiffany through her glass window. Tiffany looked at her in despair and shook her head no, signalling that she could not get the lawyer on the line.

*Oh no... Now what am I going to do?* Aurora opened her desk drawer, took out a Xanax, and gulped it down with a glass of water.

Aurora got up out of her desk chair and opened her door. She walked over to Tiffany's desk. Aurora leaned forward with her elbows on Tiffany's desk counter next to a jar of candy and moved close to Tiffany. She whispered, "You couldn't get him on the line?"

"No," Tiffany said, hesitantly. "He isn't available."

"Did you tell him it was an emergency?" Aurora said.

"I told his assistant that and she said he is available around 1:00 p.m. tomorrow."

"Tomorrow!" Aurora said.

"I am sorry," Tiffany said. "Lawyers are busy."

"I know, but it is just that I have a meeting scheduled for that time with a photographer about a cover in our magazine."

"I know, Ms. Tousey," Tiffany said as she twirled a pencil between her fingers.

"So what did you tell the assistant?" Aurora asked as she whispered more softly while putting her head closer to Tiffany's computer screen.

"Well," Tiffany said, "I told her yes."

"But I have that appointment."

"I know, and I hope you won't be upset, but I called the photographer and moved that appointment to 2:00 p.m. today," Tiffany said. "Is that okay?"

"Normally I wouldn't be happy if you changed my appointments without asking me," Aurora said as she stood up straight. "But this is a time that I will allow it." She smiled.

--

Aurora couldn't eat until the next day. She was getting better at eating more, but when she was triggered by the thoughts of Gannon, she couldn't eat. So she forced herself to get a smoothie from the café down below. She took the smoothie up to her office and kept staring at the chocolate peanut butter drink. She took sips every few minutes. *You will not let Gannon be the reason you stop eating again; you will talk to the lawyer soon.*

Aurora kept starting at the clock every few minutes to see if the time was closer to 1:00. When it was 1:00, she took turns staring at the clock and her phone, waiting for a phone call. She finally heard it ring, and her heart beat faster with each ring. She took a large breath and picked up.

"Hello?" Aurora said as if she were out of breath from running a marathon.

"Aurora, I have your lawyer on the other line," Tiffany said.

"Please put him through to me."

"Hello Ms… Aurora." Though Aurora had never taken her husband's last name, the lawyer never used last names when addressing female divorce clients. He didn't want to remind them of their husbands.

Aurora got straight to the point because she knew that lawyers charged by the hour. "If Gannon doesn't show up, will I still be able to get divorced?"

"It does not matter."

"It does not matter?" Aurora took a big breath and exhaled.

"I can tell you are a bit stressed, but I promise it's good news," he said. "If he fails to appear at the final hearing, the court will proceed without him. They would proceed without his input towards the final order and he would be in default."

Aurora seemed confused. "Okay, explain that in common English." She thought, *I guess that's why I am paying you to make my life easier.*

"If he isn't there, it doesn't matter. You can still get divorced that day."

"Okay, thank God." Aurora sighed with relief. She felt as if a rock had been lifted off of her chest. "Last, I want to move somewhere by myself. I am living with my best friend now, as you know, but I want to get my own place. I don't want to keep driving so much every day. It is wearing on me, you know?"

"Yeah, I understand, but I recommend that you don't move because of all the court documents. But if you do move, still keep the address as the current address you have now." Aurora had asked for his advice, but she knew she was going to start looking for a new place regardless. She was stubborn.

"Okay, that is all I wanted to know." She wanted to keep the call short but sweet. She had to get those questions answered right away, or she would have kept thinking about them all day. She figured, the less she could worry about, the better.

"Okay, good….. Oh, wait! I have one more thing," Aurora said. "I want to block my husband from calling and texting me. Can I do that if I want to?"

"Yes! Of course!"

"Sorry for all of the questions. This is my first divorce. But one more thing," Aurora said. "We need to schedule an appointment to talk about this pre-nup situation."

"Ah, yes," he said. "Well, your assistant can set that up with mine."

"Okay, thank you."

"At our meeting we can discuss a possible loophole."

"That's great!" she said. "Can you tell me?"

"I am sorry, but I don't have any more time. I have to got to go," he said.

--

That same day, Aurora looked into getting a new place. She

emailed Laura Hamilton, one of the realtors she knew, who put ads in Aurora's magazine. She knew that Laura would get her something nice and affordable, fast. Though money wasn't really a problem for Aurora, she just wanted a place she could pay for with cash. Aurora told Laura the kind of place she was looking for and that she would like the place as soon as possible.

--

The following morning, Aurora was sitting at the kitchen table at her and Tessa's, editing some magazine articles, and drinking her morning cup of coffee. She stared out of the window in front of her. She thought about Melih and became frustrated; this pushed her for a needed distraction.

She called Jason.

"Good morning," Aurora said. "How was your weekend?"

"It was good," Jason said. "How did ice skating go?"

She was happy he remembered that she was going ice skating, which meant he was actually listening to her when she talked.

"It was good," Aurora said as she took a sip of coffee. "Thank you."

"That's good," Jason said. "Well, you missed a good show on last night."

*He must have invited some other girl.*

"I wish I could have gone," Aurora said. "I am sorry about that…. Anyway, did you find anyone to take with you?"

"Yes." *Of course you did.*

"That is nice," Aurora said.

*Get ahold of yourself, Aurora. Even if he had invited some other woman, you are still married and crushing on Melih!*

"Well, actually," Jason said, "my sister was in town visiting her friends for the weekend, so I asked if she wanted to go. We had a nice time."

"Aw! Are you and your sister close?" Aurora said. "I remember her being the head cheerleader in high school."

Jason's sister was Aurora's cheerleading coach at a cheer camp her mom made her attend when she was in the third grade. Aurora would rather have been at home reading the newest book about Junie B. Jones.

"Yeah, we are close," Jason said. "We used to fight all of the time when we were younger, but we have become very close since she went through a bad breakup a couple of years ago."

"It is the same way with my younger brother and me." *Except my brother and I bond to get over the sad memories from our childhood.*

"So," Aurora said, "what would you like to do on our date this weekend?"

Aurora was thinking about how upset Melih had made her and was hurt thinking about Gannon. She wanted to distract herself.

"I didn't know it was a date," Jason said. "I thought we would just be hanging out."

"Oh."

"I was kidding," Jason said. "Anyway, I was thinking we could have dinner at Crandall's Peruvian Bistro. It is one of my favorite places to eat."

"I love that place! It is my favorite, as well," Aurora said. "That is the place I had cater food for the charity event."

"Nice."

"I used to treat myself to some ceviche and a glass of wine after any big test in college."

"And I went to college with George Washington," Jason

chuckled. "Wait, I thought you said you don't drink?"

"Well, I drank then, but I don't anymore," Aurora said. "Anyway, you are not that old at all. You are vintage. Not old."

"So," Jason said, "am I your new accessory, then?"

"Something like that," Aurora said. "Though I haven't tried you on yet."

"Oh, really?"

"Maybe eventually," Aurora said. "I don't know."

"This is too much pressure!" Jason said. "I don't think I can handle it."

"I am sure you can handle it," Aurora said. "You are a lawyer. Well, I was just calling to say hi. I hope you enjoy the rest of your day."

"You too."

--

Aurora went to bed that night smiling. Jason was just the distraction she needed. He was flirtatious, successful, and easy on the eyes. She was not sure if anything would come of them, but she was just trying to enjoy her life at that point and was thinking she might play the field a little bit because she hadn't been single for long and she wanted to enjoy it for a while. *Tessa is right. I need to believe in myself again. No dating.* Aurora was worried that if things got too serious with Jason, she would have to tell him that she was still married. *At least Melih knows I am married.* Melih and Jason were too tempting to her, but she was worried they would get bored with her.

*Why is it that these men find me attractive and amazing, but I still don't feel that way?* In her mind she kept hearing Gannon say, "You made me do it. You made me beat you. You deserved it. No one would ever put up with you like I put up with you."

*I know I shouldn't be dating, but I don't want to be alone. They make me feel like I am wanted. I am too depressed right now to be alone. I need a distraction. They are like a drug that is giving me life right now.* She thought that maybe attention from a guy would help her gain that confidence, or maybe Jason would only be a rebound. *Melih could never be a rebound, right?*

What scared her most was that she thought if she ended up being with Jason, she would lose her chance at being with Melih, forever.

# Chapter 15

It was a Thursday afternoon and Aurora was sitting in the waiting room of her lawyer's office. She chose to sit in a dark red suede chair, which was in the corner of the waiting room, next to the bookshelf. She crossed her legs as one of her black leather boots hit the hardwood floor. She stared aimlessly at the books on the shelf next to her. *Pride and Prejudice* by Jane Austen caught her eye. She took the book off the shelf and opened up to a page, which read, "It is a truth universally acknowledged, that a single man in possession of a good fortune, must be in want of a good wife."

"Ha!" Aurora said out loud and some of the other people waiting in the waiting room looked at her. She then looked down. *How can a book that was written over two hundred years ago have a quote that rings so close to Gannon's need for a wife? Why didn't I see it then?*

"Ms. Tousey, would you like anything?" The secretary said. "Coffee, tea, or sparkling water?"

"Ahh," Aurora said as she looked up quickly from the book. "Sparkling water, please."

The receptionist brought Aurora the drink and Aurora swallowed the carbonated water as air bubbles came out of her nose. *I don't know why I find that feeling of carbonated water burning my nose so satisfying.* She hiccupped some of the air bubbles and put her hand over her mouth.

Erik Wulfblitzen, Aurora's lawyer, opened his office door and cleared his throat as he nodded at his receptionist.

"Mr. Wulfblitzen will see you now."

Aurora got up and put the book back on the shelf. *I think I am going to read this at home later.*

"So, Erik… Any good news?" Aurora said as she walked into her lawyer's officer.

"Yes." He signaled toward one of the chairs that sat next to the table in his office. "Take a seat," he said.

Aurora sat down.

"So?" she said as Erik put the pre-nup in front of her like he was dropping a large cement block on the table. "Yikes." Aurora opened her black leather purse and pulled out her glasses, and she then started to glance over the prenuptial agreement by flipping through the pages.

"Yup," Erik said. "So, though it seems like Gannon's mom was a bit conniving, I found an infidelity clause."

"A what?"

"Well, I know that it is not usually enforced, but adultery is illegal in Wisconsin," Erik said. "It is actually a criminal offense. However, we only need to prove his infidelity for the clause to work."

"So?" Aurora said. "Are we going try to get him in prison?"

"Well," Erik said, "we have to prove that he committed infidelity, and then the pre-nup will be invalid, but you don't have to press charges."

"Well," Aurora said, "how do we prove that?"

"Well, do you have any proof of him admitting to cheating?"

"Well," Aurora thought for a moment and looked up at the ceiling. "Do text messages count? Maybe I have old voice messages, as well."

"That is perfect," Erik said. "Well, on the court date, when your husb…. Gannon's lawyer–" Aurora glared at him with a side eye. He continued, "When his lawyer brings up the pre-nup, I will point out the infidelity clause and that it is illegal in the state of Wisconsin to have an adulterous relationship while you are married. Then you can show proof by playing the voicemails or showing any messages between you two."

"So, on what page is this clause?"

"Go to page 39," Erik said as Aurora rushed through the pages. "You will see it toward the middle of the page."

"What am I looking at?"

"It says if it is proven that the male is proven adulterous, then the dowry clause will be null-in-void."

*Is my dating adulterous?* Her face became paler than the snow outside. "I have..." She said as her voice squeaked. "I have to tell you something. I have been dating someone."

"So?" Erik said.

"It's not adultery?"

"No!" Her lawyer said. "You have to have intercourse. Even if you were adulterous," Erik continued. "Read farther and it says that if the woman becomes pregnant, it must be proven that it is the child of the husband."

"This is all good to hear, but how do I know Gannon and Shazzy had intercourse?" Aurora said.

"You can ask one of them."

"Well," Aurora said, "I don't really want to message either one of them."

"Message him and ask," he insisted.

Aurora pulled out her phone and began to type and said, "No. I can't."

"Well, you either do that or you pay him a huge dowry," Erik said. "Whatever you prefer."

"Fine!"

"Make it sound convincing, like you want to get back

together or something."

"Really?" Aurora said.

"It should not be hard. You are a writer, are you not?" Erik said. Aurora rolled her eyes.

Aurora: Gannon... Can I ask you a question?

"See!" Aurora said. "It is worthless. He will never reply," she said as he heard a beep come from her cell phone. She stared at it in amazement.

Gannon: Of course! I thought you would never message me again.

Aurora: If I were to get back together with you, I would need you to answer a question for me.

Gannon: I will tell you anything.

Aurora: Did you cheat on me? Like, did you ever have sex with anyone?

Gannon: Aurora...

Aurora: You said anything.

Gannon: Are you actually thinking about getting back together with me?

Aurora: Yes, I am thinking about it but need to know the truth. Did you have sex with Shazzy?

Gannon: No.

Aurora: You never had sex with anyone besides me our whole marriage?

Gannon: Well.

Gannon: I had sex with someone else during our marriage.

Aurora: Really? Who?

Gannon: Some chick from work.

"That makes me feel even worse!" Aurora blurted out. "He had sex with someone else!"

"He what?" Erik said in shock by how fast Gannon told her. "Let me see," he said, as Aurora practically threw the phone at the lawyer. Aurora started to cry and sank back in her chair. She crossed her arms.

"What's wrong?"

"Really?" Aurora said. "For a lawyer, you really are stupid."

"Hey," Erik said. "I am sorry. I am just shocked he answered so fast." They both heard Aurora's phone ding again.

Gannon: So, will we be getting back together now?

"Are you going to reply?" Erik said.

"Obviously not," Aurora said. "I think that I have had enough for the day. I also think you have all of the evidence you need."

"Okay, I just needed proof for the…" he said, as Aurora stood up and left.

She opened the door and began to walk out of the office. She then remembered the Jane Austen book on the bookshelf. She went to the shelf and took the book.

"I am taking this!" Aurora said to the receptionist.

"But that's not yours."

"Well, I basically just helped him fight my pre-nup," Aurora said. "So, think of it as a payment for a job he owes me for."

Aurora flashed the receptionist a fake smile and left.

*All I need is Jane and me, here*, she said as she hugged the book. Then she put the sleeve of her jacket to her face and dried the tear on her cheek.

# Chapter 16

The little black dress hung on a wooden hanger on the back of the door in Aurora's office. She stared at it all day anticipating how her date would go that Friday night. Since she wouldn't have time to go home after work, she brought the clothes she planned to wear on her date with Jason. Aurora was certain she would not wear heels like the last date. After all, to her it wasn't "a date."

When it was time to get ready, Aurora put on the little black dress. She had recently bought it while shopping with Tessa. She wore her black leggings with black leather boots that went to her knees. She also put on her black petticoat that had a hole in the left pocket. She knew it should be fixed because she kept losing things in it. She didn't want to fix it because her grandmother had given it to her. It was sentimental to her.

Aurora arrived at the restaurant at 6:00 p.m. She could see from outside of the restaurant that Jason was already there, sitting at a table, when she walked into the downtown restaurant. She lifted up her jacket sleeve to look at her watch, making sure she wasn't late. The feel and look of the restaurant was similar to an older Spanish style restaurant from the 1800s, though it was Peruvian. The windows had white curtains draped on each side. The sun was gone by then, so the lighting in the restaurant was dim. It had a romantic feel to it. She saw that Jason was sipping on a glass on red wine when she walked in.

Aurora walked up next to him and touched his shoulder; he jumped up and looked behind himself.

"Oh, you scared me!" Jason said.

"Oh, I am sorry." She giggled like a schoolgirl. *Okay Aurora, grow up now. He is already ten years older than you. Don't make the age difference that obvious.*

"It is okay." He stood up as Aurora took off her coat. Her hair was tied back. A pair of pearl studded earrings fit perfectly in her small earlobes. Jason could not help but stare at her, starting from her eyes, then following the curves of her body that her black dress outlined, all the way down to her leather boots.

"Wow. You are gorgeous," Jason said.

Aurora's face grew red as she sat down; Jason pulled out Aurora's chair, then put it underneath her. *Wow, such a gentleman! I could get used to this,* Aurora thought. She said to Jason, "Thank you." Jason sat down and took a gulp of red wine.

The waiter came and showed Aurora the wine menu and asked Aurora what she would like to drink from the menu.

"No. As tempting as it sounds," Aurora said, "I don't drink alcohol. I will just have water." She could tell Jason was staring at her as she ordered. Her cheeks remained as red as his wine the whole dinner. She turned from talking to the waiter and looked at Jason. Then their eyes locked for a moment.

"So, how was work today?" Jason said.

"It was good. It went slow. I feel Friday never goes fast enough." Aurora replied.

"I agree." Jason said with wide eyes, "Wow, Aurora. You just look so gorgeous tonight."

"It must be the lighting." She smiled and they both laughed. *Why am I falling for his charm?*

Jason said, "No, that's not it. You have this je ne sais quoi." In French, that referred to a quality that could not be easily described.

"Tu parles français?" Aurora asked. It meant, "Do you speak French?"

Jason was stunned and replied with, "Pas beaucoup, juste un petit peu. J'ai étudié à l'étranger en France." It translated in English: "Not a lot, just a little bit. I studied abroad in France." Aurora was fascinated that he spoke French.

"Oh, nice. I went there during college over one winter break and took a class on French literature and learned some French." She thought, *I just learned why French was really called the romance language.*

Jason said, "Oh that's nice. The people in France seem to think it's rude if you don't speak French when you are in France." Aurora rolled her eyes.

Aurora responded, "Yeah, some Americans feel that way about speaking English in America. I feel it's so stupid to think that way, but I digress." Aurora was passionate about political matters, but didn't want to engulf the subject that soon into their relationship since this was their first real date and all, though she kept telling herself it wasn't a date. "Anyway, let's not talk about politics," Aurora said.

"Good idea," Jason said as he cleared his throat and sat up straight in his chair.

The waiter brought Aurora her water and asked, "Are you two ready to order?"

Aurora looked at the waiter and smiled. She realized she had been so engulfed in the conversation with Jason, that she hadn't even looked at the menu. She usually got ceviche, but she would not that time because she wanted to avoid having stinky breath. So, she had to look at the menu that time. "No, not yet."

"Okay, I will be back in a second."

Aurora said to Jason, "So, tell me about yourself. What are your hobbies?"

"Well, I love to work out." She thought, *of course he does. God, please tell me he is not a gym bro.* Jason continued, "I work out every day after work. I have lost almost a hundred pounds in the last two years."

Aurora thought, *the weight loss could explain his bad posture.* Aurora hated when someone had horrible posture. However, she was intrigued by Jason's weight loss. She thought that was pretty amazing. *Is this why he is single and not married with kids?*

"Wow, Jason! That is impressive. I am sure that was tough," She said.

"Yes, it was tough, but I am pretty proud of myself." She figured Jason must be pretty confident with himself if he was open to talk about something that he may have been insecure about. Aurora wished she had that confidence to tell him she was married.

"Yeah. That's awesome! I love to work out too, but I have been slacking on working out since I moved. I used to be a gym rat."

"Oh. You just moved to Madison?" She immediately felt regret for saying she moved.

Aurora started to get flustered. She didn't want to say anything wrong. "No, I didn't move to Madison. I moved away from Madison. But I am moving back soon. I have a realtor looking for a new place for me."

"Oh, what happened? Bad roommate?"

"Uhhhh…" *My ex-roommate was an abusive sociopath, to say the least.* Aurora said, "You could say that."

"Well, I don't want to pry." *Too late.* "…but my cousin told me about what happened. I am sorry." Aurora was annoyed because she didn't think that growing up in a small town would still come back to haunt her after high school.

"Wait, what cousin? Your cousin told you what?" Aurora was still trying to be coy, but she figured he knew about the divorce or her still being married.

"My cousin is Cynthia Jackson."

*Oh crap! He knows everything then,* Aurora thought. She felt sick to her stomach and felt numbness at her temples.

"She was visiting a couple of days ago, and I told her I was seeing someone from up north. I told her your name and she told me she knew you."

"Yeah, she was my best friend in high school." Aurora was still shocked that she had no idea she and Jason were connected in such a close way. Aurora lowered her head and became extremely disappointed. "So, I guess Cynthia told you everything then, huh?"

The waiter came to the table to take the order but clearly felt like he had walked up to a serious conversation that he probably shouldn't interrupt. Jason made it easier by ordering for both of them.

After the waiter took the menus and walked away, Jason continued saying, "She told me that you are getting divorced."

Aurora took a big gulp of water and thought about drinking the rest of Jason's wine. Jason reached out his hand to hold Aurora's. She stopped breathing for a second. She looked at his hand grabbing onto her fingers. His hand was warm. Hers were cold and clammy from drinking from her water glass.

Jason started to rub her hands with his thumb. "Are you okay, Aurora?" Aurora was still looking down.

Aurora said, "Yes, I am fine." She started to laugh

hysterically. "This is a conversation that you would not normally have with someone on a first date."

Jason said with a grin, "Well, technically this is our second."

Aurora ignored his cute comment and still was hysterical. She pulled her hand back and put the napkin on her lap, while folding it half, making it a triangle. She started picking at her nails, which she typically did when she felt she was in an awkward situation. She finally looked up at Jason. "So, you are okay that I am still married and not divorced yet?"

"That is correct. As long as you are okay with it, Aurora, I don't care."

Aurora smiled. "No, I am fine."

She took a big breath. Aurora was so happy that they talked about that because it was bothering her. She knew they would have to talk about it eventually if things got serious. Before the date, she played the conversation in her head that they might have about her still being married. She expected it to go a lot more smoothly, but as Aurora had learned with Gannon, nothing in life goes quite like you expect it.

Jason and Aurora spent the rest of their dinner getting to know each other. In between each bite of food, they were laughing and smiling. Aurora could not remember the last time she had an adult conversation with such a smart individual.

After dinner, Jason had the idea to walk on the path next to Lake Monona. It was one of the big lakes surrounding the city of Madison. Jason said that the lake was walking distance from his house. *That better not be an invitation to come back to your place.* Aurora drove herself and Jason down because Jason had walked to the restaurant. He said he walked almost everywhere, and his job was also only a few blocks away from the restaurant.

Aurora and Jason parked in the parking lot. Her hands were freezing from holding onto the cold steering wheel. She got out of the car and her scarf almost blew off of her. It was so cold outside, that she could see her breath when she breathed. Jason got out of the car and walked out to meet her by the driver's side door. He grabbed her hand. She stared at their hands for a moment. She still couldn't believe she was dating again. *Wait. You are not dating. This is not a date.*

Jason tugged on her right hand. "You ready, beautiful?" Aurora was blushing but it was too windy and dark for him to notice.

Aurora quickly put a stocking cap on her head and wrapped her scarf around her neck. "Yes, I'm ready now," She said but her voice was muffled from the scarf covering half of her lips.

They started walking to a path and Aurora said bluntly, "So, since we are talking about so much personal stuff on this date, how are you still single, Jason?"

It seemed like Jason was trying to avoid that conversation just like Aurora didn't want to talk about still being married. Jason said back, "Well, I wish I knew the answer to that question, too."

Aurora was expecting him to say a little bit more. She said, "Oh, if you don't want to go into it, I understand."

"No, it's not that." Jason said. "Well, my last relationship didn't work out well. I mean, it was not as bad as yours." *Ouch.* "But I was engaged and I found out she was cheating on me. I saw her texts and everything. I didn't even want to look or anything, but he messaged her when she was sitting next to me on the couch."

"Hey, no need to explain. It could be worse. I caught my husband in the act with one of my friends." She laughed out loud, but it was an awkward laugh. She remembered the abuse she had received from Gannon and she got scared about being in a relationship or anything serious again. She pulled her hand out of Jason's hand. "I just want to put my hands in my pockets. My hands are so cold."

"Are you okay?" Jason asked, concerned.

They stopped and sat on a bench overlooking the lake. The moon beautifully reflected off of the lake that was still made of ice.

"I know something is wrong," Jason said. "You can't lie to me. I am a counselor." He laughed. He probably felt very witty after that comment.

"What do you mean that you are a counselor?" Aurora said. "I thought that you said you were a lawyer?"

"Well yes, I am a lawyer, but in court they can also call a lawyer a counselor. I was trying to be funny and make light of the situation."

"Oh..." *Again, you missed his joke.*

Aurora shivered as a gust of wind and snow came her way.

"If you are cold, that is definitely something I can help you with." Jason put his arm around her shoulders while still balancing his arm on the bench. Then he tried to put his arms around her waist and pull her closer to him. "I can help warm you up."

Aurora felt his warmth and for some reason felt like all of her stresses disappeared. She found herself not being able to have the courage to talk again, like she did when Jason had held her hand at dinner earlier that evening. *Why am I so uptight! Relax, Aurora. This guy is perfect. Calm the heck down.*

Then Jason pulled her forehead to his lips, having to lift up her hat. His lips were soft and warm pressed up against her cold skin. Aurora felt like she had known him forever, or at least like they had been together for a while. She let all of her walls melt away and felt completely comfortable in Jason's arms. This was the solace that she didn't know she needed. At least then, she just needed someone to hold her. She held back her tears as she thought about how many years she had wasted with Gannon when she could have been some famous author or journalist.

"Everything is going to be okay," Jason said as he pulled Aurora closer to him. She then stood up straight and looked at him. She put her hand to his face and rubbed his beard. She loved beards and Gannon would never grow one. Aurora said, "Sorry. I love beards."

"So you are a lumber sexual, huh?" He laughed again. *He seems to laugh at himself a lot.*

Aurora was confused by his comment and said, "What is a lumber sexual?"

"You have to know. You read all of the time. I am sure you have seen it somewhere."

"Maybe I did see it somewhere, but my mind is blank".

"Well, there are guys that sport a flannel and a beard. Then the lumber sexuals are the ones fanaticizing about a guy cutting wood with an axe and no shirt on, like he is a lumberjack."

"So, like a Paul Bunyan type?"

"Precisely," Jason said.

Aurora remembered reading about it as if a light bulb came on in her head. "You are right! I saw it in a Buzzfeed article," she said while laughing, then turned toward Jason again. She couldn't stop staring at his soft lips. She continued, "I grew up in the north woods. I cannot help but enjoy looking at a handsome man with a beard."

Jason said, "If you think I am handsome, then I must be really good looking."

"Yeah, I guess you are. That is why I am still so shocked you are single."

"It is because I haven't met you yet."

"Aw," she said. "That's sweet."

"Not as sweet as you."

"Okay, sly guy, I got it." They laughed again and became silent and looked at the moon.

Jason said, "The moon is beautiful tonight, don't you think?"

"Yes, it's so bright out here." Aurora looked around. "You don't even need a flashlight to see outside tonight. The natural light from the moon makes it seem so bright outside."

"Yes, it sure is beautiful," Jason said while he was looking at Aurora.

"But not as beautiful as me?" Aurora and Jason both laughed.

Jason turned Aurora's face towards his and kissed her. Aurora kissed him back and it made her feel happy, but it wasn't the first kiss she was expecting.

*But he is not Melih.* She then pictured herself kissing Melih, and pulled back from kissing Jason again and sat there as the wind hit her face.

Jason said, "Was it a bad kiss?"

"No, it's not that." She felt numb and emotionless. Many thoughts ran through her mind. Jason kissed great, but she didn't know how to feel. When she kissed Jason, she thought about how Gannon had tainted what love actually was to Aurora. When she saw love or romance, she saw it as a tool to manipulate her. She thought kissing someone would be a catalyst to manipulating her in the long run. But what she really did not understand is why the thought of kissing Melih had popped into her head.

"Is everything okay, Aurora?"

"Yeah, I'm fine. Just tired and cold." Jason didn't seem to believe her.

"Okay, would you like to go? I can walk home."

"No, I will drive you. It's freezing and dark out."

Jason and Aurora went back to her car. She drove Jason to his house, as he gave her directions from the passenger seat, pointing where to go.

As they almost arrived to Jason's, he said, "I am right there on the left."

She pulled up to his place. He lived in an apartment building, although she was expecting a man of his age to live in some fancy house.

"You live here?" she said.

Jason said with pride, "Yes I do." He saw Aurora yawn and asked her, "Do you want to come inside to have a cup of coffee? I know you live a little bit away. This will help keep you awake and warm you up."

"No, I am fine. I will stop at the coffee shop a few blocks down."

Aurora started to feel she was sounding uptight, but appreciated the evening that they had. She was happy to be able to talk freely about her life and relationship. She also enjoyed their intellectual conversation. She realized that she did have a good time and she shouldn't let that kiss ruin anything.

"I did have a good time tonight. I mean, I had one of the best conversations I had in a while. I felt very comfortable with you," Aurora said.

Jason felt that he was already being put in the friend zone, though that wasn't the case at all. She just wasn't ready for any physical contact with a man. She held Jason's hand and she kissed him on the cheek good night. "Jason, I am fine. I had a great time tonight."

Jason still didn't completely believe her, but he took her word for it. "Okay, thanks for accompanying me tonight. I had a lovely time."

Aurora said, "I am sorry I ended it so soon. I am just tired, Jason."

"It is okay. I understand." He put his hand on Aurora's face and she flinched like she had at ice skating rink. "Just message me when you are home."

"Okay, I will. Have a good night."

Jason smiled at her and said, "All right. You too, beautiful."

He got out of the car. Aurora watched him open the door to his apartment complex and then she left. She was worried all Jason wanted was sex because he was older than she was. She thought, *why else would an older guy date a young girl like me? Does he want a trophy wife or something?*

That night, Aurora drove home feeling sad and mad all at once. Her face was red from the wind and frustration she felt for Gannon and Melih. She resented Gannon for making her feel so hurt. "You ruined my chance of ever feeling love again," she said. Jason was so predictable, but she thought that Jason was safe.

Maybe safe was what she needed.

AFTER SHE SAID YES

# Chapter 17

Aurora got to Tessa's place a few nights later, after she was done with work. She sat on the couch to watch the news and started to think that she felt bad about what had happened with Jason. She felt like she shouldn't have pushed Jason out of her car so abruptly. *He was probably just being nice, right? I don't know a good guy if I see one right now.* Aurora was upset Jason hadn't messaged her or called her. *My theory about him only wanting sex from me was accurate, or maybe he just sees me as damaged goods.*

She wondered why a guy ten years older than she was, who was successful, handsome, and charming, wanted anything to do with her.

*Maybe he only goes for vulnerable women... That is why he went for me in the first place. I am vulnerable, but I am not falling into a trap set up by a boy, again... But wait, Jason is a man. It must be different since he is not Gannon.... Oh crap, Aurora.*

She was so upset that she messaged Jason about it.

Aurora: Hello, Jason. I was wondering why you haven't messaged me to at least see how I was doing.

He never responded to her, and she regretted sending him that text because she felt needy.

Aurora waited for days for Jason to message her back, but he never responded to her text. She then called her best friend from high school to find out about Jason.

"Hey Cynthia, I cannot get ahold of Jason. Is everything okay with him?"

"Well, hello to you too."

"Oh, sorry. Hey. How have you been?" Aurora said.

Cynthia said, "Fine…. And yeah, he is fine. He was up north last weekend."

"Oh, well, he hasn't messaged me. I wonder if something went wrong."

"No, he was fine, but he dropped his phone in the lake. That is probably why he didn't respond."

Aurora said, "Well, did he get a new number?"

"He might have. Why don't you message him on Facebook?"

"I deactivated my Facebook." Aurora deactivated her Facebook every so often when she wanted to rid herself of drama and current events. Though in reality, she was really sick of seeing happy couples. It made her want to throw up.

"You guys didn't have sex, right?"

"Oh my God! Really, Cynthia?" Aurora said. "No, you know I will only have sex when I am married to someone." Cynthia should have known better than anyone that Aurora had saved her virginity for marriage because Aurora had prided herself on that in high school. Aurora's virginity had meant everything to her, which is another reason she resented Gannon because he had been so eager to take it.

Cynthia replied, "Good, I am glad to see you haven't changed."

"You know me!" Aurora said. "So, how have you been?"

"Good. Just moved back with my parents for a while."

Aurora responded, "What! Why is that?"

Cynthia said, "I got a job at our high school, as an English teacher."

"Oh! That's exciting! Congratulations."

"I know I am not as successful as you, but it is still exciting."

*Yeah, I am successful, but I am divorced…. Well, almost divorced. How exciting. I don't want anyone to be envious of me. No one wants to go through what I went through with Gannon.*

Aurora said, "So, are you still writing?" Cynthia and Aurora became friends in high school because they both loved writing. Cynthia wrote poems and Aurora wrote short stories for fun.

"Yes I am. I am hoping to put together a bunch of my poems. I already have a few agents in mind."

"Well, that's exciting."

Cynthia said, "I am not getting my hopes up, but I think it could be really good."

"I hope someone publishes you. How about I do an article about you in our magazine? Tell your agent about that and maybe it will help."

Cynthia said, "No, Rora. I want to do this on my own." Like Aurora, Cynthia didn't want to have to depend on anyone or feel like she owed anyone anything.

Aurora said, "Come on. I owe you one!"

"You owe me for what?" Cynthia said.

"You are going to get Jason's number for me."

Cynthia said, "Well, I still don't know if I want your help."

"Come on, Cynthia."

"Fine Aurora. We have a deal. In the meantime, I'll message the agents about the article and message you Jason's number."

Aurora said, "Thank you. And about the article, don't mention it."

--

Later that night, Zara called Aurora and asked her to come hang out at her place on the following Saturday night with

Zara, Sara, and a couple of their friends. Aurora was sure that Melih would be there.

"I am sorry Zara. I cannot make it."

"Vhat? Really, Aurora? Come on! On a Saturday night?" Zara said.

*If only Zara knew I am just worried that it might be awkward between Melih and me.*

"Come on, Aurora. You can't lie to me," Zara said. "Aurora? Vhere did you go?"

"I am here. Just thinking," Aurora said.

*Okay, since Dan and Tessa are hitting it off, Tessa would definitely go. So I guess if Tessa is there, she will be a good buffer and it will not be so bad.*

Aurora heard Tessa in the back of her mind saying, "You better go, Aurora. I never have time to meet guys, so now I have this opportunity with Dan... I need you there."

--

Two days later, Aurora pulled her cell phone out of her desk drawer during her lunch hour. She saw that Cynthia had sent her Jason's number.

*Should I message him now? No, I can't. What about Melih? What about my divorce? What about looking too needy? You know what, forget it. What do I have to lose anymore?*

Aurora: Hey Jason.

Jason: Hey. Who is this?

*What? How many girls is he talking to that would say this to me?* Then she remembered she was still married and wanted to hang out with Melih at the same time.

Aurora: It is Aurora... I was wondering why you haven't messaged me?

Jason: Oh, hey! I am so glad you messaged me. How did you get my number?

Aurora: Your cousin Cynthia...

Jason: I am sorry I didn't message you or try to contact you. I had to get a new phone.

Aurora: I figured since I wouldn't have sex with you that you wouldn't message me again...

Jason: Oh wow...

Jason: Just know that I am not like that. I knew you had to drive home still. So I wanted to make some coffee for you to take with. What I say is what you get. If I want something, I will tell you or ask you.

*I guess I read into that too much... Like I do with everything.* Aurora liked how straight forward he was. *I feel like the bad guy now.*

Jason: It's fine. We can just pretend it never happened. Deal?

Aurora: Deal.

--

The next morning, Aurora arrived to work and saw two bouquets of flowers on her desk. They were not the ugly yellow roses like Gannon had brought her the day after he cheated on her. All she could think was, *I am still married, and two people are sending me flowers. I know how this is going to make me look to everyone in the office.*

Aurora was anxious because she was going to be looking at a couple of new houses within a few days, and the Valentine's Day magazine special was about to come out.

Tiffany asked, like a kid on the playground when someone has a crush on them, "So, who are the flowers from,

Mrs…Miss Tousey?"

Aurora said to Tiffany, "You didn't look?" Aurora laughed. Aurora knew that Tiffany had always been nosy because Aurora was so closed about her life and never let anyone get to know her on a personal level. So, Tiffany tried to find out for herself.

Tiffany replied as she looked down at her computer and pretended to type something, "No, I didn't." Aurora didn't believe she didn't look at the cards before she got in. She gave Tiffany a peculiar look. "I really don't know whom they are from." Aurora assumed one was from Jason and the other must have been from Melih. She went into her office and shut her door. She ran to see the cards on the roses.

She looked at the first bouquet of red roses that were cut short and packed in a white box. She picked one up and felt the velvety rose petal. She then brought it to her nose to smell it. She sneezed and said, "Dang allergies." She looked around the first bouquet for the card. There was no card on the first one. "Well, that is weird."

She cracked open her office door and said to Tiffany, "Did both of these flowers have cards?"

Tiffany said, "No, only one did."

"Ha! So you did look," Aurora said.

"Ah, What… N-n-n-o," Tiffany said as her cheeks grew red and her lip quivered.

Aurora laughed and closed the door.

Aurora went and looked at the second bouquet and around it for a card, again. She found it and took it off the plastic cardholder.

*The first bouquet is because I am sorry for not contacting you the other night. The second bouquet is because you are gorgeous.*

*- Jason*

Her face became flushed as she read the card. Though no one was around for her to feel shy, she still blushed. Since she usually didn't keep flowers in her office, for some reason she wanted to keep those, though she would only keep them in her office them until the end of the day and have Tiffany put them on her own desk.

--

Two nights before Zara and Sara's party, Aurora was lying in bed, reading her new Jane Austen novel. She heard her phone chime and picked it off of the mint colored nightstand next to her bed.

Melih: Hey Aurora… I hope you have been doing well.

*Is he really messaging me? Finally?* Her heart started to beat fast as she read the message several times. She started to daydream of the moment where they stared into each other eyes at the ice skating rink. *It was as if time stopped. As if he was the person who would come save me after I was lost at sea.*

Aurora didn't respond until after staring at her phone for half of the morning. She thought of texting, *I was fine until you messaged me* or *I was fine until you triggered what Gannon did to me.* Aurora only wanted to say those things so she could look tough, but it just made her look mean.

*But that isn't me. I am not mean.*

Aurora really knew that it was not his fault because no one knew until that point, besides Tessa or Aurora's family, that Gannon was abusive. *In reality, I am scared that I may really fall for him and be hurt again.*

Aurora: I am fine…. Thank you for asking.

Melih: Well, I wanted to say sorry for what happened when we went ice skating. I had no idea what happened to you and I

wanted to give you space. I didn't know Gannon abused you...
I hope I am not messaging you too late.

*What is it with these guys and their space? The space you gave
me, Melih, was like the distance between Earth and the Sun. The last
thing I want is for you to give me space; I want you to console me.*

She wanted him to tell her everything would be all right.
She thought that if he really cared, he would have chased after
her to make sure everything was all right and express his
undying love for her. Due to her being a hopeless romantic,
she often thought that all romances should be like the love
stories you see in the movies, where one character is playing
hard to get, while the other character is running after them.
Then they both end up expressing their undying love for one
another. She thought she might have unrealistic expectations,
though with Gannon, she had set the bar pretty low.

Aurora: Everything is fine. Thank you for checking up on
me...

Melih: I am bad with messaging. Would you like to meet
for a coffee after work tomorrow?

*What is the worst that could happen?*

Aurora: I'll check my schedule and get back to you in an
hour or so.

Aurora knew she was free that night, but wanted to be coy.
Every few minutes she was thinking about responding to him,
but she wanted to drag him along by a thread, like he was
doing to her heart. She messaged Melih an hour later.

Aurora: Okay, I can meet you tomorrow after work. Just
text me the coffee shop and I will meet you there.

Melih: Okay. See you at Michelangelo's at 6.

--

She could not stop thinking about Melih all day that day. She knew one thing, that if he told her how to feel, she would freak out. She was over men telling her how to feel.

Aurora walked into the coffee shop and was hit with the aroma of freshly brewed coffee and the sound of milk frothing in the background. The coffee shop was full of hipsters and college students working on homework. Aurora noticed their awkward facial expressions and mannerisms that she mimicked as well. *They must be here on their first date.* Aurora felt her heart beat fast. Aurora looked down when she realized that Melih might see her. She went to the barista and didn't look for Melih. She didn't have to see him to know he was there. She could feel the electricity of his presence near her.

Aurora ordered a cappuccino and pulled out her money to pay and Melih came up from behind her and said to the barista, "I will pay for her drink." Melih was wearing a gray cardigan sweater and dark green jeans.

Aurora turned around swiftly and said to Melih, "No, I can pay for myself. Thank you."

Melih said, "No, please." He gave the cash to the barista and told her to keep the change. "I invited you."

*He is killing me with kindness, I see...* "Well, thank you for the drink, Melih." Aurora said as she put her hair behind her ears.

"No problem," he said with a big smile, as if he achieved breaking through her walls. "My father and my religion taught me to be generous. Even if it is something so small."

He signaled to the table where he was sitting. Aurora followed him to the table and felt herself smile as she smelled his Chanel cologne. The smell gave her goose bumps down her spine. *Don't fall for his charm,* she thought.

"Let's go take a seat," he said. *He is not Gannon. He may be genuinely nice.*

They sat down. Melih said, "So, how have you been?"

She thought to herself, *I have been a nervous wreck and Gannon ruined my idea of love but otherwise, I have been great. Thanks.* Aurora said, "I have been fine. Just staying busy with work."

"Dat is good you are staying busy."

The barista came with Aurora's cappuccino in a white porcelain cup. The art of the foam mixed with the espresso made it look like a heart on top.

Aurora said, "Yeah."

There was silence as they both realized this was the first time both of them had been alone together, even if it was in public. Both of them took drinks from their coffees. Aurora decided to speak first to break the silence. "So, why did you invite me here?" She was sure it was to clear the air before they saw each other on Saturday at Sara and Zara's house.

"Vell, I vanted to see how you vere doing." He took a deep breath. "I hawen't stopped thinking about vhat you told me about Gannon."

*Why couldn't you have called or texted to tell me that then?*

Aurora's face went white as if they were talking about someone who had just died. Melih used his hand to push back his silky dark black hair. His fingers were long, and he had a few dark hairs on his knuckles.

"Oh. It is no problem. I have been fine." Aurora took a drink of her coffee.

"Den you must be tough."

"Yeah, something like that." Aurora looked down and started dragging her index finger along the rim of the coffee cup. She knew that she had made it far since she had first found Gannon on that couch with Shazzy. Then saw a flash back of them on the couch and felt a bad taste in her mouth. She said out loud, "Just nasty." She had meant to think that.

"Vhat's nasty?"

"Oh nothing. Just remembering the lunch I had today." *Where is your filter, Aurora?* she thought. "So, I talked to my lawyer about what would happen if Gannon didn't come to court."

Melih sat up straight and his temples started to pulse. He slightly stuck out his chest as the sound of Gannon's name made him want to fight him. Melih said, "So, vhat did your lawyer say?"

"Well, basically if Gannon doesn't show up, they will just proceed without him."

Melih replied, "Vell, that's good."

"Yeah, I was worried about it. I thought I was going to have to be married to him forever."

"That would be horrible," Melih said. "Since vee are talking about your divorce, I vanted to say…. I am sorry."

"Why? You are not divorcing me." Aurora seemed confused.

"No, I am sorry about vhat he did to you." He pushed his hair back again. Aurora thought that it might be something he did when he was nervous. She imagined herself putting her hand through his hair. *Aurora, get ahold of yourself.*

Melih continued, "I felt like I could have done something to prevent it or I could have stopped him."

"No one could have stopped him, Melih. I didn't even have the power to tell anyone. He manipulated me to complete silence."

"I know, Aurora, but vee all saw how horribly he treated you. I alvays felt so bad for you. I just didn't want to interfere. Da way I was raised, vee never put our noses in anyone else's marriage. Vee all knew Gannon was spoiled growing up, but vee never knew how abusive he could have been."

"It is okay, Melih. That is how the youngest child acts when they do not get their way." Now that Aurora thought about it, she was annoyed that no one had spoken up if they saw him treating her badly.

Melih grabbed her hand now and started talking with more passion. His hands looked as soft as a freshly made bed. Melih said, "I am da youngest in my family and I am not like dat." Aurora stared at his hand as it touched hers. *Oh my God. His hand is touching mine.* Their hands linked together. It felt like putty melting in her hands. Melih continued, "He is not a man. He is a boy."

"I know. It's fine," Aurora said. *We are touching hands!*

"How are you so calm about dis, Aurora?"

*Xanax.* The conversation was starting to exhaust her. *What, do you want me to cry or something?* She was lost in her thoughts.

Melih said, "I am just shocked you are showing no emotion."

*Okay, I get the point,* she thought.

"I am tough." Aurora smiled. *Tougher than I look.*

He took his other hand and started rubbing her hand that he was holding. He took a deep breath and calmed down. "Aurora, I guess I am just upset vith myself for not doing anything."

"It's okay, Melih. You have always been sweet to me." She flashed him a smile, showing her dimples. "Don't worry." She started rubbing his knuckles. She felt that he should be the one telling her to calm down, but she was consoling him. She could see deep concern in Melih's eyes. She wondered what he was thinking. Aurora continued, "So, will I see you Saturday night at Sara and Zara's?"

Melih was caught off guard and said, "At vhat?"

He took a second to collect his thoughts, like he was in a different world. Melih looked down on his hands and immediately pulled them away. Aurora looked distraught as she was confused why Melih pulled away. Aurora didn't know then that he had never held a woman's hand before.

Melih continued, "Oh yeah, I vill be there." He collected himself and smiled at Aurora. "How about you?"

"Yes, I will be there." Aurora sighed. "I kind of have to go now because Dan and Tessa are together. Well, at least they like each other."

Melih said, "Hey! I'll be dere. Dat should make it better for you, right?"

"Is there any other reason you invited me here, Melih?"

"Ahh," Melih looked up like he was pondering a thought. "No, I just vant to see how you are."

"Well, I still have to drive home. It's getting late." Aurora wanted to make it seem like she had something more important to do.

"No problem. I will walk you to your car," he said without giving Aurora a chance to say no.

They both put on their jackets and walked to her car.

Melih put his arm around her waist. She took a deep breath in. *Stay calm, Aurora. Act natural.* She felt her heart fill with a feeling she had never felt as they walked to her car.

"You know you are so sweet, Melih…. and so handsome." *Again, you should keep your thoughts to yourself.*

"Vell, you are gorgeous. So, I tink you vin," Melih said. She rolled her eyes.

He opened the door for her and kissed her on the forehead before she got into the car. She felt excitement. It was as if she were just on the first date she had ever been on in her life. She didn't know that that feeling could ever exist again. *He probably didn't see it like a date, but I felt it was... Well, I hope it was. Was it?*

She heard knocking on her car window and she rolled it down as the steam of Melih's breath turned into vapor. "Aurora, I vant to tell you that I know I cannot change vhat Gannon did to you, but I can help you through this divorce."

"Thank you," Aurora said. "That means a lot.... But I think I should get going. You are probably freezing."

"I am." He said as he rubbed his hands together to warm them up. He flashed a warm smile at Aurora. "Good night, Aurora."

"Good night," she said.

# Chapter 18

It was Saturday morning, and Aurora and Tessa were getting ready to go house hunting. Tessa was there merely for moral support. Since they would be going to a party that night, they thought they would just spend the whole day in Madison. Aurora wanted a coffee the size of her head that morning because she had not been able to sleep much the night before. She thought of Melih putting his hands through his hair, the way his hands touched hers, the way his lips would touch his coffee cup. She wished his lips would touch hers like that.

Aurora and Tessa had breakfast at a quaint restaurant called the Wooden Chair, which was Aurora and Tessa's favorite breakfast and brunch place. It was their favorite because it felt like home to both of them. Tessa had grown up on a farm and Aurora's father always took her to a café that was similar, as a child. The place was a farm-to-table restaurant. The walls were decorated with photos from Wisconsin's farming history. To add to the décor, there was an assortment of different colored chairs at each table. Not one chair was identical. The aroma of eggs being friend on the griddle and fresh herbs filled their noses. What filled their stomachs were the veggie eggs benedict.

"So, today is the last day we may spend like this, huh, Aurora?"

"I hope not!" Aurora said as she smeared some jelly on her toast.

"Well, I feel like it is…"

"It is not like I am leaving the country, Tessa. I am moving about forty minutes from you."

"I know, but I am just worried we will not see each other or talk much, like you did when you were with Gannon," Tessa said as she looked down at her coffee cup that was nearly empty.

"I know. You have mentioned it before," Aurora said. She pulled money out of her purse to pay for the breakfast. "You don't have to worry, Tessa. Things will not be like last time."

--

They arrived at the realtor's office near downtown. The outside of the office was a cream-colored house with brown shutters and a front porch overlooking the busy one-way street. Aurora and Tessa walked inside and sat on the waiting chairs. Aurora found a stack of magazines on an end table for them to look at, ones like *Good Housekeeping*, and even her magazine. They read through them as they waited, though Tessa would occasionally look at her phone and read something on the screen and smile or giggle.

"Is Dan up this early?" Aurora said.

"How do you know th…"

"Tessa, I know you too well. You are my best friend, remember?"

"Yes. He is awake," Tessa said while her cheeks turned red.

Tessa again looked at a text on her phone and smiled. *Aw. I am so happy that a good guy finally is making her smile,* Aurora thought.

Aurora started to get severe anxiety from remembering she would be living on her own. However, she was happy for the new start and second chance at life after Gannon.

The realtor, Stacey, came in and shook both Tessa and Aurora's hands. Stacey was a blonde with long legs that she was always hiding with her pants suits. She was good at her job, which is what Aurora admired her for. Aurora really appreciated and admired hard work. They all went into the office and Stacey pulled up some listings on her computer, where she showed some places that Aurora may be interested in. Tessa was still on her phone, messaging Dan, while Stacey and Aurora conversed. Aurora saw Tessa keep smiling at her phone. Her smiles made Aurora smile.

Aurora said to Stacey, "I prefer something downtown that is close to work. I prefer that it is a house, too."

Stacey said, "What is your price range?"

"A thousand per month, but I prefer to pay in cash and not have a lease. You can pull some strings, right?" Aurora said with a smile. Stacey rolled her eyes at Aurora.

"Well," Stacey said, "I guess I can, but why cash?"

"Well, at least until my divorce is finalized. That is what my lawyer advised, so I don't need to change my address with the court."

"Ah, noted." Stacey looked back at her computer and clicked some houses to show Aurora. It showed an array of houses in her price range.

"I like that one!" Aurora said while pointing at the screen.

"But it is not very modern," Stacey said.

"So!" Aurora said. "It is right on the lake."

"Well," Stacey said, "if that is what you want."

It was a beautiful two-bedroom English style home that had to be almost two hundred years old. The bathroom and kitchen tiles were white with dark hints of blue, and it looked like it had recently been remodeled. The walls were matte white. Aurora figured the wooden floors would creek when she walked on it, but she wanted a place with history. It reminded her of the home her great grandparents had lived in after immigrating to the United States from Pomerania. She could almost smell her great grandma's apple strudel, fresh out of the oven.

"All right. I have the keys to this place. We can go see it now if you like. Are there any other ones you might be interested in?"

"No. I think this is going to be the one," Aurora said.

--

They pulled up to the home. The porch was not perfectly flat. If you were to put a marble on the porch, it would certainty roll off, but Aurora didn't mind. It had a small back yard overlooking the lake. *I could host parties back there, if I wanted to…. Ha! Don't kid with yourself, Aurora. That will probably never happen, you anti-social butterfly!* Though she was introverted, she thought she might start to change that and be more spontaneous.

They walked inside and took a look around. Aurora saw that there was a beautiful room overlooking the lake upstairs, and she imagined herself having a desk right in front of that window, where she could work and write, with a beautiful view in front of her. The kitchen was below the office room, with the same view as well.

Before she thought about it anymore, she looked at Stacey after touring the house. "So, how much for this place again?"

Stacey had a peculiar look on her face and said, "Well, it is slightly out of your price range." Aurora gestured her to proceed with telling her the price. "Also, I called the owner on our way here. He said it is twelve hundred a month and he will pay for the utilities because you are paying in cash. He doesn't normally do this for me, but he owed me a favor. I also explained your situation about the divorce and he was understanding." Aurora hoped she wouldn't have to repay Stacey back for her doing this favor, as well, but she didn't care at that point. She loved the house.

Aurora said, "Great! I will take it then."

"Perfect. I will email you the paperwork to fill out and then you can move in as soon as you like," Stacey said.

Aurora looked around and realized she regretted she would have to buy furniture. "Stacey?"

"Yes, Aurora?"

"I also need your help with something else," Aurora said.

"Of course you would," Stacey mumbled under her breath. She was unenthused with Aurora's needs, as if she didn't have a choice besides to help her on her Saturday off of work. Stacey probably didn't want to lose the chance at a spread in Aurora's magazine.

"I'm sorry. What did you say?" Aurora said.

"Oh. I said your hair looks nice."

Aurora and Tessa both rolled their eyes at one another.

"Stacey, one more thing. I need you to tell me somewhere I can rent furniture. I don't want to buy anything."

Stacey said, "No problem. I can contact the company that works for me. You know the company that I use to stage houses for your magazine?"

"No, I don't really remember. Sorry," Aurora said. "Do they owe you favors too?" Aurora tried to joke and laughed an awkwardly as she looked at Tessa. Tessa looked bored and un-amused. Like Aurora, Tessa was not good at hiding the way she felt. Stacey didn't reciprocate a laugh either. Tough crowd. She didn't seem too amused because she was already taking time out of her Saturday to help out Aurora. *Stacey's Saturdays are probably for brunch dates with her girlfriends and shopping.*

--

Aurora and Tessa spent the rest of the afternoon in museums, eating lunch, and enjoying girl time. They laughed until they cried. It reminded them of their times in college when they would come to The Union to drink coffee and study in the spring. It was bittersweet because they knew that it would be one of the last times they would be able to hang out like that for a while.

As they were walking to Aurora's car to go to Zara and Sara's, Aurora wanted to tell her about something in advance.

"Tessa, there is one thing I want to tell you before we go to Zara and Sara's to help prepare for the party."

"Okay? What is it?"

"Well, no one knows about Melih and me liking each other," Aurora said.

Tessa raised one of her eyebrows, "Oh... really?"

"Nope."

"Well. Someone does," Tessa said.

"What? Who!"

"Well, I told Dan... I didn't know it was a secret... I'm sorry."

"Wait!" Aurora said. "Now that I think of it, Melih never said he liked me, but his actions speak otherwise."

"Aurora, you are just overanalyzing the situation," Tessa said.

"Well, that is what I do."

"I know. So, just don't worry and have a good time tonight, okay?" Tessa said.

"Okay," Aurora said. "I mean, Melih and I are not in a relationship, so you are right. I am overanalyzing."

Tessa smiled as she said, "I know. I am always right." They both laugh.

"Well. It's okay. As long as no one else knows about him and me, I am fine with that," Aurora said. "It is just... You know how they already stopped hanging out with Gannon because they decided to take my side."

"Yeah."

"Well, that is why I don't want them to know about Melih yet because if something bad happens between us, then they will have to choose sides again and it is going to be extremely awkward. I don't want them to have to choose between me or Melih."

--

Zara and Sara's house had a very classic Russian set up. It looked like a sitting room of Russian royalty. Aurora envisioned their sitting room was out of a scene from Leo Tolstoy's book *Anna Karenina*. The curtains were made of white and gold silk and a chandelier hung from the ceiling in the living room. Aurora always assumed Zara and Sara came from rich families in Russia, but she never asked. *They are probably descendants of royalty.*

Since only a few people were going to be there, it was more of a casual get-together than a party. After setting everything up and helping with making party food, Aurora and Tessa changed and got ready. They both put on a pair of dark jeans and black three-quarter sleeved shirts. Tessa curled her long hair and Aurora just combed hers. Aurora was never really into doing her hair. She would usually just wash it, comb it, and then let it air dry. Aurora put her hair behind ears and put on a pair of diamond-studded earrings. As she looked in the mirror, she smiled at the reflection she saw. Gannon had once convinced Aurora she was distorted and ugly. But when she looked in the mirror, she thought she was beautiful for the first time in what felt like forever to her.

Tessa was sitting in the living room with Zara and Sara while Aurora went to the kitchen to get some snacks. As Aurora was in the kitchen, she saw Dan and Melih walk in. As soon as she saw Melih, she dropped her plate of pita chips, though she felt like she dropped her pride. The first thing Dan saw was Tessa sitting on the couch and walked to her without noticing the mess Aurora made. *Good one, Aurora!* Aurora thought to herself while grunting and mumbling things under her breath.

She saw two feet in loafers in front of her. *It's him. It's him. It's him.* She didn't want to look up.

"Hey, Rora, let me help you vith dat." Melih moved the bangs from her face and put them behind her right ear. She was craving that touch. Melih then started helping her clean up, as if he had never touched her. They reached for the same chip and his hand touched hers so softly, as if he were dragging a feather along her skin. They both looked into each other's eyes and time stopped for a moment.

Zara came into the kitchen and saw the two kneeling on the floor. "Hey, is everything okay, guys?"

Aurora and Melih both said in sync, "Everything is fine."

"Okay," Zara said, "but it doesn't look like it. Do you need help?"

Aurora said, "No, thank you. Melih is helping me. I dropped my chips. You know I'm clumsy." Melih smiled at Aurora. Luckily Zara couldn't see how Melih was looking at

Aurora and could only see the back of his head.

"Ve vill be in da living room in a second, Zara," Melih said.

Zara walked to the living room.

Aurora was biting her lips as she stared at him with an illustrious look, as if he were making her weak. *How can I ignore those beautiful chocolate eyes and-olive toned skin? Or how can I stop staring at his soft lips?* Aurora bit her lower lip.

It was too cold of a night for any of them to want to go out. They decided to stay inside reminiscing on the good old days from college and the new days with their new friend, Tessa. Zara and Sara served Russian tea and sweetened it with cherries. Melih gloated about how much better Turkish tea was in comparison.

Reminiscing reminded Aurora of their days in college, and the only thing missing was Gannon. Aurora missed the way Gannon had been in college. She wished for a second that it could have worked out because the last thing she wanted was him to be the monster he was. *Is there anything I could have done to change the way he was or prevented his anger?* Aurora came to terms that she could not change the past, to rewrite the present or the future. All that thinking about Gannon made her overwhelmed. She started to feel herself sweat and could feel her heart beat fast. Everyone could tell she was upset about something because they all knew that Aurora was horrible at hiding her emotions. Also, her face was extremely pale.

"I'll be right back," Aurora said as she stood up and straightened out her shirt.

"Hey, I-I-I gotta take a phone call," Melih said soon after Aurora stood up. "My family is calling from Turkey."

Aurora hung her head as she walked down the hall.

Melih went to the room that Aurora was in. He sat next to her as she lay on the bed in Zara's room. It reminded her of the room of a sultan. Silk pillows surrounded her as she buried her face in one of them. She yelled into one of the pillows to muffle her screaming. "Why can't you just get him out of your head, Aurora! He is not in control of you anymore."

She felt someone sit next to her. Aurora turned around and sat up, pushing him away.

Melih tried to rub her back, but quickly pulled his hand away. "Everything is going to be okay, Rora."

"Melih, stop that. Leave me alone. Please. Someone is going to come in here and find us." *Don't leave though. I want you, Melih. I need you.*

"Don't worry about it, Aurora," Melih said. "Tell me vhat is vrong. Are you okay?"

"I feel like you already know the answer to that, Melih," Aurora said. "But yes, I was just thinking about Gannon." A tear ran down her face, and Melih wiped it away. "Please don't touch me."

"I am sorry," Melih said. "I am just trying to help you relax. You know I am here for you and vant to help you through dis divorce."

"I am sorry to sound mean. I-I-I am just scared of men right now." Aurora continued, "And... I just feel stupid for ever being with him."

"You don't have to blame yourself for Gannon. You did not know he vas a monster," Melih said. He put his hand to her wet cheek to dry her tears. "Aşkım. I mean, my love." He started to stumble on his words. "Aşkım means, my love, in Turkish.... Sorry, I didn't mean... Oh dang it..."

"You have never called me that before, Melih." He chuckled at her.

"What?" Aurora said. "Did I pronounce it right?"

"Pronounce vhat?"

"Your name?" Aurora said.

"Vell. No. But dat is da cute ting about it," Melih said.

"Anyway… you are right about Gannon," Aurora said.

"Stop thinking about him. His name should not leave your beautiful lips." With his hand on her face, he rubbed his thumb along her lips. His thumb felt soft. Melih continued, "Aurora, you know I like you so much." He quickly pulled his hand away as if touching a woman were touching forbidden fruit to him.

"No I don't, actually." She could smell his masculine pheromones calling out her name.

"I am trying so hard to contain my feelings," Melih said. *You have no idea.*

"Well, you have done a great job so far," Aurora said and giggled.

*I don't know why, but I am trying hard to not kiss him right now.*

Aurora and Melih got off the bed to walk out of the room as they heard some noise in the living room. The sounds came from a man that wasn't there earlier. The voice was muffled. *Why does that voice sound so familiar?* She heard the voice getting closer. For a few moments the man stopped talking. She could hear him getting closer to her, and she heard Zara yell. Aurora could hear the stomping the man's feet made with each step he took. He was getting closer and closer. She could hear him in the hallway, and her heart started to beat faster. Adrenaline went through her veins to her brain.

"Not now," she said. She could sense something bad was about to happen. The door opened and she couldn't breathe.

"Gannon, please don't!" Aurora yelled as she thought he was going to attack her. All of her past memories with Gannon flashed in front of her eyes. She covered her face with her hands to protect herself. She thought he was going to kill her, but Gannon lunged toward Melih. She thought he was going to kill Melih. *How did he know I was here? No one invited him. Who told him about tonight?*

Gannon yelled, "I knew you guys were messin' around!" Aurora could smell the whiskey on Gannon's breath.

Melih said, "No vee veren't, bro. Calm down!"

"Melih, you already told me you liked her. You ain't foolin' me." *He told him what?* Gannon released a large amount of air from his chest and got close to Melih. Their noses were almost touching. Gannon continued, "You know what, you dirty A-rab. I am goin' to kill you." Gannon pointed at Aurora, then at his own chest. "She is my girl."

Instead of talking back by saying he was Turkish and not an Arab, he ignored that comment. Gannon was too ignorant to even know the difference between a lake and an ocean, let alone an Arab or a Turk. Melih always knew that Gannon was racist, just never toward him, until that moment.

Melih said, "Gannon, she isn't yours anymore, and she isn't mine yet, either." Melih continued after taking a breath and raising his voice, "She is nobody's!"

Aurora thought that Melih wasn't proud enough to be with her or too ashamed. She didn't hear Melih say, "Yet." She became so upset that she tried to run out of the room, but Gannon grabbed her arm.

Aurora looked in Gannon's eyes; they were red like a fire, as if the devil himself was staring into her eyes. "You ain't goin' anywhere, Aurora!"

Aurora tried to pull her arm away as hard as she could. She yelled, "Let go of me!" Dan rushed to the room and pulled Gannon off of Aurora.

Gannon was breathing heavily while clenching his fists and jaw. That was the way he used to look at Aurora before he would abuse her. Gannon tried to fight Dan, but he knew that he didn't stand a chance with him. Dan said, "Gannon, you need to go, buddy." He tried to pull away from Dan. "Come on, man. You know I am stronger than you. Don't even try to fight me. You need to leave."

Gannon pulled away and walked fast out the door, stomping his feet. As he left, he slammed the door, and the whole house shook. Then everything was silent as everyone was in shock by the situation that happened in such a short amount of time. Gannon came in like a tornado, trying to destroy everything in his path.

"I am sorry, everyone," Aurora said frantically. "This is my fault." She started to cry. Aurora was used to Gannon always blaming her. She went right back into believing that Gannon's storming into that house was her fault.

Then Melih reassured her and said, "No, it is not your fault, Rora. Just sit down." She pulled away from Melih and put her hand in front of him, meaning for him to stop.

Aurora said, "I don't want to sit down. I want to leave." She yelled, "Tessa! I want to leave." Aurora fell to the floor. Zara and Sara came in with Tessa to console Aurora, since Dan had told them to wait in the living room until Gannon was gone. Aurora's heart beat faster, and she felt a tightness in her chest. She felt like she was unable to breathe. She thought to herself, *Melih couldn't even fight for me. Am I not good enough? Was Gannon right? What the hell is wrong with me?*

Sara's dark black eyes looked into Aurora's. It was as if she were staring into Aurora's soul and knew her future. She said, "Everything is going to be okay, my love." She then hugged Aurora. Aurora never liked hugs, either giving or receiving them, but she needed one then. She needed a lot of hugs.

The guys left the room, but Melih stayed in the doorway.

As soon as she calmed down, Tessa and her went home. Dan walked them to the car and kissed Tessa on the cheek. Aurora could see it as she looked from the passenger side window. She touched her lips and remembered Melih's lips. Then it made her feel defeated again.

On the way home, Tessa turned the radio off in the car. "Aurora, I really want to talk to you about something."

"Is it something about Dan?" Aurora said.

"No," Tessa said. "It is about you, actually."

Aurora gulped down a breath of air.

"You really should stop dating for a while because you do not need that kind of drama in your life."

"You are right," Aurora said. "I am just shocked with what just happened."

"I know, and hate to be harsh, Aurora," Tessa said. "But I am your best friend, and if I do not tell you the truth, who will?"

"It is fine," Aurora said. "I know you are just looking out for what is best for me."

"I wish you could see what was best for you."

"Ouch."

"I mean, I wish you could see how much of an amazing person you are. Nice, funny, and a great writer," Tessa said. "Don't forget that. Don't forget who you are."

"I know. Gannon made me forget who I was for a while."

"And... I know you like Melih a lot." Tessa turned on her blinker to take a right turn.

"You do?" Aurora said. It was one of those times that Aurora needed to hear the truth, or she would have kept burying herself in Melih's heart.

"Well. Just be careful, Aurora. With Jason as well," Tessa said. "You have to remember that you are still not divorced."

"I know. I know," Aurora said. "I just…"

"You just need more time to heal."

# Chapter 19

Aurora kept herself busy by moving into her new place. The days following the fight at Sara and Zara's, Aurora thought about how she wanted to call Melih and yell at him for not defending her.

While she was unpacking some clothes into her new place, she had some time to reflect. *Why am I mad about Melih? I am not Melih's…. but he was right. Why am I always mad at everyone? Even the people who love and care about me.* She wanted to call and yell at Gannon too, but she knew yelling at Gannon was a waste of time because that was the kind of attention he wanted. She felt pathetic for Melih not being able to fight for her when Dan had. *But why was he so afraid to stick up for me? What is he hiding? Why is he holding back? What is wrong with me?….. You know what, nothing is wrong with me. It's them.*

*Okay….I have to stay busy. I need to write. I need to put my emotions on paper and forget about all of this.* Her writing was the best when she was mad or depressed, though she wouldn't admit it, and no one knew that about her, either. That is when she let out her real emotions and coping with life's struggles since she was ten years old, when she started journaling.

She turned her frustration and anger into writing. She took the black elastic hair band from her wrist that she has had always worn since she was a teenager to put her hair in a bun on top of her head. She always did that when she was really into writing or working hard on something.

Aurora started by typing at the head of her computer

document a title: *Leaving Your Abusive Husband*. She scratched her head as she thought. She laid out the entirety of what words she would write in her mind, like a blanket being laid out on a freshly made bed. With every letter she typed for that article, a small amount of pain left her heart and mind. The article was a way for her to cope and to get back at Gannon for what he had done to her. She was sure he wouldn't even read it because he never read her articles. *No more turning back or hiding those dark secrets now. After I write this article, I am not wasting one more thought on him.*

A box of Kleenex and many tears later, she hit send on her laptop. *Why don't I feel happy?* I feel nothing. She knew she was too nice to be revengeful, but she did what she thought was right. She used her voiced to speak for the voiceless that were in abusive relationships like her. *I just feel bad for Gannon. He is so pathetic.* She finally realized nothing she did could be equal to what he did, and she was okay with that. *I finally think I am going to be okay. I mean, I have to be. I am not hiding anything anymore.*

# Chapter 20

Aurora met up to go shopping with Tessa to get a new outfit for her divorce.

"So, what do you suggest?" Aurora said as she looked through some clothing racks. "Should I wear all black because it is like I will be dressing for a funeral?"

"No, Aurora," Tessa said. "You need to dress your best. No one wants to dress bad on their divorce day."

"How do you know that?" Aurora said. "You don't know any divorced people."

"That is true, but if I were getting divorced," Tessa said, "I would want to look my best. Show him what he is missing. Show him what he lost."

"I honestly don't care what he thinks," Aurora said. "He is dead to me. That is why I wanted to dress like it is a funeral."

"Do you want to just dress like the grim reaper then?" Tessa said.

"Why not?" Aurora said. "Do you think places still sell Halloween costumes this time of year?" Tessa rolled her eyes.

Tessa continued to talk about fashion as Aurora felt her phone vibrate. She took it out of her jeans pocket and saw she had an email notification.

She opened her phone and saw it was from *The New York Times*. *Please don't be spam. Please don't be spam.* Her heart started to skip beats.

Aurora had pitched her article to one of the editors at *The New York Times* a week earlier. She assumed they were never going to respond because they typically respond within three days. She had pitched to them several times before, but she had not pitched them a story in a while.

The one she pitched about her leaving her husband was different. It was real and raw, as if she had written with blood. She had never written about her relationship or personal life before that article. She wrote that article because she wanted to protect the world from people like Gannon, and she felt like she had to. Though she knew no matter what she would write, say, or do, nothing would be worse than what Gannon had done to her.

The email was from the assistant to the Editor-in-chief, Dean Banquet, at *The New York Times*. *Oh. My. God. I hope this is good. It must be good.*

*Hello Aurora,*

*We were deeply moved by your article that you sent us. We put it up on our website this morning and within the first hour after posting that article, it reached ten thousand shares. We project that it will reach almost one million views in this month alone.*

*Furthermore, we see that you are the type of upcoming talent we are looking for. This is the first article that we have seen of yours where you let us into your life. Many people were reaching out to us to talk with you and thanking you for writing that article. We would like you to know that we have a position open for the Assistant Executive Editor. We also know you are working with the "Happy Living Magazine" in Wisconsin, but we would like to extend the opportunity to you to interview.*

*We know a several years ago you declined the offer to come work with us, but we want to let you know that a better opportunity has become available.*

*Contact us if you are interested.*

*Best,*
*Audrey Gorgio*
*Assistant of Dean Banquet*

Aurora kept re-reading it over and over again. *What?* She put her hand to her mouth. *Dean Banquet's assistant is messaging me? No way.*

"Are you okay, Aurora?" Tessa said.

"Yes," Aurora said as her voice cracked. "Just reading a work email."

*This is exactly I need. Though I cannot leave until the divorce is finalized.* Leaving Wisconsin and going to live her dream was exactly what she wanted. She smiled and laughed. *Is this even real?* She was scared to leave, but felt that it was necessary for her to finally be happy. *Will this finally make me happy again, if I was ever happy?* She had always resented Gannon for not going to New York, and she had always beaten herself up about it. *You know what, Aurora. Stop blaming him for not going. You didn't have to say yes. It was your own fault you didn't go.* She knew that she would not let a moment like that pass her by again. *I finally have a way out of here, but what about Melih? What about Jason? But maybe I should be thinking for once, what about me?*

She didn't know if it was luck or fate. She was not the only one shocked, but *The New York Times* was as well. She opened her social media and saw messages from women thanking her for the article, messaging her "this is the push I needed to leave my abusive relationship." *I am happy I helped these people. I am happier that there are other people out there that have been through what I have been through. Not like I want anyone to go through this, I just don't want to be alone in this anymore.* Though she was ready to write about her divorce, facing the reality to talk about it to people in person was too hard for her. Her main reason for becoming a writer was so she could avoid confrontation.

"Aurora? Aurora?" Tessa said as she snapped her fingers at Aurora. "Are you listening to anything I am saying?"

"Yes," Aurora said as Tessa grunted and rolled her eyes again.

"You have been staring at your phone for the last ten minutes," Tessa said as she handed Aurora an armful of clothes. "Just try these on, please."

"Whatever you say, mom." Aurora smiled.

"Why are you so happy now?" *I can't tell her they offered me an interview. She will tell me not to do it or that it is too much of a step… But I can't lie.*

"Well…." Aurora said. "*The Times* posted an article I pitched to them." *I guess that had some truth in it… Part of the truth, anyway.*

"My best friend is awesome!" Tessa said. "Okay… After we choose you a nice divorce outfit, we can go celebrate."

Aurora walked to the fitting room with her arms full of clothes.

*You know what, I have to call them for an interview.*

# Chapter 21

Two days after she posted that article, her employees were staring at her after they all read her article. They felt sad just looking at her because behind the tough exterior that Aurora always displayed at work, people got to finally see past that. Aurora was sitting at her work desk sipping coffee from her bright red coffee mug that said, *The BOSS,* on it. She was editing articles for her magazine, with a pencil tucked into the bun on her head. Her cell phone started to ring, and she saw that it was Jason calling.

"Hello, Jason? I think this is the first time you have ever called me before," Aurora said as she continued to type on her computer.

"Hey. I just read your article! It was very powerful!" She stopped writing. "I just thought a phone call would be more personal, don't you think?"

"I mean, I guess?" Aurora said.

"See Aurora, you are stronger than you think," Jason said.

"Who said I wasn't strong?" As she sipped from her coffee mug she thought, *I am not really that strong. He must understand why I wrote that article. How can he see through me? Maybe I am getting stronger.*

"You are right," Jason said. "You are a strong and beautiful woman."

"You know why I wrote that article, right Jason?"

*I know Jason was intelligent enough to know why I really wrote the article... but Jason didn't know about the altercation at Zara and*

*Sara's that finally pushed me to write it and tell the world about my abusive relationship. I bared it all to the world. I revealed my scars.*

"Well, I have my thoughts, but I am not in the position to comment on it," Jason said.

"Do you want to know why?" *Just ask already! I wrote it to fight the inner demons that Gannon planted in my brain. Ask me and I will tell you! Why can't I say this out loud?*

"I don't want to pry, Aurora."

"I don't want to sound annoyed, but remember when you said before, 'If I want to be straightforward with you about something, I will'?"

"Well, yes…"

"So, then why did you actually call?" Aurora said. *Why am I so defensive? Maybe he actually cares.*

"Just seeing how you were doing and to congratulate you," Jason said. *Yup, he cares… At least it seems like that to me.*

"Oh," Aurora said. "Well, thank you. I am glad you liked it. I have gotten an overwhelming amount of emails and support from people."

"I figured so," Jason said. "So, let's celebrate! I will take you to any place." *Why? To celebrate my divorce and crappy relationship?*

"Maybe we shouldn't," Aurora said. *Again, on the defense. Am I my own lawyer?*

"Why not?" Jason said.

*But Tessa said hanging out with anyone would be a bad idea. It's just a celebration dinner. It doesn't mean anything, right? We are not boyfriend and girlfriend. We are just hanging out.* She figured if he really wanted to take her out, she would choose the most expensive restaurant she could think of. *Maybe that will get him to say no.*

She said, "Okay. I like this one French place by the capitol."

"You mean "L'Etoile?" Jason said.

It was the most expensive restaurant in town, and she wanted to celebrate the article. It was a nice gesture she took advantage of, not to use him but to see how nice he really was, to see if he was better than Melih, or Gannon. She could pay for her own dinner, but she wanted to test him. Though in reality, she kept looking for a flaw that he might have.

"Yes, if you don't mind."

"Of course not. I love that place. It will remind you of your days in France." *Oh my God. He is perfect and says all the right things. Why can't he just be Melih?*

She finally, for the first time in a long time, felt happy for herself. She thought she was in a dream because she had not been happy in so long. She didn't know why she was so happy in particular, but she tried not to think too much about it. *Could he be bringing me happiness? Or am I happy with my success? Or is it Melih?*

*Or maybe I am just happy with myself for once in my life.*

--

It was a Friday, a few days after Aurora and Jason's previous conversation. They would meet at L'Etoile at 7:00 p.m.

When Aurora was getting ready that night, it took her longer than expected to get ready because she could not find the outfit she wanted to wear. She kept scratching her head as if a light would go off in her head. *Why don't I ever know what to wear in front of this guy?* Aurora still had not fully unpacked her clothes since moving into her new place. She hated packing and moving. She always paid someone to unpack since she could afford it. She let the movers move the boxes to her bedroom and let them unpack everything but her clothes. *It's*

*so gross. I don't want someone touching my clothes…. Especially not
my underwear!*

She kept rummaging around her boxes and clothes
sprawled over her bedroom, like a raccoon going through
garbage. *Why didn't I keep everything on the hangers? I should have
just stuck them in a garbage bag and just packed them that way!*

Aurora had a little dress in mind that she wanted to wear.
She thought black was classy, if worn with the right
accessories. *What would Tessa wear?* She wanted to message
Tessa and ask her what to wear, but Tessa would lecture her
on why she shouldn't be having dinner with Jason. Eventually,
after dismantling several boxes, Aurora found the dress she
was looking for.

"There you are," she said, smiling and proud, as she lifted
up the bottom of the black cocktail dress to look down at her
black suede Christian Loubtion's booties. *Good choice, Aurora.*
The sleeves went off of her shoulders gracefully. They almost
slid off, but that was the way the dress was designed. The dress
length was to her knees. It also had pockets, and Aurora loved
dresses with pockets. To match her dress, she put on her pearl-
studded earrings and a pearl necklace. With the dress and the
pearls, she felt as beautiful as Audrey Hepburn in *Breakfast at
Tiffany's.* Then she put on her black leggings because it was still
cold outside, and she was too lazy to shave her legs. She put
her hair in a sleek ponytail as she looked in her vanity mirror.
She took out a tub of red lipstick and put it on her lips. She
grabbed her cell phone and took a selfie of herself. She wanted
to send a picture to Tessa to show her the cute outfit she chose
to wear. She posted that picture to her Instagram later with the
caption, "Feeling Fabulous."

It was 7:00 p.m. when Aurora arrived at the restaurant.
When she walked in, a man at the door took her jacket. The

lighting was romantic; the tables were draped with white tablecloths, silverware, and long white candlesticks with little flames coming from the tops. The front wall of the restaurant was a long wall of glass windows which overlooked the state capitol building. She found Jason at the bar waiting for her.

"You are always early, huh?" Aurora said. She then giggled as she flashed him her eyes and winged eyeliner that she was proud she was finally able to accomplish.

He turned and looked at her with his eyes wide. "Wow. Your beauty never ceases to amaze me."

"You look good yourself." She winked at him.

"Thank you," Jason said. "Ready to go to the table?"

"Yes, I am starving." This was true. She forgot to eat lunch that day and didn't have any food in her new place yet. She could have snacked after work, but she wasn't much of a cook either. Her grandma was a doctor and a working woman, just like Aurora. Her grandma always said, "I don't make money to cook. I make money to buy the food instead."

Aurora and Jason went to their table and Jason pulled out the chair for her to sit down. "Thank you," Aurora said. *Such a gentleman!*

Jason sat in his chair and took a sip of his water. He then looked in Aurora's eyes and smiled. "So, how did I get so lucky to have dinner with a famous person?"

"You had dinner with someone famous?" Aurora said.

"You are the famous person," he hit his hand to his forehead.

"I am not famous," Aurora said as she looked down at her plate as she put the napkin on her lap. "I just got lucky." *I am not famous, am I?* Aurora had felt normal up until that point. She felt like an ordinary person.

"No, I am the lucky one. You have amazing talent, Aurora."

"I guess," she said humbly. "I still feel like I have much more I want to achieve. I am not satisfied by my accomplishments."

"Why is that?" Jason said surprised.

"I don't know," Aurora said. "I just don't like to speak about my feelings. I can only write them."

"I understand." Though Aurora thought he didn't understand because he wasn't a writer. He was a lawyer, so being confrontational was probably easy for him. "I have read your work for years, and this is the best thing you have written."

*He has been reading all of my work and I never knew him, though Gannon was my husband and he could not even read a sentence of any of my work.* "Well, this is the first good article I have written in a long time," Aurora said.

"Well, it is wonderful."

"Thank you."

"You know," Jason said. "I really like you, Aurora."

"Oh," Aurora said. *Oh God,* Aurora thought. Her face went white. She looked out the window toward the capitol and saw Melih walk past the restaurant as a light post lit up the side of his face. His hands were in his leather jacket and he was looking down as he walked. *Is he thinking about me?* Her heart started to beat fast. He looked toward the restaurant. Aurora immediately looked away from the window and at the first waiter she could find. *Please do not see me.*

"Just oh?" Jason said. "That was not what I was expecting you to say." She had a great time that night, but was fighting herself to like him. She looked up out the window again and realized that Melih had walked past. *Wohooo, that was close.*

Jason said, "Aurora?" She stopped looking at the window and looked toward Jason.

"What?" Aurora said. "I mean… I like you too?" She said that because she felt guilty, as if it was her fault for leading him on and thinking about Tessa telling her to not date. She liked his company and didn't want to stop hanging out with him. She really enjoyed that night with him. He was successful, funny, and smart.

He was perfect for her in almost every way, but her only problem was that he wasn't Melih.

Maybe that was a good thing. Her brain started to fight her heart. *Look where listening to my heart got me. Why shouldn't I give this a try? I mean, I have fun with him.* Jason drinks though and my sobriety means a lot to me. *Melih doesn't drink. I don't know what to do…*

"Well, that's good." Jason responded with, "I was worried for a while that you were friend zoning me." She laughed awkwardly. *Is he right? I never thought of it that way.*

"No, of course not," she responded immediately to him as if she were trying to cover something up. She looked at him and gave him a crooked smile.

"Enough about me, Jason." She smiled at him. "Tell me about you. What have you been up to?" Aurora hated when the attention was on her. Her social anxiety couldn't handle it. *I can't believe Melih just walked past the restaurant.*

"Nothing new here. Same old same old."

"Old like you?" Aurora said with a cackle. "Ha!" They both laughed. "Just kidding…" She said.

They ordered their meals and chatted throughout the dinner. They spent the night laughing. He told her stories about clients from when he was a public defender.

He mostly stuck to talking about the funny cases because he didn't know if she could handle some of the things he had seen being a public defender. He didn't like it because that is was what made him nearly emotionless.

"You are not emotionless," Aurora said. "You are a sweet guy."

"Yeah, I just have seen a lot of stuff."

"It is okay. You don't have to talk about it," she said as she lightly touched his hand but immediately pulled away as she thought of Melih touching her hand at the coffee shop.

Throughout that dinner, Aurora never told Jason that she had gotten an offer for an interview for *The New York Times*, and she didn't want to. She was sure it would be a buzzkill to talk about it. Aurora loved the intellectual conversation she had with him and didn't want to ruin it. *Seeing Melih almost ruined this evening for me.*

*There is something about Jason tonight that is making me extremely attracted to him. I think it is because this is one of the first times a man has ever been nice to me. He is a man who isn't scared to be with me.* Maybe it was the food or the ambiance or maybe he was just perfect for her. She didn't want to believe that he was perfect for her. *If I cannot like myself, how can I like him? When she saw romance or love, she didn't notice it. Or how could he like me or love me? I don't deserve Jason. I don't deserve anyone.... Aurora, stop thinking like that! You deserve the best.*

"You are gorgeous. You don't need to say anything else if you don't want," Jason said as he took her hand into his. His hands were soft and looked like he took care of them. *Maybe he gets manicures. I should get my nails done more often, myself.*

"So, are you interested in coming over to my place afterwards to watch a movie?"

"Okay," Aurora said. "Then this makes up for my not coming after our last date."

"Deal."

They decided to watch a movie on Netflix. Jason signaled

her to move closer to him on his couch. She slid his way and he put his arm around her. She flinched and grew stiff at first, but his body was soft and felt like a teddy bear. She put her head on his chest. Mid movie, Jason stopped it.

"I have a question for you."

"Okay," Aurora said as her lip quivered.

"Can I kiss you?"

She never said no, but she closed her eyes and kissed him. It brought her back to college when Gannon asked her the same question. She knew that after she said yes things would change like it always did when she said yes to a man. Before she knew it, she was on top of him and realized that she hadn't had sex in a very long time. *What am I doing?* She jumped off of him.

"I'm sorry." Aurora had to stop and say, "I-i-i can't."

"It's okay. We don't need to rush," Jason said but Aurora could see the lust in his eyes. She bit her lip and thought, *This is not me. I have nothing against people who do this, but I know if I give myself away like this, I will lose myself again. And after all the progress I have made.*

"No, Jason, I really can't." Disgusted by herself, she proceeded to get off of him as if he was an ancient European plague she wanted to avoid.

"Okay," Jason said. "I don't want to push you into anything you don't want to do."

For a moment, she thought she wanted to have sex with him, but she didn't. *I won't have sex with a man I am not married to. How do I tell him that? That I am old fashioned? I will look pathetic.* They spent the night talking until she fell asleep with her head on his shoulder. She told him everything that night.

She woke up around 2:00 a.m. and kissed Jason goodbye.

"I have to go," she whispered. He offered for her to stay, but she insisted to go home. She didn't want to wake up the

next day and have to take the walk of shame to her car.
Though they didn't even have sex, other people wouldn't
know that. She saw enough girls do the walk of shame in
college; she didn't want to be one of them.

Aurora thought about Melih on her way home that
night. *What would have happened if Melih and I had done what
Jason and I did? Gannon would have killed us both if he walked in on
that.*

*Why can't it just be easy to be with Melih? I am just getting so
tired of it. Maybe Tessa was right… No more drama.*

Aurora barely remembered driving home that night. She
took off her clothes as she trickled up the stairs to her bed and
ended up sleeping in only her underwear and pearls.

# Chapter 22

Two weeks before Aurora and Gannon were to be divorced, she was more than ready to move on from that chapter in her life. Melih had not messaged or called her, and this drove her to start dating Jason regularly after the steamy night at his house. She wasn't sure if it was because of that night that she was staying with him or that Melih and her were not communicating. Jason and Aurora would meet every morning at *Colectivo* for coffee before they would head to work. He would usually go to a bar after work and have some alcoholic beverage to take the edge off from his stressful day at work.

She wasn't quite sure why she was with him. *Remember Aurora, Jason is the safe choice; Melih wasn't. You did right by not chasing* Melih. Aurora and Jason loved spending time with each other.

"I never met anyone like you, Aurora," Jason would say. "You are so intelligent and beautiful."

Aurora just wanted to have an older male figure in her life to cope with her dad failing as a father. Jason's friends teased him because she was much younger than he was, but he didn't care. They even gave her the nickname, "The twenty-five-year-old." Aurora thought, *I just hope he is not a rebound. I would feel so guilty. What is wrong with me?* To Jason, something about Aurora made him so happy. The way he looked at her was like everything in the world had disappeared and she was the only living being on earth besides him, though he hadn't told her.

Aurora was living life and trying to enjoy everything. She

enjoyed living on her own. She had not told Jason or anyone about the job in New York. She also had to tell her current boss she would be leaving. She was trying to avoid telling anyone, but she knew she would have to eventually. *You can't run in denial forever.*

Melih had tried messaging Aurora several times, but she ignored all of his messages. He kept telling her sorry and kept saying he wanted to meet with her.

The messages were along the lines of:

Melih: I am sorry, Aurora. I didn't mean what I said that night. I do like you, Aurora. I cannot stop thinking about you. About us! I even told all of our friends now. I am not hiding the truth anymore.

And

Melih: I am sorry Aurora for not fighting for you that night. I was a coward. I just wanted Gannon to leave. So I said anything that would make him leave. I didn't mean what I said.

She was so mad at him for not fighting for her or sticking up for her that night, even though he had said he was sorry countless times. She never heard him say, "She is not mine, yet." Even if he said that, her body was in fight or flight mode and she was on the complete defense about everything. Her stubbornness would not give into Melih easily. *Melih really means he is sorry? How do I know? Gannon said sorry all of the time and never meant a word. He would say sorry and then do the same hurtful things over and over again.* She did not believe words anymore, only actions. *Or maybe I will not respond to Melih because I feel upset on wasting months on him, waiting for something to happen between us. But it never did.*

She thought she and Melih had very strong chemistry and was upset that he gave up so quickly that night. For once in her life, she wanted someone who would not just fight for her but stick up for her as well, who would stand by her side through the absolute worst in her life. *The only one I know will always stand by my side, no matter what, is myself.*

She wanted to get some things off of her chest. She secretly wanted to hear his voice say her name one more time. She also started to feel guilty because she kept ignoring him. After she was at her home one evening watching Netflix and drinking hot chocolate, she called Melih.

"Hello," Aurora said.

"Hello, Aurora. How are you?" Melih said. "I am so happy you called."

"I am great. How are you?" Aurora said. "I figured I would give you a call after all of the messages you had sent."

"I vas not good, but now I am. Your voice soothes me," Melih said. "I am glad you finally contacted me. I am surprised for you to call."

"I am surprised too, but I wanted to talk to you," Aurora said.

"Oh. Oh no."

"It is okay, Melih."

"Ahhh, Aurora. I luh how you say my name. It is so cute." *I love the way you say mine....*

"Oh, Melih.... Don't make this harder than it is."

"Dan vhat? I am sorry but I didn't vant to stop messaging you. I never thought dis much about a girl. I keep trying to fight my feelings for you. I have tried for months. For years even. Believe me. I tried to stop dinking about you, but I couldn't."

"Melih..."

"Yes, Aurora?" *Ohhh... Say my name again, she whispered softly under her breath.*

"I don't think it is good for us to see each other anymore," Aurora said.

"But we do not see each other, Aurora."

"I mean, never again," Aurora said.

"Aurora, can I see you in person, please? I vant to tell you how I feel. I vant to tell you my reason for ewerything."

"Let's be grownups about this."

"I know Aurora, and I am sorry, but I want to change that. Just give me a chance to explain. Let me show you," Melih said. "Please."

Aurora thought to herself that if she saw Melih, it would only cause more heartbreak. *I am done with guys who don't have their minds made up anymore.* However, she did want to see Melih because she figured it would be better to burn that bridge before she left town.

"Okay, Melih. We can meet and talk, but I don't want to know how you feel anymore. It just makes this harder and more complicated."

"Okay Aurora, let us meet for a coffee tonight at 7:00. I will meet you at the same coffee shop as last time."

--

Her glasses were full of steam as she left the cold weather outside to come into the heated coffee shop. Melih was already there. She wanted Melih to wait, so she arrived late. Melih saw her as she came in because he was anxiously watching the door, waiting for her. He walked to the front to meet her as she came in. Melih touched her back as he said, "I already paid for your drink." He directed her to the baristas. "Just tell them you are here."

"Okay," Aurora said.

Aurora waited at the counter for her cappuccino as Melih sat down. Melih had a very serious look on his face. He stood up to pull out Aurora's chair for her to sit down.

"Thank you for the drink," Aurora said as Melih sat down.

After having a serious look on his face, as if he were in deep thought, Melih smiled and said, "No problem. That is the least I can do for a girl who deserves the world."

*Wow, that was romantic... but why is he doing this?* "That is sweet of you," Aurora said. "But Melih, I cannot keep..."

Melih grabbed her hand and interrupted her mid-sentence. "Aurora, I know vhat you vant to say. I know you don't vant to see me or talk to me. I know I haven't been ideal in dis situation. Especially after I told you I wanted to be by your side through dis divorce. I am sorry for the vay things vent down. I vant to be vhat you vant me to be, from now on."

Aurora stared into his eyes and didn't know what to say. Though she had been waiting for him to say that for months, she never thought of what she would say in return.

"I know you don't believe me, but I am going to prove it to you," Melih continued.

Aurora yanked her hand away from his. She spoke loudly, "Why should I give you the time of day when you could not even fight for me?" She saw people looking at them and she lowered her voice. She got her head closer to him as she spoke for only him to hear. "I mean, Melih. It hurt my feelings. Am I pathetic? Ugly? Fat? I know I am not yours, Melih. But you hurt me and dragged me around long enough."

She took a few deep breaths.

Melih just wanted to listen to her and not interrupt her. "We have been doing this for months. You tell me how you feel and then you disappear... How do I know you will not disappear on me again?"

He grabbed her hand again and said, "Because this time is different. I kept pushing you avay because I knew a guy like me doesn't deserve you," Melih said

"What are you talking about?" Aurora said. "You told Gannon that I am not yours or anyone's."

"Vell, yes I did say dat, but I said you are not mine, yet... Not like you will be my property, but I vould like you to be someding more than a friend. Someday, in sha Allah."

"What does that mean?" Aurora said. "In-sha-la?"

"In sha Allah means, if God wills." Melih continued.,"Look Aurora, nothing is wrong with you. You are perfect. Dings are just complicated vith my parents... I know if they vill ewer meet you, they vould love you."

"What? You are saying things like I am your girlfriend or something?"

"Vell, dat is the thing, Aurora. The vay I vas raised. Vee don't really have girlfriends, at least not in my family. A lot of people in Turkey do, but my family is different."

"So that is what you wanted to tell me?" Aurora said.

"Look, Aurora. I am not against courting you," Melih said.

*Courting? Like old school dating?*

Melih continued, "I just vant to do it right. I cannot control myself vhen I am alone vith you. I feel like I am a vampire and your blood is like a drug to me."

Aurora was taking a sip of her coffee as she choked up the words, "Like a drug?"

"Yes," Melih said. "It's just dat..."

"Melih, I understand you are a conservative person but... So...So what do you want to do?"

"Vell, I vant to start hanging out more vith you. But vee need to meet in public because I don't want anyone to think anything bad about you," Melih said. "I have a lot of respect for you. I don't want anyone to say you and I are..." Melih started to struggle to say the next word because he didn't feel comfortable saying it.

Aurora finished his sentence and said, "Having sex?"

"Yes, that."

"Well Melih, you are in luck. I believe sex is for marriage." As Aurora said that, she remembered Jason and the fun time she had been having with him. It was like Jason didn't even exist until that point. She felt extremely guilty. Whatever Melih was saying, Aurora started to block out because she felt bad for what she did with Jason. She didn't want to be like Gannon and be a cheater. Though Aurora and Jason never said they were exclusive. *For people at Jason's age, if you were dating regularly, are you considered boyfriend and girlfriend? Aurora didn't know the rules, but she felt guilty nonetheless.*

Melih pulled on her hand as he saw she was not paying attention to what he was saying. "Rora, are you okay?"

"What?" Aurora blinked and shook her head from the shivers that went up her spine.

"I said, are you okay?" Melih said.

"Oh yes. It is just... The caffeine rushed to my head too fast. That's all." She pulled her hand away from Melih, crossed her arms, and put them around her stomach, rubbing her fingers against her ribcage. "Melih, I think I am ready to go home."

"Are you sure you are okay?" Melih said.

"Yeah, I am fine," Aurora said.

"You are right. You have a long drive home. I should let you go." *Right... Melih doesn't know I live in town now.* So she decided not to tell him and used it as an excuse to leave early.

"Sorry, Melih. I am tired. I had a long day." She got up and put on her coat before he had a chance to offer to walk her to her car. He got up quickly while grabbing his jacket and walked fast to catch her.

"Let me valk you to your car."

"No, I am fine," Aurora said.

"I insist."

"Fine."

He walked her to her car and they didn't say a word. He could feel her tension.

It felt like the longest walk in her life.

He opened her car door after she clicked the unlock button on her car keys. "Promise me you are okay?"

Annoyed, Aurora said, "Yes, I am fine."

"Okay, I vill message you before I go to bed tonight. I vant you to know that you are the first thing I think about before I sleep," Melih said. "I promise I will talk to you more now." Aurora started to shiver from the cold and her jaw jittered. "I guess you are cold…"

"Yes, I am pretty cold."

"Can I…" Melih said so quietly it could have been mistaken for a whisper.

"Can you?" She said.

"Can I have a hug, Aurora?" Melih said as she stared into his eyes.

"M-m-may you have a hug?" Aurora said back in confusion.

"Vas that too straight forward?"

"No. I was teasing. You should have said 'may' instead of 'can.'" *Could you be any more awkward?* She looked down and shook her head at herself.

"Vell?" Melih said as he slowly put his hand under her chin to lift up her head.

"Yes!" She took and big gulp and she said, "Yes, of course you may hug me. I would love that." Aurora's heart stopped as she tried to breathe in the cold winter air. *If only he knew I longed to feel his heart against mine.*

His hug felt warm and she could feel his heart beat through his leather jacket. His warm lips touched her forehead. She could feel his stubble beard scratch her forehead. She felt like they hugged for an eternity. She didn't want to let go and neither did he.

"Well, Melih," Aurora said as she slowly let go of Melih and slowly slid her hands along his ribs when she pulled away. They stared into each other's eyes for a moment in complete silence. "Melih, I should go."

"Okay," he said as he put his hand to her cheek. "Good night, Aurora." She got into her car.

She looked at him in the rearview mirror as she drove away. *Did that really just happen? Did he really tell me all of that?*

# Chapter 23

A few days later, Aurora was watching *Dirty Dancing* on Netflix one evening, wrapped up in her white fleece blanket, sipping on a cup of chamomile tea.

Aurora heard her phone ring. *Dan? Why is he calling? He rarely calls me.*

"Hey, Aurora," Dan said.

"Hey?" She said has she untangled her phone cord.

"Can I talk to for a second?"

"Sure," Aurora said. "What's up? Is everything all right?"

"Yes. Everything is great. I was seeing how you were doing," Dan said. "I know you had a rough night the other night."

"I am still shook up, but it's okay."

"Well," Dan replied, "I want to tell you something."

"What is it?" Aurora said.

"I am calling you for Melih." Aurora's heart stopped when she heard his name. "Do you remember the night you cooked for us and made that yogurt salad with sugar instead of salt?" Dan said.

"Of course!" Aurora responded with excitement, like she knew an answer on *Jeopardy*. "He was the only one who complimented it when everyone else bluntly said they hated it. But that was years ago. Why are you bringing this up?"

"Yeah, well," Dan responded as he laughed, "we all hated it, but Melih kept raving about it and saying he loved it."

Aurora became silent. "Again, why are you telling me this

now?"

"I don't know. I am just sick of him not saying anything." Dan continued, "I only decided to speak up because I saw the look in his eyes that he had when you walked out of the living room back to Zara's room." *So he doesn't know about Melih and me meeting at the coffee shop?*

"The night Gannon showed up?"

"Yes," Dan said.

Aurora heard a man with an accent murmuring something in the background on Dan's end.

"Who was that?"

"Oh, no one," Dan said.

"Come on. Why are you calling for Melih, though? Isn't he right next to you?" Aurora said. "I know he is there with you. I can hear him."

"Oh no…"

"Oh yes…." Aurora said. "Would you mind putting him on the phone?"

"Melih?" Dan said to him on the other end.

"Hello, Aurora…" he said as if he were a puppy that had just been caught ripping up its owner's shoes.

"Why did you want to call me? Or why didn't you tell me when we had coffee? You can talk to me about anything, Melih."

"Well," Melih said, "it actually vas Dan's idea."

"Oh."

"Vell, Dan wanted me to call because…" Melih hesitated.

"Just tell her!" Dan whispered loudly in the background.

"Tell me what?" Aurora said more loudly.

"Vell, Dan noticed dhat vhen you got up to go to da bedroom at Zara and Sara's…"

"Noticed what?"

"He saw the look in my eyes when I saw you were sad and you walked away."

"So?"

"Vell…. he knows."

"He knows what?"

"He knows…."

"I got that he knows already."

"Ouch!" Melih yelled.

"Are you okay?" Aurora asked.

"Yes," Melih said. "It vas just Dan punching me to make me tell you." He continued as he choked on the words, "To tell you that I like you."

"You like me?" Aurora said. *He likes me.*

"Yes, Aurora, and I have since college." Melih said. "Freshman year, to be exact."

"Really?! For that long?"

"I knew it all along!" Dan said in the background.

"But I thought you were best friends with Gannon then…." Aurora said. "How could you hide that from Gannon?"

Melih and Dan both started laughing.

"Aurora…" Melih said. "Dan and I are best friends."

"Really?" Aurora said. "But what about all of the times you and Gannon hung out?"

"I did it because I felt bad for him. Everyone thought he was narcissistic and a know-it-all. But no. I'm not good friends vith him now, and I never have been." Dan continued, "Don't you remember that vee didn't go to your wedding?"

"Well, you said you were in Turkey," Aurora said. "Dan said he couldn't go."

"Dan said he couldn't go because one of his relatives was sick. Neither of us vanted to go to the vedding because vee didn't really like Gannon and couldn't bear to see you two marry."

Aurora said, "Really? Why didn't you two tell me?"

"I didn't feel I had the right to tell you then," Melih said. "Vee only hung out with Gannon because you vere our friend, Aurora. Dhat is vhy it vas easy to stop talking to Gannon once you left him."

"I remember that after you got married and before, Melih always wanted to make excuses to hang out with you guys," Dan said in the background. "It was only to see you. I mean, Melih never told me that, but I am sure that is the reason."

Dan said while smiling as he took the phone, "Hey again... Melih, I am going to step into the other room for a second."

Aurora remembered how after she left Gannon, Melih ignored her and tried to push her away. She said, "Well, after I left Gannon... Why hasn't he tried harder? I mean he kisses me on the forehead and acts like he likes me, but I don't know why this has to be so difficult."

"Because, Aurora."

"Because why?" Aurora said.

"Because you are still married. You know that Melih is old fashioned and he is also worried his parents would not accept you."

Aurora replied, "Why is that?" She was feeling upset at herself for wanting so much from Melih when she was still married. "Why can't he tell me this himself?"

"I have no idea, Rora," Dan said. "He is probably just shy to bring up a woman to his parents. He said that the way he was raised, when a man talks to his parents about a woman, he wants to marry her. He is probably too shy to tell you. He has never even talked to me about girls before."

"Oh, wow," Aurora said. She swallowed a gulp of air and almost choked. Thinking of getting married again made her sick.

"You okay, Aurora?"

"Ah yes. I am fine. Thanks for telling me all of that, Dan," Aurora said. "That was a lot to take in."

"Yes, but I think it will help you understand him more – or his actions – and who he is."

*That call was so weird, right?*

# Chapter 24

Two weeks before Aurora's divorce, she felt a constant pressure in her chest, worse than what she was used to feeling. She took extra Xanax and worked out more, but nothing would take the pain from her chest. She did not know why it made her feel more anxious rather than happy. She just wanted that court day to be over with. She just wanted to feel relief, but she knew she would not have that burden lifted from her chest until after she was divorced.

She was sitting in her office at work, sipping on her morning coffee, as she looked out her window and thought about what she really wanted to do with her life. She knew that when she was divorced a lot would change because she had many big decisions to make. She needed to choose between Jason, Melih, and being alone. *Well, I cannot have everything, right? That is how life seems to play out for me and the people around me.* She had yet to interview for that job in New York, but she wanted to. She dreaded that she would have to resign from her position at the magazine.

She picked up the phone. *You can do this. You can do this.* She began to sweat. She dialed the number of Dean's assistant at *The New York Times. You can do this. You got this.* Aurora took in a big breath of air.

"Hello, this is Aurora... Aurora Tousey." She let her breath out.

"Okay," the assistant on the other line said. "How can I help you?"

"Well," Aurora said, "you emailed me about the assistant editor position opening up for *The New York Times*?"

"Oh yes," the assistant said. "I remember now. Mr. Banquet and one of the owner's daughters requested for you specifically to be interviewed."

"Really?" Aurora said. "The owner's daughter?"

"Yes," the assistant said, "but that is all I know."

"Well," Aurora said, "am I able to do an interview? Are they still interested?"

"Yes, they are," the assistant said. "Let me check Mr. Banquet's schedule." She continued, "Are you available tomorrow around 10:00 a.m. for a conference call?"

"Yes!" Aurora said. "Yes, of course. 10:00 a.m. Eastern Standard Time?"

"Yes. I will email you the details for the call."

"Please call my personal number directly," Aurora said. "No one here at my office knows I am interviewing for a job yet."

"Okay, no problem."

Aurora said to herself, *I guess if anyone asks tomorrow, I will tell him or her I am on a business call for a new set designer or something. I don't want anyone to think something is up. I mean, I don't know if I will get the job. Why would they want me?*

--

That night, Aurora could not sleep. The more Aurora thought about leaving to go to New York, the more she didn't want to interview for *The Times* position. *You are just trying to psych yourself out, Aurora. Snap out of it.*

The more Aurora thought about anything, the less likely she was to do it. It was like when Aurora would shop and find a nice shirt or a pair of shoes that she really liked. She had so much excitement to get that new shirt or those new shoes. *I worked hard for this; I deserve this,* she would think to herself. The longer she shopped in that store and looked at other things, the more she would think about why she didn't want it or didn't need those shoes or that shirt. This would lead her to end up leaving the store without anything.

She did the same thing with any big decision in her life. She didn't know what would be the shoes or that shirt she left in the store. Would it be Melih, Jason, or New York? If she would defeat her self-doubt for something she was passionate about, then she knew she would know she was doing the right thing. She felt that way after she left Gannon. She did the right thing, and she hoped she would feel the same way after the next big decision she made after her divorce.

Aurora didn't like change because she didn't like the unknown. So, if Aurora would think about something too long, she wouldn't do it unless she was really passionate about it or really wanted it. Then nothing would stand in her way to get what she really wanted deep down inside her heart. She was always testing herself to see what she really wanted. If she still wanted something hours after telling herself she didn't deserve it, want it, or really need it, then she knew that thing was meant to be for her.

She didn't like that she could not predict the future or that she might fail at getting the job and her dream of ever working for *The New York Times* would be ruined for her. Aurora was her own biggest enemy and critic. Later in life, she would come to terms with knowing that there was nothing she could have been done to change the outcome of her and Gannon's relationship or the way he was. Even if she had believed in his "artistic talent," he would not have changed or been a better spouse.

In Aurora's career, she strived for the unachievable and achieved it. In her personal life, she settled and never strived for someone she liked or deserved. That is why she stayed with Gannon for as long as she did.

*But I want to change that way of thinking.*

--

As she walked to the coffee shop that next morning to meet Jason for their morning coffee, she started to realize that she had no idea why she kept meeting with Jason, but Melih hadn't called or tried to talk to her in weeks. *But Melih "promised" he would be by my side through this divorce.*

As she sat at the table and people in suits were running in to pick up their coffee and read the morning paper, she felt like all of the people around her were moving in fast-forward.

"Aurora?"

"Yes?" Aurora said as she stared at her cup of coffee, thinking about her interview, Melih, and her divorce.

"Why are you so quiet this morning?"

"What do you mean?" she said as she was sweating from her temples that had their own heartbeat.

"I don't know," Jason said. "It just seems like you have something on your mind. You didn't even eat your chocolate croissant. You usually eat that in one bite." He laughed.

"It is nothing," Aurora said as she sat up straight. "I just have a stressful meeting with my boss." She took a bite of her croissant to prove to Jason nothing was up.

"Oh, okay," he said. Then Aurora wiped her buttery hands with a napkin.

She graced Jason's hands with hers and said, "Everything is

okay." She felt guilty, as if she were living a double life. *I am lying to myself.*

"All right," Jason said. "I will take your word for it…. So you were out drinking late last night?" Aurora took a sip of her coffee.

"Yes, I was," Jason said. "You know that I was drinking to destress."

"But it was a Monday night," Aurora said.

"The earlier in the week, the better, huh?"

"Not really," Aurora said. "You know I do not drink anymore."

"I know," Jason said. "I am sorry about that."

She gave him a smile. "I just wish you could just drink less."

"I wish that for myself, too."

After she left the coffee shop, she thought, *I don't know if I am annoyed with Jason and his drinking or just overly stressed this morning. Is it about Melih? Why won't Melih just call me? What is wrong with him? I need to tell Jason the truth about Melih. Wait, no I don't. What if Melih never talks to me again?*

--

She put her hands to her face. *Aurora, snap out of this boy drama and focus on this dang interview.* She took several breaths and tried to resume working, but she could not focus. She kept organizing the articles she needed to edit, and her stationary set on her desk.

One hour went by and Aurora received a call. She let it ring a few times while she calmed down and caught her breath. With every ring, her heart beat faster.

*This is big, Aurora. This could change your life.* She released a big breath of air and picked up the phone.

"Hello. Good morning." *Oh my God.*

"Good morning, Aurora," Dean Banquet said. "So, you used to intern for us?" Aurora coughed as she cleared her throat.

"Well, yes," Aurora said. "But I was writing for you too. I mean, I still freelance for *The New York Times* on occasion."

"Yes." Dean said. "Of course…. So, do you mind jumping right into the interview questions?"

"No," Aurora said. "I am ready whenever you are."

"What do you read? What are you currently reading now?"

"I read *The New York Times*, of course." Aurora said. "But I also read women's fiction, history books, romance… I basically read anything, but right now I am reading through Jane Austen's books."

"Right. She is one of the classics," Dean said. "Why do you want to work for *The New York Times?*"

"Well," Aurora said, "It is my dream. As you know, I shut down an editor position with you once before, and it is definitely something I do not want to again. I deeply regretted that. Working for *The New York Times* is my dream job, and I know that now better than ever."

"By why work for us?"

"I just love everything about *The New York Times*," Aurora said. *Oh God… What am I even saying? I just want to get the heck away from Gannon and this city, which is tainted with horrible memories from my past, and most likely my future.*

"I love it too, but if you could change one thing about *The New York Times*, what would it be?" Dean said as he kept firing off the questions like a machine gun.

"Well," Aurora said, "I feel you need to focus more on hiring some younger staff to have their voices be heard."

"Well," Dean said, "we have *The Edit* now, for that."

"I know," Aurora said. "But I do not think that is enough outreach because it is only a newsletter. Maybe have more positions available to younger writers?"

"Noted. But if we were to hire you, we would be hiring a millennial. A 'young person.'" He flipped over a paper in front of him, then wrote something down. *Maybe he didn't like my answer.* "Anyway, what is something you are most proud of?"

"Doing this interview today."

"Really?"

"Yes," Aurora said. "It took a lot of courage to get to this point and to finally make this call and try to really pursue my dreams… It was something I should have done a long time ago."

"That is a good answer," Dean said. "Is there anything else you would like to add to the interview today?"

"No," Aurora said. "Well, I want to add that if you give me this opportunity to work for you, I promise I will not let you down. This is what I want to do."

"Well," Dean said, "those are all of the questions I have for now." *That was quick. Why did I make all of this anxious excitement for this short interview?*

"Thank you for taking the time to do the interview with me today," Aurora said.

"You're welcome," Dean said. "We will be in touch."

"I look forward to…" She heard the click sound as he hung up the phone on the other end. "…hearing from you." She sighed.

*We will be in touch? Was he not interested in me? Of course he isn't,* she grumbled as she put her head to her desk.

# Chapter 25

Aurora continued to hang out with Jason, as Melih avoided her. *Is Melih scared of showing me his true feelings and then his family may not want him to be with me in the end?* Though she knew seeing Melih too much would make her never want to leave to go to New York City, if she got the job. Aurora could not avoid her own thoughts because she was always thinking about Melih. She wanted to be with him. She wanted to be holding his hand and going on dates and kissing him. Melih had told her that he would be "whatever she wanted him to be" and "I will help you through this divorce." But she knew that was too good to be true. His actions spoke louder than his words. *With Melih, you have to read between the lines, right? I mean, I cannot figure him out.*

Things were simple with Jason. Not just simple but easy. He had his life together. Things were not complicated, but that kind of simplicity made Aurora bored. Jason had been very supportive through the whole divorce process. Aurora started to learn that that was not a justified reason to stay with Jason. *You had pity for Gannon. Do not have pity for another man. Look where it got you.*

One evening, Aurora was at Jason's having dinner. Like many Wisconsin nights, it was windy and cold. You could hear the wind whistling outside as it moved its way up and down the street. Inside his apartment you could hear mushrooms simmering in a wine reduction. The aroma smelled sweet. Aurora wanted to take her fork to try to steal a mushroom from the simmering pan.

"Don't touch it! You have to wait to have the full effect of all of the flavors at once," Jason said, after he took a sip of his glass of wine. Aurora was staring at his red wine stained lips. She rolled her eyes. *He is literally always drinking something. Doesn't he care I am trying to maintain my sobriety? Ugh.. Whatever...*

He poured the reduction over a mouth-watering chuck steak, grilled to perfection, with a side of fingerling potatoes tossed in a garlic butter sauce. The smell was intoxicating.

"I love that you are a great cook because I am not," Aurora said.

"It is okay, I have had your pancakes once. They were not bad," Jason said.

Aurora brought up a subject that she had brought up many times. Whenever it was brought up, he would always change the subject. It was a dark and problematic time in Jason's life he did not want to talk about. It was dark like the chocolate covered strawberries Jason pulled out of the fridge. He placed them on a plate with whipped cream and put them in front of Aurora.

"Thank you for the dinner. It was amazing. Like always." It was one of the best meals Aurora had ever eaten, but the conversation they would have after dinner left a bad taste in her mouth.

Jason said, "I figured you would like it."

"So, Jason," she paused and thought about whether she should bring up a certain topic he would not want to talk about. "I just don't get how a handsome guy like you is still alone."

"I am not alone, by the way. I am with you, am I not?" Jason said. "Aurora, why do you always have to say that? It is not a compliment. A guy at my age should not be alone."

Jason quoted the word "alone" with his fingers. He sat down and took another drink of his wine. Aurora watched him drink as the wine went down his throat and he gulped it down.

"Oh wow!" Aurora said with sarcasm. "I am surprised you set down your glass of wine for a second."

"Excuse me?" Jason said.

"You are always drinking something when I am around you. I am surprised you stopped for a second."

Jason said, "Are you just trying to find something wrong with me? Or does my drinking actually bother you?"

"Both. Maybe... I don't know," Aurora said as she threw up her hands. "I just don't get why you would be alone and you know I am sober, and you always drink in front of me."

"I am sorry," Jason said. "You never told me."

"I have given you hints, but you don't want to listen to me. Just like everyone else. It is like I don't exist to the world," Aurora said. "From your defensiveness over the drinking, was your last break up that bad, Jason?"

"Well, was yours?"

"Excuse me? Eff you, Jason!" Aurora wanted to cry but instead she gave him a hard stare.

"Ouch. Your words hurt me so much. Not," Jason said.

"Why are you so crabby? What's wrong with you?"

Jason slightly raised his voice. "Nothing is wrong, Aurora. You were the one acting crabby, *and you* just keep bringing up something I don't want to talk about."

"You can talk to me," she said, though in her minding she was yelling at him. She was good at faking her emotions. She had been a great actress in high school plays.

Jason said back, "Look, Aurora. I will just tell you the truth now because you will never let it go."

"What is it?" Aurora said.

"Well, you know my ex fiancé cheated on me," Jason said. "Not just that. She got pregnant from another guy. She didn't tell me until he was two years old. I thought he was my son."

"I am so sorry," She said. Aurora was shocked by the news and actually felt bad for him.

"No, you are not. You just want to find something wrong with me," Jason raised his voice and threw his hands up with disgust. "We always talk about you and your stupid divorce and your life. All. Of. The. Time."

"So, *now* the truth comes out," Aurora said.

"Guess so," Jason said. "I also want to tell you, since we are telling all of our secrets. I will never have kids or get married, either. Not to you or anyone."

"Oh, well that's good to now."

"My ex ruined it for everyone. Just like your ex is ruining your present right now," Jason said. "If you want to leave me for that, then leave. I will never marry you, or anyone."

Aurora yelled, "I never said I wanted to marry you!"

"Then why do you always act like a wife to me?"

"What the heck are you talking about?" Aurora said.

"You just always nag on me!" Jason said.

"Again, what are you talking about? I don't care about what you do," Aurora said.

"Okay then, you can leave."

"What? Just like that?" Aurora said.

"Yup! Are you happy now? Now you found my imperfection, as well!"

"But I was supposed to leave you," she said but did not realize she was speaking out loud.

Jason said shocked, "Wait, you want to leave me?"

Aurora fired back, "You just told me to leave. Why do you

care?"

"Well, I was mad at you and annoyed, but I don't want you to leave me, or to leave you at all."

"I don't take threats anymore," Aurora said. "Been there. Done that. Wrote about it."

Jason tried to grab Aurora's hand. "Come on, Aurora. I was just mad." *That sounded like the same line Gannon used to say.*

"I am sorry, Jason. I can't do this," Aurora said as she put on her boots. "I don't see my future with you either, Jason. I have to go." She grabbed her coat, purse, and keys, then left. She could hear him saying her name as she left. She slammed the door behind her.

This conversation with Jason made the decision of what Aurora would do after her divorce a lot less complicated. She felt like she was living a double life with her being with Jason and wanting Melih. *Glad Jason is out of my life now. But I am just scared of being alone. Why am I so scared? Do I think no one will ever want to be with me? Am I damaged goods? What if New York fails? I will have no man to fall back on? I will have no one. I will be alone. What is wrong with me? Why do I feel like I need a man?*

She felt she needed support from a male figure, like she had felt her whole life, just like seeking her dad's approval as a little girl, then Gannon's as an adult, though she was easily capable of handling anything life threw her way. *I am making my life much more difficult than it needs to be.* Aurora was a lot stronger than she thought.

Aurora knew that night that she had to take that job in New York. She knew if she stayed in Wisconsin, she and Melih would get together and she would be in the same routine. She already turned down a great job and opportunity once for a man; she wasn't going to do it for a man she barely knew. Yes, Melih had been her friend for several years and he made her

feel things she had never felt before, but she didn't know him
personally. He was always private about himself.

*What is with all of these guys and their secrets?*

--

The next morning while Aurora was at her office desk
drinking her coffee and checking her emails, she got some
news that pushed her to call her boss. She told him that she
needed to meet him for lunch and that it was urgent. She knew
that if she didn't message him right away, she might change
her mind, so that was why she had to act fast.

It was lunchtime and Aurora was sweating everywhere. She
hated confrontation more than anyone.

Aurora called, emailed, and messaged him several times
that Monday morning. He only agreed to the lunch because
she was very adamant about meeting, and she was never that
push, with him. This is why she needed to start looking for a
new person or maybe even two people to take over her
position. Aurora was a force of nature and would do whatever
she could to get a job done.

Aurora met Mr. Fratzenburg at L'Etoile, the same
restaurant that Aurora and Jason had gone to. She chose it
because she knew it would be a business expense and Mr.
Fratzenburg could afford it. She walked in and smelled duck
glazed in butter and heard silver clinging on plates as people
ate their food. She told the hostess who she was there to have
lunch with for a business meeting. They immediately knew
whom she was there to meet. The hostess probably thought
Aurora was an escort, knowing the bachelor, Mr. Fratzenburg,
though Aurora ensured the hostess she was there for a business
meeting. Nonetheless, the hostess brought her to the table.

They walked passed men in suits chatting about politics and the stock market.

Mr. Fratzenburg winked at the hostess and Aurora rolled her eyes. Then he flashed Aurora his white Hollywood smile. "Hello Aurora, long time no see. How is my favorite publicist?"

"Really?" Aurora said back in a snappy way as she rolled her eyes, "Uh, I am the editor-in-chief of your magazine." *How many employees does he have and actually remember? His assistant probably had to tell him my name fifteen times for him to remember it.*

He responded back, "Oh, yeah. So how are you? What's up with you? I see you are not wearing a wedding ring." She looked at her hand and put it on her lap and pretended to adjust the napkin on her lap, so it would no longer be the topic of conversation.

Aurora sassed back, "Is that the first thing you see on a woman? If they are married or not? But you cannot even remember my job title?"

He laughed. Aurora was much different as a business professional than she was in her personal life. She didn't let people beat her around. He obviously did not hire her for her charm, but he liked a girl with sass and she took work very seriously. He respected hard work.

"Anyway, what is so important that you had to meet today? You are lucky I was in Madison today."

The waitress brought out some water and wine for Aurora. Aurora looked at the wine and shook her head no. A man then came behind her with the lunch.

He then looked at her and smiled. "Oh sorry, I already ordered for you." *Of course you did.* He continued, "My assistant called your assistant and told her what you liked."

She looked down at a plate of Bouillabaisse and smiled, which included Aurora's favorite: mussels. She then said, "Well, close enough. I do like mussels."

As he was cutting up the chicken in his Coq au vin, he said to Aurora, "So, what were you going to say that is so important that we had to meet for lunch?"

"Well…" Aurora now sat down her silverware and took a drink of water. "I don't know how to put this lightly, but I am giving you my resignation." She then pulled an envelope out of her jacket that had her letter of resignation inside.

Mr. Fratzenburg put his silverware down and thought for a moment. He looked shocked and then pushed the envelope away. "No, I can't accept that."

"Well, you don't have to, but I am resigning."

"But you can't."

Aurora responded, "Well, why is that?"

"I don't have anyone to replace you." He was only thinking about his magazine as he said it. It wasn't that he would miss her as an employee or that she was great at her job.

Aurora said back, ignoring his upsetting comment, "Well, I want to leave within a month from now. I don't know how logical that is, but I will help you hire and train someone until I leave." She also knew that whomever would replace her would have large shoes to fill. She didn't want to leave in a bad way. Working for the magazine offered her many opportunities, leadership, and learning experience.

"But I will give you a raise or whatever you want to stay."

Aurora said, "I can't."

Mr. Fratzenburg said obnoxiously, as he stuffed some food into his mouth, "I mean, what's the rush?" He took a gulp of the scotch in his glass to help flush down the food. Aurora stared at him as he ate like an animal. *Does he have any manners or does he not respect me at all?* He then continued by saying, "Was the breakup that bad?"

Aurora rolled her eyes and said in an aggravated tone, "That is extremely unprofessional to bring up my personal life, which is none of your business." She then took a few breaths to contain herself. "The truth is I took a new job. It was the job offer I turned down before I built this magazine with you. Well, by myself, if you think about it."

"The job at *The Times*? You mean that liberal paper?"

"Oh, come on, Mr. Fratzenburg. I know you are smarter than that. They were not always liberal."

"I know. I am just kidding. I was kidding about the relationship thing too." His sympathy did not sound genuine with the arrogance in his voice. He continued, "Well, congratulations. That is a great. I am happy for you."

"Thanks."

"So, I guess we should start looking to hire someone as soon as possible because they have big shoes to fill." She felt like she had his blessings to leave, but that didn't matter to her anyway because she was going to go regardless.

"That's true," Aurora said as she signaled for the waiter to wrap up the rest of her lunch. "Let's get to work then, shall we?"

# Chapter 26

The next week, Aurora was walking to her home after work. The sounds of leather boots scraping and heels clicking against the pavement surrounded her. She pulled out her phone from her pocket to scroll through her social media pages as she walked on State Street. She had to keep looking up every few seconds to make sure she wasn't walking into anyone. After walking for a few moments, she saw Melih walking in front of her. She looked down and stared at her phone, like no one around her existed. *Please don't notice me. Please don't notice me. Please don't notice me.*

Melih looked both ways before he crossed the street and saw Aurora in his peripheral vision. He stopped and turned around. *Oh, come on.*

"Aurora?"

"Oh, hey Melih," she said as she looked down again. *Dang it.* "I didn't see you there."

"I have messaged you many times and you have not responded," Melih said. "Is every-ding okay?" *I am just in a crisis and don't know what to do with my life.*

"Yes. Everything is fine," Aurora said. "But I never received any messages from you. I would have responded."

"You know vhat? It doesn't matter," Melih said. "It's just that… I missed you," He mumbled.

"You what?"

"I missed you, Rora."

*I missed you too. I feel like melting in your arms after you said you've missed me, but I can't tell you that.*

Melih said, "Vell, if you are not doing anything, you want to go to da steepery and get a tea?"

"Well."

"Vell...yes?"

"Okay," Aurora said. "But only because I love their raspberry bubble tea." She smiled as she looked down at her Purple Dolce & Gabbana sling backs.

They arrived at the teashop and a waft of freshly brewed Persian tea and homemade sweet sticky buns wrapped around her nose. Her cheeks were red and windburned from the icy wind outside.

"Hey," Melih said as he smiled at Aurora. "You can get a seat vherever you like and I vill get your tea."

She went to a table in the front of the teashop so she could people watch from the front window. She took off her gloves and set them on the table.

She took a moment to stop looking out the window at the people walking by, to check out Melih as he waited in line. She bit her lip. He turned around. She waved awkwardly at him. *Aurora, really?* She felt that he giggled to himself for catching her. He walked up to the table.

"Thanks for the drink." She flashed him a smile as she fluttered her eyelashes like a butterfly.

Melih set down the drinks.

"Let me help you with that, Rora," he said as he helped Aurora take off her coat. As he was doing that, he said softly to Aurora, next to her ear, "My pleasure." Goosebumps went down her spine as the word pleasure dripped from his lips. She felt like he had said it in slow motion and the sound was prolonged in her ears.

The way his soft voice felt on her neck, it was as if he were kissing it, but his lips never touched her skin. She could feel each strand of her hair stick up, one strand at a time. She had not felt that kind of sensation before. She didn't know what that feeling was, until that moment. *Wow... This is love. Or is this lust? It must be love, right?*

He sat down and she stared at her iced tea. She used her straw to play with the black tapioca pearls in the bottom of her cup. She didn't want to look into Melih's eyes because she didn't want to face the reality of the way she felt about him. She wanted to be strong, but every moment she could feel her heart beating faster and heavier.

She then looked at him. "Melih..." She could not resist looking into his dark brown eyes that looked like the night sky with all the stars and the moons of all of the planets. *How have I not seen him like this before? This is different from the day he caught me at the ice skating rink. I should tell him I will be moving to New York.* But after the way she was feeling at that moment, she didn't want to tell him anything.

"Yes, Aurora?"

She stopped with what she was about to say. She wanted to put herself first for once.

*No matter what happens between us, I will move to New York and take that job...Even if you are irresistible... God help me.* She sighed as she looked down at the black tapioca pearls in her iced milk tea.

"Aurora?"

"Oh," Aurora said. "I am sorry. I had a busy day today."

"It is okay," Melih said. "So you vill be divorced next week, right?"

"Yes," Aurora said. "And. I. Can. Not. Wait." She threw her hands up in the air with excitement and everyone around her stared at her like she was a crazy person. Melih raised his eyebrows.

"Vell, I vould like to come with you. I don't vant you to be there alone," Melih said.

"Well, I won't be there alone. I will have my lawyer and my family said they are coming, but I guess I can't count on them. Tessa also has work that day, so…"

"Perfect. I vill come. I want to be there for you. I know dis probably may be hard for you."

"I will be fine. All the hard stuff has passed, to be honest," Aurora said. "Unless his lawyer fights the evidence, we are contesting the pre-nup."

"I am sure they vill lose. I have been praying for dat," Melih said. "You know, you are a lot stronger than you dhink."

Aurora smiled at Melih and said, "Thank you." She sucked some of the tea and one of the pearls through her straw. She struggled to suck it up, even though the straw was wider than most straws.

"You are velcome. You vent through a lot with Gannon and never told anyone." Melih sighed. "I just vish I could have done something."

She then said, "It is okay. Everyone keeps saying that, but no one could have done anything because no one knew." Aurora was slightly annoyed because she had heard it a million times from so many people.

"I know, but it is different for me."

Aurora was intrigued but confused. "How is that?"

"I liked you since da first time I saw you in Zara's dorm room."

"What?" Aurora felt nostalgic.

"Remember my saying I liked your shirt?" Melih said. "Yeah, it was an awkward compliment, but I remember that. I didn't know how to react." Aurora laughed. "I actually don't remember the shirt I was wearing."

"I remember it vas a blue blouse and you had your hair tied back." He touched his earlobe with his thumb. "You vere vearing the same pearl earrings you have on now." Aurora used her thumb to rub the pearl earring on her right ear, wishing she were rubbing his hands. Then she sucked up some more tea through her straw.

Melih went on, "See. I could have done something. I could have saved you from him. Dhere vere so many times I vanted tell you I liked you, but I just couldn't do dat to you."

Shhhh, was the sound she made as she put her finger to her lips.

"It is fine. Everything is already determined by God, right?" Aurora said. "Wait, why did you say you couldn't tell me you liked me?"

"Well, you remember the first time you and I had coffee alone?" Melih said.

Aurora looked up towards the ceiling. She did that a lot when she was thinking. She then said, "Yes, I remember."

Melih said nervously and hesitantly, "Vell, it was someding I said then... Like, my parents 'would love you' or something like dat."

"Yes," Aurora said. "I remember very well."

Melih stroked his hands through his hair as he looked down. He looked worried to tell Aurora something, as if it would change things between them forever.

She said, "What is it, Melih?" Aurora knew that something was wrong by his behavior.

Melih said hesitantly, "Vell, the reason I never said anyding in college about liking you or why I tried to push you avay after you left Gannon....Uhh.. because..."

"Well, what is it, Melih?" Aurora was getting annoyed

because she was feeling anxious and didn't really like suspense.

"Vell, I just didn't think my parents vould ever approve of you."

"Well, why? Am I not good enough?"

"No, no, no, Aurora. You are perfect," he said as he took a drink from his tea. *He thinks I am perfect.* "You are a great person, Aurora. I guess I never thought to be vith someone who vas not Muslim or Turkish. I never asked them though.... Because I thought that they would not approve.... My family are wery proud Turkish people."

Aurora was confused, "What do you mean by very proud?"

"Vell, my family loves Turkish history. Turkish people. Da Food. Baklava. Coffee. The kabob. Everything related to Turkey." Aurora didn't know what to say. Melih continued, "They just like everything Turkish. They really like Turkish people too. My dad always told me how he vanted me to marry a Turkish girl. Dat is his dream."

"Okay, so why can't you tell them?" Aurora said. "I mean, why are you telling me now?"

Melih said, "Vell, I can. I am just scare d-hey will say they do not allow it. I do not want to disobey my parents in any way."

"Melih, you don't have to tell them."

"Vell, I vant to. The next time I see them, I vill tell them about you." He then grabbed her hand. "I promise I will." *Is he going to propose to me or something? I am so confused...*

Aurora really wanted to tell Melih then that she was moving to New York. That way, it would make things easier on them. They could move on before they fell too hard. "Okay, tell them." *What? Why did I say that? She wanted to hit her hand to her forehead. I am always thinking with my heart.*

"I vill," Melih said with a smile, while rubbing his thumb

against her hand.

The rest of the night they spent talking and laughing, and they fell harder by each second. It was as if the walls finally came down between them. It took them years to get to that point. Aurora let Melih walk her to her car and he hugged her and kissed her on the forehead. His hug was so warm, and they both wished that time would stop and they could hold onto that embrace forever.

Aurora went to bed that night crying because she was sad that she would be leaving eventually, and she didn't know how to tell Melih. Every time she looked in his eyes, she became lost. She didn't want Melih to tell his family about her because she knew that things would change once she moved. She wanted to build a new life somewhere else. She also knew that she really needed to take time by working on herself and being alone.

--

Toward the end of the week, Aurora and Tessa decided to meet for lunch. Tessa was off that day and came to hang out with Dan when he was done with work. Tessa and Dan were seeing each other whenever they could. Tessa wanted to move into the city and get a job working as a dentist there. Even if she and Dan did not stay together, Tessa would make any excuse she could to come to Madison.

Tessa and Aurora met at a soup and salad restaurant for lunch because Aurora loved a light lunch. The restaurant had a hipster vibe to it. Aurora loved those types of restaurants; she thought that hipsters always knew about the hip and healthy things to eat. Aurora also never really liked eating a big lunch; she wanted to eat something light. That is because when she was too full, she would become tired within an hour after returning back from lunch. Aurora never liked that afternoon slump because she didn't have time to take a nap.

They got their food and sat down. Aurora took a bite of her avocado chickpea salad. She had a disgusted looked on her face and pushed the bowl away from her. *This is not appetizing at all.*

"Hey, I gotta tell you something," Aurora said to Tessa.

"Oh boy," Tessa said. "What is it?"

Aurora laughed. "Why do you assume it is something bad?"

Tessa shrugged her shoulders and put her hands up, signaling that she didn't know.

Aurora continued, "Well, you know that article I wrote a while ago that went viral?"

"Yes."

"Well, *The New York Times* contacted me about it."

"And?" Tessa said.

"Well, I got a job offer from them," Aurora said.

Tessa said, "Hmmm."

"Why aren't you happy for me?" Aurora said. "This is a big deal."

"I am happy for you Aurora. It's just…"

"Just what?" Aurora said proudly, as if she were a peacock fluffing up her feathers. "I will be the assistant editor-in-chief."

"That is awesome, Aurora," Tessa replied with a concerned voice. "I am truly happy for you, but as your best friend, I have to be honest with you."

"About what? You should be so excited for me, but you are always honest with me," Aurora said as she threw up her hands in agreement. "All right, say what you want to say."

Tessa said, "I am excited for you, like I said." Tessa then hesitated for a moment as Aurora waited for her reasoning.

Tessa continued, "Why don't you just slow down, Aurora? You need a break. Why do you always make big decisions?"

"I never make big decisions for myself," Aurora responded with pity.

Tessa responded and said, "You married Gannon on a whim. That was a big decision."

"That was one time! Come on."

"Maybe it was once, but that one time really affected your life," Tessa said. "So, I am just saying you should think about it. That's all."

"I have thought about it," Aurora snapped back. "I always resented Gannon for never taking that job at *The Times* a few years back. I don't want to miss an opportunity like this again. I want to start over and make something for myself."

"Aurora," Tessa said, "can't you do that here, though? You are already a well-known writer."

"I just want to do this for me. I need a change. I have been in this state my whole life. I need a change." Aurora looked down and then sat up straight and proud.

"But..." Tessa said before Aurora interrupted her.

"But you know my not making a big decision is not me, Tessa. I don't slow down. I go big or I go home. That is why I am leaving. I don't give up on anything. Even if I hate something, I try to fix it and make it bearable. Gannon treated me like crap, but I tried to fix him. I thought it would make things better. I revamped the magazine and made it a gold mine. I turned down *The Times* before. I am not doing it again. I am doing this for me. It is the. First. Time. In. My. Life. I am doing something for me."

Tessa responded, as if she were playing devil's advocate, "Okay, but do you think you won't get burned out?"

"No, and if I do, I know I always have good friends like you to come back to."

"Yes, you do. I just don't want to lose you again!" Tessa exclaimed. "That's all. Gannon hated when you and I spent time together. It is like I finally got you back, and now I am losing you again. You are my best friend."

Aurora started getting sentimental. "Look, Tessa, my grandma once told me that anyone would be lucky to make one good friend that could stick by their side forever, through the nasty divorces, heartbreaks, and sickness. She said that is the most cherished gift to have a friend like that. A friend that stays by your side. Your friendship is a cherished gift to me. You are still and will always be my best friend. I can come back and visit, or you could come and visit me. They are putting me in this fancy loft. It is furnished and everything."

Aurora pulled out her phone and showed Tessa the pictures of her new loft in New York City.

Tessa then said as she let out a big breath of air, "It looks amazing. I am happy for you. Just don't forget about me when you are super famous." Tessa sat back and laughed.

"Of course not," Aurora said. "Anyway, how are you and Dan?"

The rest of their conversation consisted of Tessa talking about Dan. It was the first time in a while that Aurora had seen Tessa so smitten by someone.

# Chapter 27

It was the day of the divorce and Aurora could not sleep the night before. She was up all night worrying about what would happen if Gannon didn't come to court, even though the lawyer had reassured her several times they would be divorced regardless, if he showed up or not. However, she was still anxious about that and the nasty pre-nup. She would be anxious until the judge hammered down his gavel for the last time.

Aurora took a Xanax about an hour before her court time to calm her nerves. She unbuttoned her black suit jacket as she felt it was hard to breath. She wanted to undue her bra, too because of the tightness she felt in her chest, to make it easier to breathe but she didn't. She met with her lawyer about thirty minutes before the court appointment for a briefing. The lawyer tried to calm her down, but the lawyer's attitude made him lack any real emotion toward her. Maybe he thought she was being dramatic or he felt that he had been through so many divorce cases that hers was a piece of cake.

"Aurora," her lawyer said in a monotone voice, "everything is going to be okay."

"Why are you so calm about the conversation?" Aurora said.

"Well, I have done many divorce cases," he said. "Yours isn't that bad."

*Ouch, but I guess that is reassuring to know that people had have it far worse than me I do,* Aurora thought.

"I would say what you said hurt my feelings, but then again, I hired you to be honest and not sugarcoat anything."

"So, I assume the pre-nup will be brought to attention and when it is, Gannon's lawyer will try to detest against it." He continued, "But there is no need to worry. He will not win."

He pulled some files out of manila folder he had in his briefcase. He then showed the text messages of him saying sorry and admitting that he cheated on Aurora. She felt sick to see the reminder of Gannon's deceit.

Her lawyer said, "Well, are you ready to go in?"

"I mean, I am anxious. Like really anxious," Aurora said. "But I have waited months for today. Maybe years."

"Well, it sounds like you are ready then."

Aurora walked into the courtroom as if she were walking through the gates of Hell and Gannon was the Devil sitting in the front of the courtroom. She saw Melih there in the courtroom on her left as she walked in. *I will just pretend I didn't see him and run out of the courtroom when this is all done with.* She could tell from her peripheral vision that they were both staring at her. She had a confused look on her face and continued to look down as she walked toward the front of the courtroom. Aurora saw her parents sitting at the front of the courtroom, right behind the tables, where the attorneys and clients would enter and sit. *My dad is probably here because my mom forced him to come. Or maybe he actually cares now.*

Aurora thought the benches looked like church pews. She took a seat. She saw Gannon to her right and remembered how weeks leading up to the divorce day, Gannon was messaging and calling her and begging her not to get a divorce. *I could have blocked him from contacting me, but I just wanted to torture him.* She was shocked to see a grown man act so pathetic when he didn't get what he wanted. The judge got to the stand and called their case.

Aurora then looked at Gannon's side and saw that none of his family or friends were there for him. He was too into himself to ever keep any real friends. Aurora almost felt herself feeling bad for him. Gannon's family probably thought he was pathetic and a failure as well. His parents didn't really care much for Gannon since he decided not to attend medical school to "follow his dream as an artist." She was always above his level but never wanted to admit it to herself because of her pity for him. Aurora had so much passion in her bones; she could never stand still and was always thinking about what she could do next. Gannon tried to trample that part of her but luckily; she got out before it was too late.

As soon as Gannon saw Melih, Gannon flipped him the middle finger. Melih laughed at that and just looked away, as if Gannon were some garbage he found in the street. Aurora could hear her dad keep saying under his breath and grunting, directed toward Gannon, like a bull ready to hit a matador: "I want to kill that little punk." *Too bad you were like him when I was growing up, Dad.*

Aurora couldn't remember how many Xanax she had taken beforehand. As soon as the judge walked into the courtroom, everyone in the courtroom rose. The judge was gray-haired, tall, and had bad posture. His demeanor was tough. *This judge looks intimidating.* The judge sat, and the rest of the people in the courtroom sat.

The judge asked both Aurora and Gannon to state their names and addresses.

"Which one of you is the petitioner?"

"I am," Aurora said and sat up straight and cleared her throat. "I am, your honor." Aurora looked anxiously as the stenographer typed everything verbatim on her small typewriter.

"Aurora, were you married to Gannon McMaster on November 6th of 2018," the judge said, "in Auburn, Alabama?"

"Yes, your honor." Aurora's hands shook and she poured herself a glass of water from the glass pitcher in front of her.

"Did you live with your spouse following that day, in Madison, Wisconsin?" Aurora choked back a tear and took a drink of water. *Why are these questions so hard for me to answer?*

"Yes," Aurora said. "Yes, your honor."

"On October 23rd, did the breakdown of your marriage occur?" A flashback of Shazzy and Gannon on the couch flashed back in her mind and she flinched.

"Yes."

"Can you describe what caused you to file for divorce?" *Years of abuse and lies.*

"Ah…" Aurora said. A tear ran down Aurora's face.

"Counselor Wulfblitzen, can your client describe the event that led her to divorce?" Aurora looked at Gannon and saw him looking down but smiling, as he knew it tortured her to speak of that night.

"Your honor, these questions are a bit invasive. As you can see, my client does not f…." Aurora started to shake like a volcano about to erupt.

"I caught him cheating on me with my friend that night!" People in the courtroom gasped. Aurora said, "That doesn't even include the years of physical, verbal, and mental abusive I suffered up to that night." The judge's face was emotionless.

"So, is you marriage inevitably broken?" The judge said in a monotone voice.

"Absolutely. Obviously," Aurora said.

"I need a yes or no, Ms. Tousey."

"Yes, your honor," Aurora said. "Yes."

Mr. Redding, Gannon's lawyer, began to speak, and Aurora slouched back in her chair and her brain felt foggy.

"I found an infidelity clause," Erik said as Aurora snapped back into reality and sat up straight. "On page 36 in the third paragraph."

The judge licked his fingertips to help him flip through the pages.

"Okay," The judge said. "Do you have your evidence?"

"Yes, your honor," Erik said as he brought up the manila folder and took out the photos of the text messages Gannon had sent Aurora. The judge looked over them.

"Mr. McMaster?" The judge said.

"Yes, your honor?"

"Can you come up here a moment?"

"Yes, your honor."

"Did you send these messages to Ms. Tousey?" Gannon looked back at his lawyer with fright in his eyes.

"Objection!" Mr. Redding said.

"On what grounds?" The judge said.

"I have not seen this evidence before the trial," Mr. Redding said.

"Sustained," the judge said. "I will allow this evidence. Though you may have not have seen this evidence, your client is acting like he has."

"Again, Mr. McMaster," The lawyer said as he cleared his throat and took a drink of water from a glass cup. "I also want to remind you that lying under oath is a federal offense."

"Y-y-yes," Gannon muffled.

"Excuse me?" The judge said.

"Yes. Yes, I sent them." Again, the people in the courtroom gasped.

"You may be seated," the judge said.

"Well, I know that it is not usually enforced, but adultery is illegal in Wisconsin." Erik said. "It is actually a criminal offense. My client will not press charges if the pre-nup is taken off of the table and not valid. Not to mention, she was under duress."

"Counselor Redding, do you have anything to add?" the judge asked. Gannon's lawyer and him were whispering to one another. "Counselor Redding?"

"No." Redding gave a stare at Gannon, like he was weak. "No, your honor."

"Fine," the judge said. "I deem this prenuptial agreement invalid."

"Yes!" Aurora said out loud as she fist pumped the air.

She then sat down, and the last thing she remembered was the judge hitting his gavel for the last time. When he hit his gavel to the wood, it sounded like the crack made from a lightning strike during a thunderstorm. It made her jump. She was waiting for the rainbow to come after the storm during court that day, but then she remembered Melih and Gannon were in the same room at once. She could feel blood rushing to her temples and her heart pounding as if it were going to make her chest and head explode.

Aurora had a few brief words with her lawyer and immediately ran to the nearest bathroom she could find. She ran out of the courtroom door as if she had just escaped from the gates of Hell. She wanted to avoid everyone, and she did. She ran to the last stall. She put her back against the yellow-tiled wall and crouched to the floor and cried. She pulled her knees to her chest and cried like she had never cried before. They were tears of joy and adrenaline. She felt a huge burst of euphoria and newfound freedom run through her veins. She was so happy to finally be free from Gannon. She got up and looked in the mirror and saw mascara streaks dribble down her cheeks from her eyes. "Oh my God. I look like a raccoon." She then laughed hysterically at herself. She rinsed her face with water.

She called her mom on the phone. She took some tissue paper to dry her face and wipe the excess mascara off her face.

"Hey baby girl. Where are you?"

"I am in the bathroom down the hall," Aurora said in a quiet voice.

"You are in where?" Her mom said louder.

Aurora said with an annoyed, loud voice, "Don't say it out loud!" She then realized she was being loud, took a deep breath, and quieted her voice. My emotions are all over the place right now. She looked at her hand and tried to steady it, but she couldn't stop shaking. "Mom, I am hiding in the bathroom. I want to leave, but I don't want to talk to anyone. Help, me leave. Please. Without anyone seeing me. Please," Aurora pleaded.

"Honey, I will be there in a second. Just stay there. I will find a way for us to leave without anyone seeing you."

Aurora hated asking people for help, but she felt like she had no other option at that point. She just got a divorce, which was enough for her for the day. She didn't want to deal with any more drama or confrontation.

"Aurora, where are you?" Her mom Elizabeth whispered loudly.

"I am in the last stall."

"You need to hurry up, kiddo. You have a dark-haired man out there asking for you. He is pretty handsome."

"Melih?"

"What?"

"No one. It is nothing. Never mind."

"I am just saying, I wouldn't kick him out of my bed for eating crackers." *Gross!*

"Mom!"

"Sorry. Is there something you want to tell me now?"

"No! Not now," Aurora said frantically. "I will tell you when I am out of here."

Aurora's mom peeked her head out of the door, looking both ways as if she were on a top-secret mission or about to walk across a very busy highway.

"I feel like a sleuth. How exciting!" Her mom whispered.

She then popped her head back in the bathroom. "The coast is clear," her mom, Elizabeth, said. "Go left and run straight out the exit entrance. Your father and I will meet you at your new place. Then we can go get lunch." *The last thing I can think about is lunch...*

Aurora quickly got out of the bathroom and went left. She ran down the hallway, almost tripping over her own feet. She then ran down to her car. Started the engine and peeled out of there as fast as she could. She went home and waited for her parents to arrive. As soon as she got home, she went straight to her bed and fell on it like she was falling on a cloud.

She made the sound, *aaaahhh* with relief. "This is it!" Aurora said while yelling into her big fluffy white comforter. "This is freedom!"

# Chapter 28

Though she had not had a drink in a while, she was craving a glass of celebratory champagne. *You do not need a drink to reward yourself with. Besides, it will make you feel worse afterwards or you will do something that you will regret later on. You are not in college anymore.* It was the norm to drink in Wisconsin, for all things in your life, literally everything. No one ever made excuses or needed a reason to drink, but people who didn't drink were expected to have a reason why they were not drinking. Aurora still chose not to drink. She just waited for her family while she sat in solitude.

While Aurora was lying on the bed on her belly, she contemplated her next move in life, with her face in her bed. She was proud to be divorced from Gannon. Though the way Aurora was raised, it was Taboo to tell anyone if you were divorced. *I really don't want to talk about divorce, but how else can I protect others from people like Gannon?*

Aurora walked downstairs to make herself a cup of coffee, wondering why her parents were taking so long. She blew on her coffee to cool it down. She looked out of her kitchen window and looked at the lake. She took a sip of her coffee. *I cannot believe I am this young and have gone through so much already. Maybe I should write a book about divorce since I have the divorce fresh in my head. Why not just start now...*

She walked up the stairs and sat her coffee on her desk next to the right of her computer mouth and Parker pen. She sat down and tied her hair in a bun on the top of her head. She looked out the window and could see trees that were bare of leaves but lightly dusted with snow. *I am sure this view is beautiful in the fall, too... Too bad I won't be around to see it.* One tear fell down her face and she wiped it away with her sleeve.

Without thinking for another second, she pulled a legal pad from her desk drawer and put the Parker pen in her hand. She heard people calling and messaging her phone. She chose to ignore it because she wanted to skip talking to anyone at that moment. She knew if she thought about it too much, or any longer, she would never write that book. She put the pen to the paper, took a deep breath, and started to write her outline. She wrote a title on the top of the legal pad: *How I Survived an Abusive Marriage.*

Her pen started to write on the legal pad like fire and brimstone.

After about fifteen minutes into writing her outline, she heard someone knock on her door. "Come on, I just got into writing this! Aurora said." "Oh no! I forgot my parents were coming here." She ran down to open the door and let her parents in.

"Aurora, what happened to your hair?" Her mom said.

"Ahh. Nothing," Aurora said as she shrugged her shoulders. "I was just writing."

"Oh, it's another one of the weird quirks that makes me love you so much," her mom said as she embraced Aurora for a hug. Aurora stood there like a stick person as her mom wrapped her arms around her. Aurora was not so keen on hugging because she didn't get hugged much as a child. She was awkward when someone would try to give her a hug, unless that someone was a boy that she loved. Aurora's mom tried to squeeze her tighter, but Aurora pushed away.

"Mom!"

"Sorry. You know, I love you so much and I am so proud of you," her mom then responded and put her hands on her hips.

"I know, mom."

Her dad Charles said, "Well, your place is nice. How much are you paying for it?"

"Enough," Aurora said. She did not like talking about money.

"Allll rightly then," Her dad said back.

"So... let's eat. Where do you guys want to go?" Aurora said.

"Any place I can get a burger," her dad said.

"Of course," Aurora said.

"What?" Charles said. They all laughed out loud because her dad would always say he wanted a hamburger any time someone asked where he wanted to eat.

"Okay Dad, whatever you want."

They ended up going to this burger joint called Milwaukee's Best; they sold many types of beer, Bloody Marys, and burgers.

Aurora always got a burger with an egg on it; her dad would always have a burger with onions and mushrooms sautéed in butter. Her mom got a grilled chicken sandwich and some fries with blue cheese dressing. Aurora's mom didn't care what she ate as long as she got some fries with blue cheese dressing to dip them in. Aurora always thought that what her mom ate was weird, but never said anything to her.

"How does it feel to be divorced?" Charles said.

Elizabeth nudged Charles' arm and whispered to him, "Don't talk about the divorce."

"Mom, I can hear you... It is not a big deal," Aurora said. "Dad, it finally feels like I am free from a man's grasp." She made a fist in her hand and held it in front of her face. Her mom looked down at her food with eyes as wide as the darkness that filled Aurora's heart from her childhood.

*I feel strong to sit across from my father and say that to his face, but I doubt he will get what I meant. I have been free from my father, but now I'm free from Gannon.*

"How's your job going? Anything new happening lately?" her father said.

Aurora said hesitantly, "Well…. there kind of is."

"What is it?" Aurora's mom said.

"Well," Aurora said. Her heart rate started to beat faster, and she could feel the sweat grow on her forehead under her bangs that were swept to one side. She took a gulp of water; her fingers became wet from the perspiration on the water glass.

Her dad then motioned with his hand for her to continue.

"Well, I got a job offer in New York."

Charles snapped back quickly, "New York? Doing what? Why would you leave your job here? You need some stability in your life."

"This new job will give me stability. They already have a place there for me."

Her mom interjected and said, "Then what will you be doing? Will you ever see us?"

Aurora said back, rolling her eyes, "Yes, mom. I will visit you two and you can visit me."

"Well, you know your dad hates flying."

"Okay, then you two can drive. It wouldn't kill you to take a vacation every once in a while."

Her dad then said, "We will see. So, what will you be doing there? Are you sure you want to do this?"

Aurora replied, "Yes, I am sure. I have been thinking about this for the last few weeks. I should be moving there by the middle of April. That is about a month or so."

Charles said, "Okay, but what about your job here? Didn't you basically make that company what it is today?"

"Well, more or less, and I did get paid a lot to do it, but Dad, it is a magazine that only elderly people read in waiting rooms at the hospital. It's not enough for me. Now I am training someone to take over for me... Anyway, I want to write something real."

Charles responded back quickly, "Can't you write here, though? Why do you need to leave?"

"My friend, Tessa, said the same thing," Aurora said. "They want me to be there to work. I can and will travel a lot, but they want me based out of New York. I will be staying in Manhattan. Dad, I am going to be the Assistant. Editor. In. Chief. for *The New York Times*."

"How? You are still so young." *Uhhhh.*

Aurora said, "I know. People tell me that all of the time. Then once they see my work ethic and what I am capable of, they forget my age." She took a drink of water. "Anyway, there have been people far more successful than me at even younger ages."

"Okay, well I am proud of you, Aurora." Aurora's dad never told her he was proud of her. This made her very happy inside, but she didn't want to show it too much. So, she just smiled and wiped away a tear from falling down her left cheek.

"Thank you, Dad."

"Yes, baby girl," Aurora's mom said as she smiled and squeezed Charles's arm. "Your father and I are always proud of you."

When her parents took her back to her place, she opened the car door and said to her parents, "You guys going to stay for a while?

Her mom replied, "No, we both have to work tomorrow."

"It is not even dark outside yet," Aurora said. "Why don't you just stay the night? It's a long drive."

Her mom replied, "Sorry baby girl, we can't." Both of her parents got out of the car and hugged her. Aurora only remembered her father hugging her once as a child. As she got to her porch, she looked back and waved to her parents.

As soon as she saw her parents drive away, she grabbed the keys from her pocket, then her phone. She saw how many missed calls and messages she had. She had one call and a text from Tessa and several from Melih and Gannon.

Gannon was telling her that they could always reverse the divorce and they had six months to decide. "Nope. Nope. And nope." She said out loud to herself. "Delete. And. Block."

The messages and calls from Melih were asking where she was and why she left right away. Aurora's boss messaged her and told her she could take off work that day. She rolled her eyes as she read that message. *I just got divorced. Sure! I will come right in... You really think I would be coming in? Of course I am not going to work. Just another obvious reason why I want to leave.* Tessa had called as well, and messaged Aurora to see how the divorce went. Tessa said she would be there that night for moral support, though on the inside all Aurora wanted to do was write that night and be alone.

Aurora called Tessa as she was lying in her pj's in front of her tv, wrapped up in a white fluffy throw blanket.

"Okay," Aurora said. "You can come over, but we are getting Chinese food. I need some unhealthy comfort food."

"It's a deal. I will buy it for us," Tessa said. "How was the divorce?"

"Well, it was good because I am divorced," Aurora said. "But... It was so... awkward"

"But why awkward?"

"Well," Aurora said, "Melih was there."

"Yeah?" Tessa said. "But you told me he was coming. How is that awkward?"

"I pretended I didn't see him... Oh! And when Gannon saw Melih was there, he flipped him off."

They both laughed.

"But what else happened?" Tessa said.

Aurora took a sip of her chamomile tea.

"Well, when the judge finally announced we were divorced, I ran out afterward. I hid in the bathroom, so I could avoid them."

"Wow," Tessa said. "That is awkward."

"I had to call my mom to come get me and sneak me out. So, how are things with Dan?"

"Really good, actually," Tessa said. "I will have to tell you all about it in person."

"It must be serious then," Aurora said. "Anyway, I am happy for you, but you don't need to tell me anything too personal. Dan is like a brother to me, you know."

"Yes," Tessa said. "But I am your best friend."

"Tell me whatever you want," Aurora said. "I can't promise I won't cringe at the gushy love stuff."

"I am on my way to another class now," Tessa said. "I will tell you about all of the gushy love stuff when I see you tonight." Tessa continued, "I am sure you are excited."

"Well. Not really," Aurora said. "But I could take any type of distraction right now."

Aurora put on her fluffy gray slippers, grabbed her tea, and went upstairs to put on her favorite gray hoodie with "UW Madison" on it in big red, bold letters. She then tied her hair in a bun on top of her head and went back to her desk to continue to work on her outline. After working on her outline a couple of hours, she started to type her book. Her outline wasn't finished either, but she figured she would end up changing her outline along the way.

Aurora didn't realize what time it was until her coffee was cold. She looked out the window and saw the white frosted sky turn into an icy blue, pink, and purple sunset.

Tessa sent Aurora a text that she would be there around 7:00 p.m. Aurora continued to write until Tessa got there.

Tessa got to the house and knocked on the door. Aurora jumped out of her chair. She was easily scared, and the book she was writing triggered her into fight and flight mode. *Writing this book is going to be harder than I thought.* But she resented Gannon so much and wanted to tell the world how disgusting of a human being he was. Her hatred for Gannon is what kept her going.

Tessa came into the house and stomped the snow off of her shoes on Aurora's rug. She had her backpack on and two white plastic bags with Chinese food in them. Aurora grabbed one of the bags and peeked inside it.

"Is this mine?"

Tessa responded, "If it has a white box with an L on it, then yes, it is yours." Aurora looked inside and saw General Tso's chicken with low mien noodles.

Aurora said, "How did you know what I wanted? I thought we would order delivery."

"You have been ordering the same thing for years. You literally never order anything else," Tessa said.

"Very good, my friend. Thank you." Aurora put the food on the coffee table and waited for Tessa to take off her jacket. She pulled her food out of the bag and went to get plates out of the kitchen. Aurora pulled her own chopsticks from the silverware drawer. They were porcelain white with blue Chinese writing on the end. She felt very proud of the fact that she could use them.

Aurora came back and sat on the couch next to Tessa and turned on the TV. Aurora said, "Let's put something on Netflix or I can rent any movie."

Tessa said, "Whatever you like." She continued by saying, "Too bad we won't be able to hang out like this when you are in New York."

"Well......." Aurora responded as she picked up the remote. "I was thinking we could watch a chic flick." She started scrolling through the movies on her TV. "Speaking of New York, how about *The Devil Wears Prada*?"

Tessa responded, "Sounds good to me."

Aurora said, "Even if I am going to New York, you can come visit me."

Tessa said with a whiny voice, "I know, but it's not the same and besides, you know I hate traveling."

Aurora smiled at Tessa and said, "But I am special."

"Yes, you are."

Aurora commented, "You are never sentimental like that. That's not the type of friendship we have. You better stop before it gets weird." They both laughed.

Tessa replied embarrassed, "I know. You are right." Tessa then had an epiphany as if a light bulb had gone off in her head. "Wait! I am being the emotional one now? That has always been your job."

Aurora said, "I know! Jeez! Leave the emotions to me, why don't ya?" They both laughed.

"I am sorry, Aurora. It just sucks having your best friend leave you. Especially since we are hanging out again."

"Tessa, this is different, and you know that. I can come see you any time. You can come see me whenever you like."

Tessa laughed as she said, "We are starting to sound like a married couple in a long-distance relationship." They started laughing.

"You are right."

They both laughed again. Tessa continued, "Let's watch the movie."

They were halfway through the movie and full from Chinese food.

"Well, Dan and I are getting pretty serious," Tessa said.

"I figured so. I am happy for you."

"Thanks, but I am scared. I haven't been in a relationship in so long, I feel like I don't know what I am doing. I don't want to lose him. You know?" Tessa said.

"I don't think I am the best person to ask for relationship advise," Aurora replied. "But believe me. I know Dan. You will not lose him. Or I will beat him up."

Tessa looked at how small Aurora was and laughed. "As intimidating as you sound, I think you would lose to Dan in a fight."

"That's true, but Dan would never hurt a fly. I know he is a jock, but he is not like all the other jocks. He is intelligent and not a bro." Whenever Aurora called someone a bro, she meant they were a guy who only cared about themselves and their looks. They also would go to the gym a lot but always skipped leg day.

Tessa looked down at her plate of rice and said, "Well, maybe I am insecure."

"Come on, Tessa." Aurora rolled her eyes. "I don't know why you would be insecure. You will be a dentist soon and you are intelligent and pretty."

Aurora was getting annoyed that Tessa was talking bad

about herself. Tessa was one of the most intelligent and best-looking people she knew, though Aurora was biased. Tessa intimidated many men because of her beauty, brains, and success. Aurora always thought that it was their loss for not being with her. Many men thought that they didn't stand a chance with Tessa. But with Dan, Tessa had met her match. Her equal.

"You and Dan are perfect for each other. Don't overthink it. You will be a dentist soon and he will be a lawyer soon. You are going to be a power couple," Aurora said.

"See! How can we have conversations like this when you are in New York?"

"You see that, Tessa." Aurora pointed her finger and said, "That is a phone. You can call or text me whenever."

"I know, but it's different. I just need to succumb to the fact that you are moving. I mean, I am really proud for you. So, you are famous now, right?"

"No, I wouldn't call myself famous," Aurora said. "Maybe someday, but I am not striving to be famous though. I am striving to be happy."

The rest of the night, Tessa and Aurora spent talking about their future, past, and present. They reflected on how their friendship had made it through a lot.

Aurora struggled to sleep because she could not stop thinking about Melih and how bad she felt for just running away from him like that. She told herself she would talk to him about it. She also told herself that she would tell Melih she would be moving to New York.

--

Dan arrived to the house the next morning and knocked on

the door. Aurora opened the door, still in her pajamas. Dan looked at her clothes. "Are you coming to lunch with us dressed like that?"

"What?" Aurora said. "I am not going to lunch with you guys. I don't want to be the third wheel."

"But…" Dan started to say.

"Come on, Dan. You know I will." Dan pulled out his phone frantically to text someone. "What's the rush? Is someone dying?"

"Ahhhh…" Dan said, as he quickly grabbed the phone from his pocket. He then looked up from his phone and put it back in his pocket quickly because Aurora was trying to see whom he was messaging.

Dan continued, "No, Aurora. No one is dying. It was just a thing I had to send to one of my classmates."

Aurora rolled her eyes and said, "I'm not buyin' it." Dan took off his boots as he walked out of the doorway into Aurora's place.

"Nothing is wrong," Dan said. His cheeks got red, as he looked up at Aurora with an awkward smile.

"Okay, lover boy, I was just joking." She laughed. She softly slugged his arm to let him know she was teasing him because Aurora thought he was acting a bit uptight.

"Well, your place looks nice," Dan said.

"Your princess is getting ready upstairs. She will be down in a second. You can take a look around if you want." He looked around the house and saw Aurora's kitchen.

"The view is beautiful, Aurora."

"Wait! Let me show you my office upstairs!" She grabbed his arm and dragged him up the stairs.

"Sure, I'd love to see it," he said sarcastically as he rolled his eyes.

She showed her the room and he saw an array of papers crumpled up on the floor. Dan said, "Are you writing something? Or did a tornado come through here? The last time I checked, we live in Wisconsin, not Kansas." They both laughed.

"Well, I am writing something," she said humbly. She never wanted to gloat.

"Good for you, Rora!" Dan said with excitement. "What is it about?"

"Divorce…"

Dan replied, "Oh…"

Aurora said back, "Yeah…"

Dan did not know how to console her without bringing up what Gannon did. So, they just remained silent and went back downstairs. Dan sat on the couch and waited for Tessa. Dan was not normally a patient man. He wanted to yell up the stairs and ask Tessa if she was ready, but since they were in their honeymoon stage, he didn't want to rush or annoy her.

Dan and Tessa insisted that Aurora come with them to lunch, but Aurora insisted that she should stay home. Aurora thought it would be a win-win situation. This would also give Aurora some more time to work on her book, while Dan and Tessa had their alone time. If Aurora went a day without writing, she would feel like she had forgotten something and would not be able sleep. If she weren't writing something for work, she would write in her journal. Sometimes both. It was her go-to to destress. In addition to that, Aurora knew she would go crazy if she had to sit and be the third wheel. *Noooo, thank you,* Aurora thought

Moments later, Tessa came down the stairs with a pep in her step and smile on her face that Aurora had never seen before. *Wow,* Aurora thought. Aurora smiled and stood up, almost pushing them out of the door.

Aurora yelled to them as they walked off the porch and she wrapped her gray cashmere cardigan around her to brace the wind, "Well, you cats have fun!" *Cats?*

Tessa rolled her eyes as her face became red. Aurora laughed at what she had said to them and walked back inside. She then went back upstairs to work on writing some more of her book.

When Dan and Tessa were enjoying their lunch, Dan brought up the idea of inviting Aurora along for their evening. Dan said, "We could eat anywhere. Then afterwards, go downtown to dance or hangout."

Tessa was getting confused as to why Dan was so persistent on inviting Aurora out with them. She wasn't an expert, but she knew that he was not being completely honest when he said, "I just feel bad for her because her divorce was yesterday." Tessa just decided to brush it off, then texted Aurora insisting she should go out with them. Tessa was just worried Aurora would feel like a third wheel.

Aurora agreed after both Dan and Tessa messaged her, persuading her to hang out with them. *Well, they won't stop annoying me. I guess I will go. I need a break from writing, anyway,* Aurora thought.

# Chapter 29

Aurora, Dan, and Tessa walked to the restaurant together that evening for dinner. Dan looked at his phone right before they walked into the restaurant. The restaurant was called Dos Rancheros. The hostess welcomed and addressed them by asking if anyone else was coming and where they would like to sit.

Dan interjected frantically before the hostess could finish, "Oh, we are meeting someone here."

"Oh, okay." The hostess continued, "Do you know where…."

Dan interrupted her again, "Yes, we know where he is sitting." Dan pulled out his phone to look at it.

*He?* Aurora thought. *Am I going on a blind date?*

Aurora whispered to Tessa, "What does he mean by he?"

Tessa shrugged her shoulder as she said, "I have no idea, Aurora. You know as much as I do. Maybe this is why Dan has been acting weird all day and looking at his phone." Tessa seemed to be as confused as Aurora.

Dan was talking with the hostess in between texting someone, so he did not notice what Aurora and Tessa were talking about.

"Seriously, Tessa?" Aurora said in surprise. She whispered more quietly, "You don't know who we are meeting?"

"I swear," Tessa said.

"You ladies ready to sit down?" Dan said to them as he looked up from his phone.

Not realizing how long they had been whispering, they both said "yes" at the same time.

They followed Dan to the table. As she got closer to the man, Aurora could see the back of his head. The man's hair was shiny and black. She saw the man run his fingers through his hair. *Oh my God. Don't tell me.* She rolled her eyes to the back of her head. As soon as Dan said hi, the man turned around.

It was Melih.

"Hey guys!" Melih said with a huge smile on his face. He stood up and pulled out Aurora's chair for her to sit down.

"Thank you, Melih," Aurora said as she gave Dan a peculiar look.

Tessa whispered to Dan, "So this is why you wanted her to come so bad? You know she is moving to New York. Why would you set her up like this with Melih?"

Dan grabbed Tessa's hand from under the table and smiled as he said, "I promise I will tell you about it all later.... But wait, Aurora is moving to New York?"

"Yes, but don't say anything. I will tell you about it later."

Dan pulled Tessa's hand to his lips and kissed it. She then rolled her eyes because she didn't think it was good for Aurora to be seeing anyone, even though she didn't want Aurora to leave for New York. She didn't want a man to be the reason she would stay.

Tessa said to Melih like she was a detective, "So, Melih what are your plans with Aur..."

Dan interrupted her and said, "Yes, Melih, how was your day?" Tessa grunted.

"Ah, good. Just enjoying my day off," Melih said. "I didn't know you two vould be joining Dan and me. Dis is a nice surprise."

Aurora rolled her eyes. *Is Dan trying to play matchmaker?* Aurora thought. She felt like she was in an awkward position because she had not returned Melih's calls or texts and had hid from him after the divorce hearing.

"Well," Aurora said, "we are just as surprised as you are."

Melih looked at Aurora and smiled. "So how are you doing today, Aurora? Is your phone not vorking?" She took a deep breath in, *He smells so good.*

"Yes it is," Aurora said. "Why would you think that?"

"Oh, I thought it wasn't," Melih said. "Since you haven't been returning my messages or calls, I just thought...."

"I am sorry. I just was so upset yesterday," she said to him softly, so Dan and Tessa couldn't hear her. "I didn't want to see or talk to anyone." Aurora stared at Melih's hand, which was a centimeter away from hers. He looked down too and immediately pulled it away.

"It's okay. I understand," he said while looking into her eyes, as if he were lost at sea.

*What are you doing, Aurora? Stay strong. Ignore his beautiful smile, smell, and hair. Oh. My. God. He just put his hands through his hair again. It's making me weak... How can a man look so beautiful and handsome at the same time?*

The rest of the dinner was full of awkward silences. Tessa was upset Dan had hidden something from her and Aurora was mad at herself for hiding things from Melih. She was hoping that their going out to dance would relax some of the tension, though Aurora didn't want to be around a lot of people. She promised that she would go out for a little bit because she had promised Dan and Tessa she would. She was only was staying out with them because she wanted to spend time with Melih, now that Melih had moved passed her avoiding him. Aurora thought avoiding Melih was easier than

telling him the truth about the day before and that she would
be leaving for New York. She had promised herself days before
that the next time she saw Melih, she would tell him that she
was moving to New York.

They went to a Latin American dance club that night
because Aurora liked to dance to the music. When they walked
in, Merengue music played on the loud speakers. The smell of
sweat and the sight of hips swaying and bodies touching had
Aurora feeling a sense of comfort and happiness. Aurora loved
to dance to Latin American music because no talking was
required. Your bodies did all of the talking for you. Tessa didn't
like dancing but Dan did, so he danced with Tessa and her two
left feet.

Melih and Aurora sat at a table. The passion between them
was a fire that the whole ocean would not be able to put out.
They were not saying anything to one another. Aurora didn't
dance yet because she was waiting for Melih to ask her to
dance because she knew how talented of a dancer he was. She
also wanted to feel his touch against her body. She craved the
softness of his skin touching hers and the smell of his sweet
sweat.

Aurora and Melih sat at one of the tables surrounding the
dance floor. As she was waiting for Melih to ask her to dance,
another man came up to her. He was cute, short, had black
hair, green eyes, a big white smile, sun kissed skin, and the
shiniest black leather shoes she had ever seen. She thought he
looked like a more muscular and shorter version of Enrique
Iglesias, or maybe the lighting was just that good. Melih sat up
straight and flexed his arms and jaw muscles as he listened to
him talk to Aurora.

"Hola, Linda," the man said. "Do you want to dance?"

"I am not Linda," Aurora said shyly. "You have the wrong

person."

"Oi, no." Aurora noticed his Colombian accent because she had Colombian friends in college. "Linda means beautiful."

"Oh." Aurora giggled like a schoolgirl as she looked at Melih, to see if he was paying attention. Testosterone raged through Melih's body.

The man said, "So, is this man next to you your novio?"

"No," Aurora said as she sat up straight. "He is not my boyfriend."

"That's good," he said. "So, I was wondering if you would like to dance with me?"

Melih interrupted them and said, "She and I vere just about to dance, actually."

Melih put his hand out for Aurora and said, "Shall vee?"

Without saying yes, Aurora took his hand and he spun her around the dance floor as they swung their hips with their bodies intertwined. But they were still not touching. They had all of the eyes in the room on them, and Tessa stopped dancing for a moment when she noticed.

After a few songs had passed, Tessa had to pull Aurora to the side and tell her, "What are you doing? You shouldn't be flirting with him. You are leaving." Dan and Melih took a seat at one of the tables.

"Tessa, I know." Aurora hesitated. "I just.."

"You just what?" Tessa said.

"You are going to think I am crazy, Tessa."

"What, Aurora? Tell me."

"Well, I like him a lot," Aurora said.

"Well," Tessa said, "I figured that much."

"Oh, you did?"

"Come on, Aurora, I am your best friend." Tessa then started to laugh. "Also, you are not great at hiding your emotions."

"That is very true," Aurora said as she laughed with Tessa.

"You know, it's just that you are leaving. Though I don't want you to leave, I also don't want to see you give up your dreams again for a man." *She keeps saying the same thing over and over again. She knows I am stubborn.*

"You don't have to worry. I am taking that job."

Dan put his arm around Tessa and said to them, "What are you two talking about?"

"Nothing," Aurora said as she looked down.

After their feet were sore and they became tired, they got into Dan's car and he drove everyone back to Aurora's apartment. Dan and Melih got out to walk them to the door.

They said good night. Dan hugged and kissed Tessa. Aurora saw them embracing and hugged Melih. This was the first time Melih had seen Aurora's new place.

"Oh," Melih said. "Thank you for da nice night, Aurora. Let's get brunch tomorrow, okay?"

She squeezed him tighter and said, "Okay."

She then stopped hugging him and said good night. She walked into her house. Tessa came in shortly after that and Aurora said, "I am getting brunch with Melih tomorrow."

"Oh. Okay." She and Aurora started to walk up the stairs after taking off their jackets and shoes. Tessa continued, "You going to tell him?"

"I will tomorrow. Good night, Tessa."

"Good night, Aurora."

Aurora showered and got ready for bed. Then she texted Melih.

Aurora: I had a great night with you tonight. I love dancing with you.

Melih: I love it as well.

Aurora: Good. I am glad.

Aurora: Well, I will meet you at the Flapjack at 10:30.

Melih: Ok, Pretty Lady.

Melih: Can't wait to see you.

Aurora: Good night, Melih.

Melih: Good night.

She put her phone on mute then set it on her nightstand after she set her alarm. She stayed up for hours thinking about how she was going to tell Meih she was leaving. *Why can't I just stop thinking about this?* She didn't want to ruin their connection. She was wondering how she could look into his kind eyes and tell him she was leaving. She kept replaying scenarios in her head until she finally fell asleep.

# Chapter 30

Aurora walked into the Flapjack and heard the sound of bacon sizzling on the griddle and pancakes being flipped. She smelled maple syrup and heard people laughing and sipping on their coffee. The Flapjack was a breakfast and brunch restaurant known for their pancakes, but her favorite thing on the menu was the eggs benedict. It typically came with ham but Aurora never liked ham, so she got tomatoes and spinach as an alternative. The restaurant walls were mint and blue, and covered with pictures of pancakes. There were brown wooden tables and chairs scattered throughout the restaurant.

Aurora's favorite meal of the day was breakfast, but her favorite meal of the week was Sunday brunch. It is something that she had always enjoyed since she was a little girl. She just hadn't done it in a while. Her father used to take her and her family out after church for Sunday brunch. That was a tradition that stuck with her. If she were not making brunch at home for a guest, she would go have brunch by herself at a restaurant. It was comforting to her.

Aurora went straight to the hostess and Melih tapped her on her shoulder from behind and said in his mellow sweet voice, "Good morning, Aurora. I got us a table." She felt like the entire restaurant became quiet, but it was only in her mind.

She turned around and looked up at Melih and smiled at him. His jet black hair was swept to one side and he had on a dark gray cashmere sweater with a white collared shirt underneath it. He also had a pair of light brown corduroy pants on and brown leather oxford shoes. After she realized she was checking him out, she snapped back into reality and said, "Thank you."

"Shall vee sit?" Melih said as he signaled to their table next to the window, which overlooked downtown.

Aurora nodded her head yes and followed him to their table. He pulled out the chair for her. Melih then sat across from her and opened the menu.

As he was glancing through his menu he said, "So, did you get my texts last night?"

"No. I didn't look at them yet." She continued, "What did you say?" She took the phone out of her jacket pocket.

He looked at her and said, "Nothing important. Just seeing if you wanted to invite Dan and Tessa?"

She put her phone back in her pocket. She didn't know why he wanted to invite other people until she remembered that Tessa stayed at her house the night before and then Aurora felt selfish.

Aurora then said, "I can call Tessa to join us."

"No need. I messaged Dan this morning and he said he and Tessa were going out for brunch as well."

Aurora said, still feeling embarrassed and selfish, "Here?"

"You look like someone died, Rora. It's okay. Just relax," Melih said, laughing. "I vanted to spend time alone vith you to be honest." Aurora's face started to turn red. *Aww.*

"We are not alone here," she said. "There are other people in the restaurant."

"Vant me to tell them to leave?" Melih started to stand up and Aurora grabbed onto his hand. She felt the sparks and warmness go from her hand straight to her heart.

"No!" She smiled at him but quickly pulled her hand from his. "You don't need to."

"I am just kidding," Melih said.

"I know." Her eyes opened as if she were a kid who had just arrived at Disneyland for the first time.

The waitress came to the table and they both ordered coffee. They told her what they wanted to eat for breakfast. Aurora ordered what she usually ordered, a veggie eggs benedict.

"I vill have the same as her," Melih said to the waitress.

"Anyway, did you have fun last night, Melih?"

"Of course I did."

"So," she said, "what do you think about Tessa?"

"Oh. She is wery nice. She dances like she has two left feet."

"Yeah, I am the artistic one in our friendship."

Melih said, "Have you only been friends vith her for a short time?" Aurora remembered how Gannon had never wanted Tessa around, but Gannon never declared that to his friends.

"Oh," Aurora said, "Tessa is my best friend and has been since the beginning of freshman year in college."

"Oh vow! Really? I cannot believe ve never met her if she vas your best friend."

"Well, Gannon didn't like her," Aurora said as she crossed her arms. "He probably didn't like how she saw through his bull crap."

"Vee all did. You don't have to explain anymore. We don't need to talk about Gannon. He doesn't deserve our breath."

She looked and Melih and smiled, "Yes, you are right." *He is probably sick of hearing about Gannon.*

"The outside of your new place looked very nice."

Aurora took a sip of her coffee and then said, "Did you see inside?"

"No, of course not," Melih said. "I didn't look inside out of respect for you and your privacy."

"Oh, that's nice. Why is that?"

"Common decency?" Melih said. "Vell, maybe it is my culture or my religion or the vay I vas raised. I don't look into the house of someone else because that is their personal space. You know? I also vasn't invited inside last night."

She almost choked as she said, "You what?"

"I meant to say," he then put his hand to his forehead after being embarrassed by the comment he had just made, "I vill only look into someone's house if I am invited in. I didn't mean anything else."

"I figured so. You are very respectful."

"And Aurora, for me," Melih said, "sex is for marriage." *Thank God he said that.* Though she assumed he wouldn't be that kind of guy, but after her experience with men, nothing surprised her. Melih continued, "I also have a lot of respect for you. I vould never do that to you."

"I am so happy you said that." Aurora looked at him and smiled with a sigh of relief. "I feel the same way. By the way, that is a deal breaker for me with a guy."

"Vell, I am glad ve got this conversation out of the vay." They both laughed. The waitress came with their food and they started to eat. As soon as Aurora took her first few bites, she saw how happy she was with Melih, but she remembered she had to tell him that she would be moving to New York.

At the same time Melih and Aurora both said in sync, "I have to tell you something."

"What is it?" Melih said.

Aurora pointed at him and said, "You go first."

"Vell, my dad is really sick, Aurora. I may have to go back to Turkey for a vhile," Melih said. "My mom really needs me there and my older sister has kids and cannot be vith him all da time. My mom is so emotional, too." Her heart then sank to her stomach. *I thought he was going to say he loved me. Silly me.*

"Oh wow, Melih." She took a big sigh with a concerned look on her face. "I am so sorry, Melih." She was concerned for her future with Melih and concerned for Melih's father. "Well, Melih, I guess I have something similar to tell you."

"Oh, Aurora!" Melih exclaimed, "Is your dad not going vell?" Aurora put her hand to her forehead. *He is too innocent.*

"Well, no," Aurora said. "My dad is fine. I meant that I am going to be leaving too."

"Leaving to vhere? Is everything okay?"

"Everything is fine." Aurora sat up straight and said, "Everything is great, actually." Melih was staring at her, waiting for her to continue, and she said, "Well, I am moving to New York. I got a pretty good job offer after one of the articles I just wrote."

"Vell…" Melih said. "Dat is good, but vhere will you be working? Vill you be a journalist?"

"Not really a journalist but somehow, I assume," she mumbled humbly but he was listening close enough to understand her. "I am going to be assistant editor-in-chief at *The New York Times.*"

Melih said shocked, "You are not too young for dat?" *If I hear that one more time!*

Aurora rolled her eyes. "Everyone says I am too young," Aurora said. "But they know I am a hard worker and my writing skills. I turned down an editor position with them once but Ga…. Well, I got married and never pursued it."

"Vell, I am happy for you," Melih said as he looked down at his coffee. "Vow, Aurora.. That is amazing news."

"Melih, I am sorry though."

"Why is that?" Melih replied.

"What about you and me, Melih?" She could handle a long-distance relationship between Wisconsin and New York, but she didn't think she could handle his being so far away.

"Vhat about us? You haven't left yet, and I haven't left yet. We can still hang out now," Melih said. "Anyvay, I am sure that if vee are meant to be, Aurora, nothing vill get in da vay of dat." Melih took a deep breath as if he were going to say something very serious but he held back and said, "Aurora, I can come visit you, too." Aurora thought that he was going to say something else.

"Yes, I was thinking we could visit each other but you are going to Turkey for a while," Aurora said. "That is pretty far away."

"Yes, that is far avay, but love can overcome all of dat distance."

Aurora said with a screech in her voice, "Love?" Aurora could not wrap her head around why he had said love, but she had been waiting for him to say it.

"Yes, Aurora. I love you." He looked into her eyes and smiled. Aurora felt like she couldn't breathe or speak when the words came from his mouth. Still shocked, she looked in his eyes and tilted her head to the side, like she was examining him. He said, "I thought it was obvious."

"Not really. You went a while without talking to me." She didn't think he showed he loved her because he talked to her on and off for months. "Or did you forget about that?"

"That is because I love you, Aurora."

"That makes no sense to me," she responded, shaking her head. "Because I love you and I think about you day and night. I always want to see you. E-e-ever since the first time you took off my jacket at the coffee shop, I couldn't stop thinking about it. I didn't feel you felt that way. I thought this was a one-sided love."

"Really, Aurora? I felt it far before that. Since I first laid eyes on you, but I didn't know that I vas in love then."

"Yes, Melih." *Perfect Timing....* "We love each other, and now we are leaving one another. That doesn't help us. Love has only brought pain to my life."

"Aurora, I am not Gannon," Melih said. "I am different. I vant you to pursue your dreams and I vill always support you in vhatever you do."

"I guess I don't need anyone's support." She continued, "I made it this far on my own; I don't need anyone's permission." *Why am I getting so defensive... It's like I want to push him away.*

"Aurora..." Melih replied in a very silent voice as if he were embarrassed by how she was acting. Aurora then realized the way she was talking to him and felt guilty.

"I am sorry, Melih. I am screwed up from since I was a child. I don't even know how to love." She laughed hysterically and continued, "Are you sure you love me?"

"Yes, and you do know how to love, Aurora." He took her hand as he looked into eyes.

"How do you know?" she replied.

"You are doing it right now."

She smiled at him, and he smiled back.

# Chapter 31

Melih with the subject, "This is what my boring day looks like." Though she was excited for the day ahead of her and did not think it would be boring at all. She thought it would be full of fun and exciting new beginnings.

Melih called her.

"Hey, Beautiful."

"Hey, Melih."

"Guess I will catch you for a late dinner around 7:00?" Melih said.

"Sounds perfect," Aurora said. "Enjoy your day and see the city."

"Look at the photo I just sent you," Melih said. He sent a selfie of him with Times Square in the background with the caption, "Already one step ahead of you."

"Enjoy your time," Aurora said. "I have some work to do before my lunch. Check out the photo I just sent you." She sent a picture of her living room and view, with the caption, "This is my office space for now."

"Vow!" Melih said, "Is dat your new place?"

"Yes, Melih, but really, I need to work for now. I am sorry. Talk to you later."

"Talk to you soon."

--

It was 12:30 and the car was waiting outside for her. The

driver was holding a sign showing "Miss Tousey" in bold font. *That's cute.*

She said to the driver in an annoyed voice, "I am Aurora."

"I am sorry, Madam." Embarrassed, he said in a light British accent as he opened the door for her. "We must get a move on." She slid onto the black leather seats into the back of the black car with tinted windows.

Aurora said to the driver, "Where are we going, Mister?"

"Paige. Paige is my last name, but you can call me Edward."

"Okay, Edward," Aurora said. "Where are you taking me for lunch?"

The driver responded, "We are going to meet Mr. Banquet at Jean-Georges."

"I bet this will give L'Etoile a run for its money," Aurora muttered under her breath, as she thought about how whenever she would meet her old boss, they would always go there.

Aurora arrived at the New French-cuisine restaurant and smelled duck roasting in a wine butter reduction sauce. She heard silverware scraping against plates and the sound of a knife slicing vegetables. The ambiance made Aurora feel like she was walking into a modern version of Julia Child's kitchen. She could see Dean Banquet sitting at a table. She felt nervous as soon as she saw him, and her cheeks grew flushed. The hostess took her coat and brought Aurora to the table. *This is the big moment*, she thought.

Dean stood up and reached out his hand to shake Aurora's.

"Nice to meet you, Mr. Banquet," Aurora said. She felt like they shook hands for two minutes.

"Likewise," he said as he smiled his cheeky smile. "You can call me Dean." He was wearing a gray suit and a dark blue textile tie. Aurora was also wearing a suit. It was dark blue with a white blouse underneath with a pussy-bow.

"Well, Aurora, we don't have much time," Mr. Banquet said. "I only have an hour. So, I did the honor of ordering for you."

Aurora replied, "Well, thank you for meeting with me." The waitress came and almost poured wine in a glass and Aurora signaled that she didn't want any.

"So, Aurora, tell me, how are you liking the city?"

"I love it. I have been here a few times. I lived here for a while when I interned a couple summers."

"Oh!" Dean replied. "That is right!"

"Yes, that was before you were working here," Aurora said as she took her napkin and folded it into a triangle on her lap.

"So, I heard you ran the *Happy Living* magazine and revamped the whole thing. That is impressive. *Good Housekeeping* probably would love you to work for them, as well." He laughed, and Aurora echoed an awkward laugh.

"Well, I am sure they would love me, but they are not *The New York Times*."

"I am glad you took the position. I am going to get straight to the point here. I hired you because I have been following your work and you are an underdog like me. I believe in your work, and I know your previous boss very well. He was always raving about you."

"From *The New York Times*?" Aurora said as she raised her eyebrows.

Dean replied, "No."

"Oh, you mean Mr. Fratzenburg?" *What? How does he know him?*

"Yes, the George Clooney look alike. He is a big investor who is always throwing parties. I have been to a few of them myself. However, the parties are not really my taste."

"Well, he is a bachelor and acts like one," Aurora said.

"That is very true." Dean took a sip of his wine. He continued, "So, like I was saying, you are an underdog like me. You have only an undergraduate degree and have found success. That and the Ochs-Sulzberger family was looking for someone who is younger because we are in the computer age. So, essentially, we know how hard you work and one of the members of the family loves your work. She also just went through a nasty divorce."

Aurora took a sip of her water as Dean continued, "Don't worry about your age, though. Mark Zuckerberg was only twenty when he created Facebook." *Finally, someone who doesn't say I am too young!*

"Oh!" She laughed and raised her water glass to toast herself, "Well, I guess that is good for me."

A few waitresses arrived at the table with the food. Dean had ordered Aurora a roasted Maine lobster, which came with a side of artichoke gnocchi tossed with a sweet onion Meyer lemon sauce.

"Wow. This looks almost too good to eat," Aurora said as she saw every piece of food that was perfectly set on the plate, resembling a work of art.

"Bon Appétit!" their waitress said.

"So," Dean took a sip of his wine and said, "you are going to be here permanently beginning next weekend?"

"That is the plan."

"Very well," he said as he drank the rest of his wine. "Well, it was nice meeting you in person. I have to go."

"What?" Aurora said, shocked, "You didn't eat yet."

"I ate before you came here. I am a busy man. You will be like this once you move here," Dean said. "There is no time to stop in this city because the world is always moving."

"Ah, okay. Well nice to meet you." She flashed him a smile as the waitress came with his coat and he walked out of the door. She muttered to herself, *I wonder if I am paying for this, or if it is already paid.*

The waitress came and Aurora asked for the bill because she wanted to be early for the next item on her itinerary. The waitress said that the meal was already taken care of. Aurora finished up what was left of her meal and walked to *The New York Times* building. The walk there reminded her of when she had been an intern. She was so happy she had been given the opportunity again. During that walk, she knew she was exactly where she wanted to be.

Aurora was able to meet Melih at 7:00 for dinner that night. They met at a restaurant called Mu Ramen. Customers sat at large brown maple wooden tables with benches. They reminded Aurora of picnic tables. The ceiling was covered in stringed lights and the walls were made of brick. She loved the feel of the place, which she had found from Google.

"I am sorry this was a bit of a drive here to Queens, but I thought it was worth the drive because I wanted to try authentic Japanese ramen noodles – not like the noodles my dorm mate used to eat out of a Styrofoam cup in college, then leave the empty cups out and not throw them away," she said as she looked at the menu to choose what type of ramen she wanted.

"It is no hassle," he said as he looked up from his menu and smiled at her.

"So, how was your day today, Melih?" Aurora said. "I am sorry you came all of this way to New York, to not even spend much time with me."

"Don't worry, Rora. Dhere is plenty to see in dis city,"

Melih said. "I did all of da stuff tourists usually do. I went to Ellis and Liberty Island, too."

"Oh yeah? I remember vising there as a teenager with my grandma," Aurora replied. "My great grandma and grandpas's names are on one of the giant marble slabs outside."

"Oh, really! How cool," Melih said. "Vish I knew beforehand. I could have searched for da names."

Aurora said back, "I thought it was cool when I first saw it too, but I think it is normal for people to find that someone in their family was an immigrant. Everyone in this country is the product of an immigrant, unless you are a hundred percent Native American."

"Very true," Melih said

Melih and Aurora ordered their food. They each got traditional miso ramen with chicken fried in tempura on top, an egg, and scallions. Melih tried to use the chopsticks. Aurora was trying hard not to laugh at him. He then asked for silverware.

"You know," Melih looked at Aurora and smiled, "I missed you today."

"Aww," Aurora said. "I missed you, too." *I was so busy, I never had the chance to miss him, but I don't want to tell him that. I feel guilty, but I am happy for the job position I have. I worked so hard to get here.* She felt starstruck. She thought at first that the job was like a newborn baby, but then she realized it was far more precious than that. She felt so happy about it, and it was all she could think about.

"Aurora, it is going to be so hard being vithout you," Melih said. "I vaited too long to be with you. I am sorry." Aurora slurped up some of her noodles and made a splash. *How romantic and attractive I probably look right now.* Aurora then wiped the miso broth off of her chin.

"Melih, it is okay," Aurora said. "There is nothing we can do now. We just need to move forward."

Melih looked disappointed with what she said. *He is falling hard for her me, but it's like I am putting my heart on hold.* She wasn't doing it on purpose. It was out of defense against men and for her not wanting to let anything get in the way of her future.

"I guess we are just at a bad time," Melih said, as in agreement with what Aurora was thinking. "I mean, you are moving. I am going to Turkey."

Aurora looked sad and said as she grabbed his hand, "Melih, it's not like that."

"But it is, Aurora."

"Okay, Melih, Aurora said as she put down her chopsticks to grab his hand. "Can we not talk about this? Let us just enjoy this time together."

Aurora loved Melih. She just couldn't push herself to really show it. She had never felt the passion for anyone like she felt for him. She would freeze as she felt butterflies flutter in her stomach every time he walked into a room, or the way he smiled at her, or the way he said her name in his Turkish accent. Everything about him drove her wild. It hurt her to act cold to him, but she wanted to make things easier on herself when she moved.

Aurora heard her cell phone ring and saw "Sabrina Assistant" on the screen.

"Hello?"

Sabrina said, "The editors are calling for an emergency meeting."

"Really?" Aurora rolled her eyes and said, "On a Friday night?'

"Guess so."

"Well, is Dean going to be there?"

"Well," Sabrina said hesitantly. "No."

"Okay then, it can wait until tomorrow. I am having dinner with my boy…" She stopped with what she was about to say. She looked at Melih and smiled and her cheeks flushed. She was going to call him her boyfriend to her new assistant, whom Aurora barely knew. They had never declared themselves as boyfriend and girlfriend. Aurora continued, "It is Friday night, Sabrina. Go out and have some fun."

Sabrina replied, "Staying home and reading a book is fun for me."

Aurora laughed. "You sound too much like me," Aurora said. "Enjoy a book. Have a good night, Sabrina." Before Sabrina had time to say anything, Aurora hung up.

Aurora looked at Melih and said, "Sorry. The editors wanted to meet now, but I already met with them today." She grabbed his hand again and continued, "Tonight is about you and me."

The gesture reassured Melih that things might be fine after all.

"That makes me happy," Melih said. "I thought I was losing you for a second."

"No, of course not!" Aurora declared. "Even if we are not together, I will always be with you, in your heart."

"Same here."

"So, tomorrow I am meeting with the editors for a brunch meeting, and then I will be free the rest of the day," Aurora said. "Maybe you can plan a nice day for us?"

"I know the city as well as you or even less, but I can try."

"Actually, I will email my new personal assistant to plan a nice day for us." She just wanted an excuse to say her "new personal assistant."

"I am glad you are so important. I vas nervous I had to plan the day for tomorrow." They both laughed. Melih continued, "I probably vould take us for gyros and shopping. Is your assistant from New York?"

Aurora thought for a second. "Well, I cannot remember where she is from. But if she is a personal assistant here, I am sure she can help plan a day for some tourists." They both laughed.

Melih interjected and said, "I would like to take you to a Turkish restaurant tomorrow night. It will be nice to have a taste of home."

"But you will be going home soon."

Melih responded, "I know. I should have said that I want you to try a taste of my home."

"Whatever you like…. Anyway, I have a romantic evening planned for us tonight. Let's go get a coffee."

"That sounds like an amazing idea."

Melih and Aurora finished up what was left of their noodles and Melih paid for the bill. They grabbed a coffee from a nearby coffee shop before hailing a cab.

"To the Brooklyn Bridge!" Aurora waved her hand. "Please."

They got out of the car and started their walk. They both looked at the beautiful lights that were draped around the wires on the bridge. Aurora wrapped her right arm around his left arm as they walked. There was a light breeze that came from the East River, which made her get closer to Melih and hold on tighter to his arm.

"Are you cold, Aurora?"

"Yes." She was shivering and her teeth were jittering. "How could you tell?" She giggled as she looked in his eyes and looked away. He squeezed her mitten-covered hand close to his heart.

"Here you go." Melih took off his scarf and wrapped it around Aurora's neck.

"Thank you, Melih," Aurora said. "I have a question for you."

Melih replied, "What is it?"

"Well," Aurora said. "I was wondering, why are you so nice to me?"

"Aurora," Melih said. "You deserve da world."

"You are so sweet, Melih." *And your lips look as sweet as sugar.*

He turned her around and gave her a hug. He kissed her forehead, while an old grumpy man behind them was angry that they had stopped in front of his path. The two then continued to walk as the man behind them muttered something to him.

"I guess vee are not in da Midwest anymore," Melih whispered to Aurora. "I guess people are not as nice here."

"It is okay, Melih," Aurora said. "You have to get used to it if you are going to be visiting me." She giggled.

"But do I have to?"

Aurora rolled her eyes and Melih laughed. Melih continued, "On a serious note, Aurora, you vere not treated nice for a long time. Now that I am treating you dis way, you have become shocked, like you don't deserve it."

"Yes," Aurora said. "I am still healing, but you are helping me heal, Melih."

"Dat is good, but you don't need me, Rora. You are stronger than you think."

"Maybe I am." She shrugged her shoulders.

"You are," he said. Melih stopped again and turned to look at her. Melih studied Aurora's lips as he thought about kissing her. As he hesitated to go in for a kiss, they begin to walk again when the old man behind them grumbled past them.

"Thank you, Melih."

"Thank you for vhat?" Melih said.

"For being here with me," Aurora said. "This job and New York have been the biggest thing that has ever happened to m,e and you have been nothing but sweet and supportive."

"Do not tell me thank you. I keep telling you dat you deserve dis and more. You have to believe dat."

"I do," Aurora said. *I mean, do I really believe that, though? Maybe I still do not know what I deserve or if deserved anything at all.* "You promise we will still see each other, Melih?"

"Yes. In sha Allah."

"What does that mean?"

"You mean, in sha Allah?" Aurora nodded yes and Melih continued, "It means, if God wills."

"Yes, if God wills it. If it is meant to be." She squeezed his arm and pulled it tight to her. "It is meant to be."

Aurora and Melih spent the next day touring the city after having breakfast at her new place. He was shy to go to her place at first, but after eating a croissant with Aurora, as he watched her laugh and smile, he couldn't have been happier. That night, as they ate at the Turkish restaurant, they both thought of how they were sad that they could not predict the future. Aurora didn't know if they would be able to stay together after he went to Turkey because she didn't know when he would be back, or how his family would react to her. She just wanted to enjoy the time she had left with him. Both Aurora and Melih wanted time to stop, but it seemed to them that it was only going faster. It had taken them so long to get to that point, that they were scared to let go.

# Chapter 32

Aurora dreaded going to work on that last Monday before she left for New York. She was over her job there and was ready to leave. In her mind, she was already in New York. Aurora continued to work, though she did not want to. She only continued to stay there and work hard because she was worried her boss would say something bad about her if she didn't work hard until the end. She was really tough at work when it came to getting stuff done. Sometimes, she would regret being from the Midwest and being too nice. She knew she wouldn't be able to do that in New York, or people would walk all over her.

That last week of her being in Madison was bittersweet. She was so happy that she was renting the furniture in her house, so she would have an easy move. She had a lot of packing to do, but she hated it, so she paid someone to come and pack up her clothes. She thought to herself that if she had the money, why would she not pay someone to do the packing for her? She also knew that packing might make her rethink her decision to leave Wisconsin. Aurora felt her heart torn between Melih and New York. She had fallen hard for him to the point that every time she thought of him, her heart would ache when she thought of him away from her. She would think to herself about how upset she was about the poor timing of their relationship.

Tessa told her that she was taking her out to eat for a going away dinner. Though Aurora wanted to spend her last few nights with Melih, she accepted the offer.

Tessa picked up Aurora. As Aurora got into the car, Tessa said, "So, where would you like to go?"

"Let's get a cheeseburger. I am craving some comfort food. Nothing like eating your feelings away, right?" She and Tessa both laughed.

"I will take you wherever you like," Tessa said with a smirk on her face. It was dark, so Aurora couldn't see the face she was making. If Aurora had seen her face, she would have known something was up.

Aurora and Tessa arrived at Zara and Sara's place. Aurora said, "What are we doing here? You know where we are, right?"

"Yeah, we just need to go inside for something quick."

"For what?" Aurora replied. "I will just wait in the car."

"No, it will take me a few minutes. I have to help Zara with something."

Tessa started walking toward the house and yelled back to Aurora, gesturing her to follow her. "Come on, Aurora!" Aurora soon saw Tessa disappear as she went inside.

"Okay. Fine," she said. *I just want to eat, though I won't see them for a while*, Aurora thought. "I will just go in," she mumbled.

Aurora knocked on the door and opened the door and everyone inside yelled, "Surprise!" *Oh God... Well, this is nice.*

Aurora was not a big fan of surprises, but she was happy they had done something like this for her. She saw some of her friends from work and some other old college friends.

Zara and Sara had been planning a surprise party for Aurora that whole last week. So, Melih wanted to be in on planning the party. Everyone knew about the relationship between her and Melih, but no matter how hard he tried to plan the party,

Zara and Sara insisted on taking control of the situation.

Zara told Melih, "You Turks do not know how to party like us Russians, da?"

He agreed that he really had no idea about how to plan a party. He only wanted to do everything that he could possibly do for Aurora, even if he didn't know how to do it.

As Aurora ate and made her rounds to talk to everyone, she could see Melih always smiling at her amongst the people.

When Melih saw Aurora no longer wanted to talk to anyone, he took Aurora out on Zara's balcony, overlooking the street. He looked at her as she watched the vehicles passing by. They both stood there in silence. He grabbed Aurora's hand and warmed it up for her.

He said, "I am really going to miss you."

"I know," Aurora said as she stared at his hands rubbing hers. "I'm going to miss you, too." She continued, "Let's just be quiet now. I want to pretend time is stopping, just for a while." Melih put his arm around her and pulled her close, as he kissed her forehead. *Ahhh, I hope he will kiss my lips just one time.*

"Aurora," he said. "I vant to ask you..."

As soon as he said that, she put her index finger to his mouth and said, "Don't say it."

"No, it's not what you think," he replied. "I know you vere probably thinking that I am going to ask you to stay, but I'm not going to do dat." Melih said with hesitation, "I mean, I vould love for you to stay, but dat is not what I vanted to say. Let alone...."

"Well," Aurora replied. "What did you want to say?"

"I just don't va..." he said. "I just don't vant you to forget about me."

"There is no way I could forget about you."

Melih said, "That makes me happy, because there is no way I vill ever forget about you."

He then took his arm from around her and put his hand in his pocket. He pulled out a little black box. She thought, *Not again. Not before I go to New York…. Not again.*

He took out a white gold chain link bracelet that had a diamond heart attached to it on one of the chain links. He didn't get on one knee as he opened the little black box. He said as he put the bracelet on her wrist, "This will help you remember me."

She took a big breath of relief because he hadn't proposed to her. Aurora thought he was going to. She didn't want to be put in that type of predicament.

"Wow, Melih," she said. "I don't know what to say." *This bracelet is beautiful. He is beautiful.* The street light made his face glow, and Aurora thought he looked like a Greek god.

"You don't have to say any-ding." They embraced.

"I don't need this to remember you, though," she said. "You will always be in my heart. Even if we are not together, I will never forget you. Nor could I ever forget you."

*I just hope he will not be the one that got away. I don't know if I can be committed to somebody who is not at least living by or near me. I guess if you want to be a successful woman, you cannot have it all, can you? I will just have to come to terms with knowing that being married may not work out for me…. Especially with Melih.*

# Chapter 33

Aurora loved her job in New York and how powerful it made her feel. She had finally found herself. She felt like she was on top of the world. *I still feel like I am missing something because my heart feels empty. I have been alone in New York for too long.*

Melih visited Aurora a few times after she moved there, and she visited him. This went on for a few months, but they never became exhausted by one another. Their passion for one another never diminished until it all came to a complete halt once Melih had to go to Turkey.

Aurora started to grow impatient from waiting for Melih. Though she didn't have time for any relationship, she still waited for him and hoped he would run to New York to be with her. She knew that was too good to be true, but she kept lying to herself. He promised Aurora he would return, but his dad was a lot worse than he had anticipated.

Aurora asked Melih to tell his family about her, but he would keep saying, "I vant to wait until my father is better."

Melih was on vacation from work and had been in Turkey for a few weeks. Then a position at his company became available at the branch in Istanbul. He took the job, as he knew he would be in Turkey for a while. He didn't want to tell Aurora about this, but he had to. After being in Turkey for a month, he called her.

"Why would you not tell me you got this job sooner?" Aurora said over a phone call, as she sat on the couch in her Manhattan apartment, overlooking Central Park.

*I will just FaceTime him. When he sees me, that will change his mind.*

*Melih refused your FaceTime*, the phone read.

"Melih, why won't you at least let me see your face one last time?" she cried.

"I can't. It vill just..."

"Please," Aurora pleaded. "I have been waiting ar..."

"I can't," he sighed. Though he never said it, he thought asking her to come to Turkey was out of the question because she was not ready for that type of commitment. He saw she was married to her job and he respected that.

"I am sorry, Aurora," Melih said. "I don't know vhen I vill be back. I know I should have told you sooner, but I didn't vant to hurt you." *Hiding this from me has hurt me more.*

"You know what, Melih?"

"Vhat, Aurora?"

"You didn't hurt me," Aurora lied as she said that and hung up the phone. She didn't want Melih to hear her cry. She then threw her phone across her apartment and it cracked on the floor. She sat crying on the floor for hours, alone. She wasn't crying because she was sad, she was crying because she was frustrated. She yelled out through her tears, *why can't I just have it all like they do in the movies? The money, the career, and love! Why can't I have those things?*

Aurora knew that nothing she said or did could change the situation. She had just started her career and was not about to leave for Turkey. He couldn't leave his father, who was suffering with Pancreatic cancer. The doctors were certain Melih's father would die; they just had no idea when. Just as time was not on Melih's father's side, it was not on Melih's or Aurora's, either.

"Why did I waste all of my time on him?" she kept yelling

at herself. She was mad at herself for weeks because she had put herself in a position where she was with a man on the other side of the world.

*Now I know how Carrie Bradshaw felt when Big left her on their wedding day.*

--

Aurora struggled to move on from Melih and tried keeping herself busy with the book she was writing. It was one of the only things that kept her sane in that concrete jungle. That book was her lifeline. After six months, Aurora finally finished and published her book. She made *The New York Times'* best-selling list. She wanted to leave Gannon, that dark part of her past, in the past, but she knew it was a part of who she was. She could not run or hide from it, though her publicist tried to. Though Aurora thought about publishing it under a pen name, she would think, *I am not a victim and I will not let people treat me as such. I am not a victim. I am a survivor.* After the book tour and speaking events, Aurora grew accustomed to talking about her divorce and the abuse she had gone through. This helped her to heal. That is what pushed her to be the strong woman she was.

At every book reading she read at, she would always look for Melih, in hopes that he would be there to surprise her. Any time someone walked late into a room, her heart would stop beating and she would look up from her book and look at the person who walked in. She always hoped it would be Melih, but it never was.

Aurora thought to herself one day at work while staring out of the glass window of her office overlooking New York City, *I thought nothing could hurt more than not being with the person you* love. *Then I found out the hard thing was that you could hurt much more than that. You and that person love each other so much that it literally hurts to breathe because they bring the air to your body. You don't even want to open your eyes because they are not in front of you. All you want to do is be together so badly, but it is impossible. Then you get so angry and sad because there is nothing you can do. That is the worst pain that there is. Not having the one you love. None of the abuse Gannon did to me hurts as much as not being able to be with Melih. I wish I could turn off my mind and stop thinking about him. I wish I could just move on. I wish I would just erase him from my mind, but he is engraved into my memory.*

# Chapter 34

*Six months later…*

Aurora's loneliness brought her to dating again. She could not find anyone her age that was not intimidated by her success. They always ended up breaking it off with her. She grew thick skin. *I don't need a man*, she would mutter to herself. *I will just adopt a kid if I want one.*

One night, at a party of one of her work colleagues, she was introduced to a very successful businessman named Anderson Scotts. He was a real estate mogul and was ten years older than she was. She did not intimidate him. He was one of New York's most eligible bachelors, and was notorious for breaking the hearts of many women. After Aurora caught his eye, he was smitten. Aurora knew how he was, so she ignored his advances. He would send her flowers every day without knowing she was allergic. This made her so annoyed that she went to his office and walked through the door without knocking. His office was full of other businessmen. She looked at all of them in shock before storming off in embarrassment. She stomped her way down the hallway.

While she was almost to the elevator, Anderson stopped her.

"So?" he said while laughing. "This is how you announce your love for me?"

"Believe me, I am not in love with you. I just want to let you know I am allergic to flowers, so please stop sending them."

"Okay." He then looked at her with a smile. "I can do that. But couldn't you have just called me to tell me that?"

"I do not have your number."

He looked at her and chuckled. "I can change that."

--

She had his number but he didn't have hers, though he could have easily got her work number, as he had her office address already.

So, everyday after she went to her office he started sending her a different book – not just any book, but first editions of books she had written about in one of her articles, "Books I Could Never Get Sick of Reading." For almost a week he did this, then she felt determined to call him.

"Aurora?" He sounded surprised.

"Hey, Anderson," Aurora said awkwardly.

"You can call me Andy."

She couldn't say anything.

"Aurora? Are you there?"

"Yes," she said shyly. Almost whispering he said, "Okay, we can start dating."

"What was that?"

"We can start dating!" She said louder. "Sorry, didn't mean to be so loud." She laughed nervously. Then he laughed too.

"I didn't notice you were loud." He chucked. "Text me your address and I will pick you up at seven to take you to my favorite Italian restaurant, Olio e Piu, in Greenwich Village."

"That sounds amazing, to be honest," she sighed in relief. "I am craving carbonara."

--

Once they began going steady, the paparazzi started to follow her around and take pictures of her. She didn't like that type of attention. After they had been dating a little over year, Aurora wanted to take a vacation to get away for a while. Luckily, her boyfriend owned homes all over the world, so he offered to take her wherever she wanted to go.

She chose Turkey, and they went to his home in Istanbul.

Though she never told Anderson that she had chosen that city because she thought that fate may bring her to see Melih, she never saw him. She tried to hide her disappointment, but Anderson noticed her sadness and suggested she stay at his condo on the Princes' Islands to have some alone time. The Princes' Islands is silent, with the light sound of the sea breeze. All motorized vehicles are banned, making the islands an oasis of peace and quiet. It was just what she needed.

As she walked into the condo, there was a photographer and someone recording her walking in. *How did the paparazzi get in here? I left the country to avoid them.* Aurora looked to the ground and saw there was a line of little white candles. *Wait. Those are not paparazzi.* She followed the candles, which lead to the living room, overlooking the beach. There in the living room, Anderson was standing there in a heart made of candles. She walked to him as he grabbed her hand; he got on one knee. *But you are not Melih!* She started to cry. She was shaking.

"Though I am on one knee now, you are the only woman who has been able to keep me on my toes," Anderson said. "Aurora, will you make me the happiest man alive and be my wife?"

"Well…"

Aurora hesitated for a few moments, which probably felt

like a lifetime to Anderson. She thought of the moment Melih had breathed on the back of her neck in that tea shop. She laughed aloud at the hysterical situation and how she had gone all the way to Turkey in hopes she would see Melih. *I cannot believe I believed in that fairy tale.* Aurora knew that Melih had never tried to contact her and probably never would. Her laughter then turned back into tears. She cried and covered her mouth.

Anderson stood up to hug her and dried her tears and hugged her close. Aurora said as she cried, "Yes, I will marry you." She felt like her heart had left her chest. She felt it would be gone forever.

She decided that she would leave her heart in Turkey, for Melih.

--

After being back in Turkey, Melih's family could see how lonely he was. They tried to hook him up with a Turkish woman, but he said no, just like he said no to the many women who wanted to marry him. He eventually told his family about his love for Aurora. They were upset that he hadn't told them sooner. He said he had never told them because he was worried they would not approve. His family persuaded him that if he still loved her, he should try to contact her. While his father was on his deathbed, his dad said he wanted his son to do whatever would make him happy.

His father said in Turkish, "All I want is for you to be happy."

Melih had the opportunity to work in New York City after he accepted a promotion. He took that opportunity as fate.

Melih's father passed away, and Melih stayed with his

family for a few days, then rushed to New York City to find Aurora. After going to her office, he was directed to her assistant, where he explained he was an old friend of Aurora's and had something important to tell her. That is when he found out that she was on a vacation with her fiancé. His heart sank to his chest when he heard that word.

"Look! Aren't they cute!" Aurora's assistant said as she pulled out her phone to show him a picture. Her assistant seemed to be more excited about it than anyone.

Melih felt as though he had been stabbed in the chest. He couldn't breathe. After the time it had taken him to come back, he said, "I should have expected this."

Melih wiped the sweat from his forehead. He sat down, almost falling.

"Are you okay, sir?"

"Yes," Melih said. "I just had a long flight from Turkey."

"Turkey?" Her assistant looked shocked. "I am sorry, who are you?"

"Yes. I am Melih," He said. "But it is pronounced Me-lee." He continued, "How do you know me?"

"Miss Tousey said you were a good friend of hers."

"A friend…" He muttered. *I guess it is my fault I was ever only "a friend."*

"Mr. Anderson and Ms. Aurora are in Turkey right now!" her assistant said. "Aurora always said it was her dream to go there, then that is when he proposed!"

Melih smiled, as if he still had a chance to be with her.

Melih said to the assistant, "Can you give me Aurora's personal number?"

"I don't really know you. What is your again name?"

"My name is Melih."

"Oh. My. God. I remember who you are now."

She quickly wrote down Aurora's number.

"I know how much you mean to her," the assistant said. "I mean, she never told us, but we figured that you were the man that got away from her. She always talks about her friend Melih."

*Again with the "her friend," he* muttered to himself.

--

After Aurora got back from Turkey, Melih sent her a package at work. The photo was of them together right before he left to go to Turkey, and he also left a note, which he had delivered in an envelope. Without even opening the package, she immediately hid it in her desk.

She then looked at the engagement ring on her freshly manicured hand.

She put her right hand to her heart as tears ran down her face. She wiped the tears from her cheek. *Why is he coming now? Why now?*

The next day, he called her. She let her phone ring a few times before she picked up.

"Hello…Aurora." *I missed the way he says my name.*

"Hello, Melih."

"So, you were in Turkey?"

"Yes," Aurora said. "How did you know I was…"

"The heart alvays finds vays of knowing dhings," Melih said. "But to be honest, your assistant told me vhen I came a few days ago."

"Oh," Aurora said. "So you know, then?"

"Know vhat?"

"That I am engaged?"

"Yes, Aurora," Melih said. "Did you read da note I gave you

and see da picture?"

"I never knew you gave me a picture or even a note."
Aurora hesitated. "T-t-to be honest, I never looked." She
opened her desk drawer to pull out the envelope. "I can look
now."

"No! Don't."

"Why not?"

"A-a-ah can vee meet for coffee tomorrow?" After Aurora
was silent, Melih continued, "What do you think?"

"Okay."

"Okay vhat?"

"Okay, let us meet tomorrow at noon. There is a café
outside of my office building." Aurora said as she laughed, "I
am sure your heart knows where that is too."

"Yes. If you are dhere," Melih said, "I will find it." Aurora
smiled so big her cheeks started to hurt.

"Aurora, before you hang up," Melih said, "can you vait
until tomorrow after vee meet to open da envelope?"

"Okay, Melih," Aurora said. "See you tomorrow then."

She arrived at the café and got a seat in front of the window
and waited for him. She was so anxious, and she showed up
early. She saw a couple next to her on a date. The man
grabbed the woman's hands and they smiled at each other in
silence. It reminded her of the first time they had met alone for
coffee in Madison, years earlier. She then remembered the
time when Melih had taken off her coat at the tea shop. She
rubbed the back of her neck, as she could almost feel him
whisper words against her neck. Shivers ran down her neck.

"Hello, Aurora," Melih said, as she almost jumped out of
her chair. He rubbed her shoulder assuring her everything was
going to be okay. "You still like cappuccinos, right?"

"Y-y-yes," Aurora said. "How do you remember?"

"It is hard for me to forget anything about you."

"Melih," she said, "I want to tell you something."

"Vhat is it?"

"You cannot just show up." Aurora clenched her jaw. "After this long."

"Vell, you did."

"I did what?"

"Showed up," Melih said. "You know vhat....Nevermind."

"Just tell me."

"Just read the letter and you vill know. I vant to tell you dat I love you, Aurora." *Yes. Say my name. Wait...*

"Don't say my name," she thought out loud. "It is too late, Melih." She then ran out of the coffee shop while holding back tears. She dried her tears before she walked back into her office building and stood up straight.

She went to her office and opened her desk drawer. She opened the envelope faster than a child opening up presents on Christmas. She found a picture of her and Melih in New York right before he had left to Turkey. She then looked in the envelope, looking for a note. She turned over the photo.

*I know the real reason you came to Turkey.*

*When he said "I showed up" at the coffee shop, he must have meant to Turkey.*

She was supposed to meet Anderson for dinner that night, but she told him she could not because she wasn't feeling well. She kept re-reading the note that Melih had put on that picture. Aurora could not sleep that night. She kept staring at the photo of her and Melih that she leaned against the lamp on her bedside table.

--

The next day after work, she showed up to Melih's house, unannounced. She took off her engagement ring and put it in her pocket, then knocked on his door.

"Aurora. Vhat are you doing here?" Melih said. "How did you find out vhere I lived?"

"How did you find out where I work?"

"Vell, it vasn't dat hard to track down your job." Melih knitted his eyebrows in curiosity, "But how did you…"

"Well, I have my ways," Aurora said. "The heart always has its way of finding things."

He looked down.

"Melih…" She touched his cheek and made him look her in her eyes.

"Yes, Aurora."

"You were right."

"About vhat?"

"About why I went to Turkey."

"Vhy, Aurora?"

"To see you," she muttered.

"To vhat, Aurora?"

"To see you," she said as she whimpered. "I went to Turkey to see you."

"Aurora, I am sorry I never came back to the states sooner." She grabbed his hand.

"It is okay, Melih." He rubbed ring hand and looked down at her ring finger.

"Vhere is the engagement ring, Aurora?"

"Melih," Aurora said. "I don't want to be engaged to anyone besides you."

"Really?" Melih said.

"Yes," She cried and said even louder as she laughed. "Yes, Melih." He dried the tears from her face.

He pulled her close and held her in his arms.

He puts his lips next to her ears and whispered, "I love you."

She looked him in the eyes, with tears falling. She stood on the tips of her toes, pulled his face to hers, then kissed him.

# About the Author

Kaya Gravitter was born and raised in Northern Wisconsin. In 2016, she moved to the Florida Panhandle, where she works as a marketing manager and freelance writer. Kaya has articles published in *The Huffington Post*, *Yahoo News*, and several other media outlets. She received a BA with a double major in Political Science and International Studies from the University of Wisconsin – Stevens Point, where she was the editor-in-chief for the diversity newsletter and campus blog.

Kaya realized she loved to write stories when she was only twelve years old. She told her teacher she wanted to turn her story into a play, which was eventually acted out for the school. Kaya's love for writing and her life experiences led her to write this novel for the women speaking out against their abusers and for the women who still haven't. Though the novel is fiction, Kaya hopes this novel helps many women who are going through abusive relationships, PTSD, or eating disorders.

How you can connect with Kaya:

Twitter / @KayaGravitter
Instagram / @Kaya.Gravitter
Facebook/ Kaya Gravitter

CPSIA information can be obtained
at www.ICGtesting.com
Printed in the USA
LVHW090101280519
619241LV00001B/17/P